THE WITCHES OF THE GLASS CASTLE

Gabriella Lepore is a powerful new voice in young adult fiction. Born in Cardiff, she took a degree in Cultural and Media Studies in Bristol and later went on to work as an assistant nursery teacher in her home town. In 2010 she began writing full time and is currently working on a sequel to *The Witches of the Glass Castle*.

THE WITCHES OF THE GLASS CASTLE

Gabriella Lepore

Book Guild Publishing

Sussex, England

First published in Great Britain in 2011 by
The Book Guild Ltd
Pavilion View
19 New Road
Brighton, BN1 1UF

Typesetting in Meridien by
SetSystems Ltd, Saffron Walden, Essex

Printed in Great Britain by
CPI Antony Rowe

A catalogue record for this book is available from
the British Library

ISBN 978 1 84624 591 6

Prologue

ADDO VIS VIRES

Mia gasped for unpolluted air, but the opaque purple smoke poured into her mouth and shot down her throat, filling her lungs and suffocating her. As she scrambled up the rickety step ladder, amber flames licked at her legs like the hot, venomous tongue of a serpent.

'Dino!' she cried, choking on the thick fumes. She clung to the wooden step ladder, her slate-grey eyes scanning her surroundings. But she could see nothing beyond the flames and smoke that engulfed the stone-walled basement.

Mia covered her mouth and nose with the sleeve of her crimson cotton cardigan. Her eyes smarted in the stinging toxic air, but she forced them open. They streamed, partly from the smoke, and partly from tears of dismay.

'Dino!' she called out again, her voice hoarse and strangled.

And then her brother ruptured the flames, diving for the step ladder and pushing her up to the hatch door.

In a scuffle they burst into the hallway, wheezing and sputtering. The hatch door slammed shut, encasing the blazing basement. Mia staggered to her feet, but her legs buckled and gave way. As she fell forward her palms impacted with a smack against the cold, wood-panelled floor.

Dino lay several feet away, clutching his head with both hands and writhing in pain.

1

Mia crawled to him, impulsively reaching out to him.

'Get away from me!' he bellowed. His dark-brown eyes were riddled with anguish.

Mia shrank back, afraid of him for the first time in her life. Although he was only a year older than her, his barbed, authoritative voice suddenly seemed to propel him to decades her senior. Even his face no longer seemed like the face of a seventeen-year-old boy, but more like that of a grown man.

Dino let out an excruciating wail. His fingers clawed at his head as though he were trying to burrow his way inside the skull.

Dazed, Mia called out for help. But it was futile, as she knew that nobody was home. She and Dino lived with their mother and their aunt, but neither of the two women had been home when the power had cut out. Mia and Dino had gone down into the basement to investigate the problem. And that was when the explosion had happened.

But much to Mia's surprise, she heard the sound of footsteps pattering down the staircase. She wondered if the sound was a delusional hallucination, but then a recognisable form appeared in the hallway.

'Aunt Madeline!' Mia sobbed, still sprawled out on the wood floor. 'There's a fire in the basement. Dino's hurt!'

Calmly, Madeline crouched over her nephew as he seethed in pain. He continued to grip his head, his chocolate-brown hair darkened from sweat.

Mia pushed her own hair back from her face, freeing strands that had been stuck to her tear-stained cheeks. The brunette shade was identical to her brother's.

'He'll be OK,' Madeline confirmed in a distinctly unruffled tone. She placed her hand on Dino's brow, her fingers cluttered with colourful rings. Giving him a brief glance, she rose to her feet.

'Cassie!' she called for her sister, but with no real urgency; it was more offhand than anything.

Mia listened to the footsteps and watched from her ground-level vista as her mother trotted on to the scene. Standing beside each other, Cassandra and Madeline were like mirror images. Both were attractive, with wild red hair and bright-blue eyes. Only from their dress sense was it apparent that Cassandra was a little more conservative than her free-spirited sister. Both women wore the same blasé expression on their poised faces.

Dino let out another gut-wrenching howl of agony. 'Get away from me! All of you!' he barked.

'What's happening to him?' Mia wept. She reached out to him again, but he swiped her hand away aggressively.

'He's going to be fine,' Cassandra said in her usual motherly tone. 'Maddie, darling, perhaps you should take Dino upstairs while I talk to Mia,' she suggested – although it was more of an order than a request.

Madeline nodded her head and hauled Dino to his feet, guiding him through the hallway. He stooped over and stumbled into the wall with a thump.

'Oops!' Madeline chuckled light-heartedly, aligning him back on course to the staircase.

Once they were out of sight, Mia returned her focus to her mother. 'There's a fire in the basement,' she blurted out. The words seemed to jumble in her mouth as she spoke.

'Don't worry,' Cassandra replied nonchalantly. 'It'll burn itself out.'

Mia paused, utterly bewildered. 'No. It's a . . .' she stuttered, trying to explain herself, '. . . it's a huge fire. There was an explosion. I lit a candle and it . . . it just blew up. The entire basement is on fire.' She waited for the severity of the situation to sink in for her mother. But it didn't happen.

'Yes,' Cassandra said smoothly. 'I understand. Did you read it aloud? The writing on the wall, I mean?'

Mia's head whirled. There had been writing etched into the stone wall: ADDO VIS VIRES. And she had read it aloud

– not because she had thought it to be of any relevance, but merely because she had considered it strange. Why would such peculiar words be engraved on to her basement wall?

'Did you, Mia?' Cassandra pushed.

'Yes,' she admitted, confused as to whether or not she should be feeling accountable for something disastrous. After all, what repercussions could there possibly be for reading out some nonsense words?

'Oh, good,' Cassandra responded pleasantly. She helped her daughter upright and carefully steered her into the living room.

With her legs still trembling, Mia collapsed on to the cushioned, beige couch.

'Oh, no!' Cassandra sucked in her breath abruptly. At last her reaction seemed appropriately fitting. 'Mia,' she went on, 'there's a rip in your new cardigan!'

Again, Mia looked bewildered. But it had nothing to do with the cardigan.

Mistaking her expression, Cassandra continued, 'Don't worry. I'll sew it for you. It'll be as good as new. You'll see.'

Mia gawped at her, astounded. She simply couldn't fathom why her mother was so concerned about the cardigan when there were clearly much greater issues at hand.

With a reluctant sigh, Cassandra took a seat on the couch. She lovingly stroked her daughter's hair. 'You are fine. Dino is fine,' she asserted unwaveringly. 'Everything is happening just as it should.'

'But the basement?' Mia whispered. Her usual peach complexion was now ashen.

'Let me explain this to you as best I can. You were destined to go to the basement today. Actually,' she corrected herself, 'today, tomorrow, yesterday – I suppose it doesn't matter. The only thing that matters is that the writing was on the wall. And I mean that in both the literal and the metaphoric sense.'

4

'What does it mean?' Mia asked shakily. She didn't dare speak the words aloud again; all of a sudden they felt like a lot more than just words.

Cassandra took off her own cardigan and draped it over Mia's shoulders. 'Loosely translated, it means, "To give power,"' she clarified. 'It's Latin, I believe.'

'What sort of power?' Mia murmured. Her heart was pounding in her chest so violently that she felt as though it might burst out of her at any moment.

'The power which was already yours. Your birthright. Myself, Aunt Maddie, Dino, you, we're all entitled to it. And now is your time to take it.'

All of a sudden Mia felt short of breath. She wrapped her hand around her throat. 'Take what?'

'Power, my love,' Cassandra said each word meticulously. 'You're sixteen now. You're old enough to use it. I suppose you could think of today as a sort of rite of passage.'

Mia dropped her hands to her lap. She noticed that they were shuddering. She was scared. Scared by the explosion, scared for her brother, and even scared of her own mother.

'Mia,' Cassandra said, smiling gently, 'you're a witch.'

1

The Glass Castle

The narrow streets of Silver Brook were eerily deserted and quiet. In fact, they were surprisingly quiet for such a bright summer's day. Only one car chugged along the winding road – a rusty blue station wagon. Of course, it wasn't exactly a vastly populated town, so the roads were never congested like they often were in the larger cities. Silver Brook was, for the most part, surrounded by mountains and forest, but the warm summer months tended to bring out the locals, sending them on day trips or picnics. Not today, however; today was different.

With an impromptu swerve, the clapped-out station wagon veered off the main road and pulled on to a parched dirt track. Pebbles and clumps of dried mud crunched under the weight of the bulky tires. The car rattled along at a leisurely pace, closing in on an archway of trees, all of which seemed to bend quaintly towards each other, creating a sort of tunnel.

Cassandra drove into the tunnel, and at once the glare of the afternoon sunlight vanished. 'This brings back memories,' she remarked to her sister, who sat in the front passenger seat picking at her chipped, orange nail polish.

'It certainly does,' Madeline agreed. 'It wasn't all that long ago that our mother was driving us here.'

'Strange now to be taking my children,' Cassandra added. 'Perhaps our time here was longer ago than we think.'

'Longer than I'd care to admit!' Madeline said with a hoot.

From the backseat, Mia listened curiously to her mother and aunt's conversation. Right now everything seemed like a mystery to her. She wasn't even completely clear on where she was going. All she knew was that she and Dino were being sent away for a while. Of course, her mother and Madeline hadn't exactly used the words 'sent away', but that was the general gist of it.

Mia blinked against the bursts of sunlight that sporadically broke through the trees. She squinted, trying to glimpse beyond the tunnel, but the bright light between the gaps blinded her. She looked away quickly, almost as though she'd been burnt by it.

Sitting beside her, Dino showed no reaction or interest whatsoever. He stared straight ahead, his eyes locked to the back of his mother's head, fixated on her mane of fiery red curls. Where Mia displayed a wide-eyed curiosity, Dino's mentality was that of a condemned man. It was as though he already knew what was beyond the tunnel – or at least what it represented. And it symbolised the end. To him, the tunnel was a portal of rebirth into a life that he did not want. And consequently, the end of the life he had.

Mia wanted to speak to him, to share her own thoughts and anxieties, but she didn't dare. His dark eyes were icy and warded her off.

She tried nonetheless. 'Dino?' she said quietly.

He didn't respond. He kept his focus on Cassandra's hair.

Mia sighed. Dino was no stranger to a sullen mood, but ever since the basement his occasional mood swings had evolved into a permanently remote and cold disposition. Unlike Mia, Dino was experiencing some agonising side effects. From what she could gather, he was still tortured by the severe pain in his head. It had lessened, but it had by no means gone. Of course, nobody knew the full extent of his suffering because he had barely spoken in days.

Suddenly Madeline let out a piercing shriek, cutting through the tension in the back seat. 'This is it!'

'This is it!' Cassandra repeated, matching her sister's enthusiasm.

Mia sat up a little higher in her seat as the tunnel of trees opened out into a rolling meadow, dotted with buttercups and lush green grass. The sun beamed vibrantly, somehow more dazzling than it had been in town.

'Cassie!' Madeline gushed. 'It's exactly as I remember it.'

'Yes,' Cassandra agreed amiably. 'It's nice to see that some things never change.' She kept her concentration on the dusty road, but she glowed with a new energy.

Madeline twisted in her seat, leaning into the back of the car. 'Do you see it? Do you see the castle?' she asked her niece and nephew.

Mia peered out the car window. At the far end of the meadow was a magnificent stone castle. 'Yes, I can see it,' she said, looking back to her aunt.

Madeline and Cassandra both let out a whoop of delight.

'What about you, Dino?' Cassandra asked, her eyes still on the road.

Dino gave a heavy sigh. He glanced half-heartedly out the window. 'Yeah,' he muttered gruffly.

The two women cheered again.

'I've been waiting a long time for this day,' Cassandra rejoiced radiantly.

'Me, too!' Madeline sang out in a high-pitched squeal. 'You're so grown up.' She smiled fondly, but more at Mia than Dino. 'And now our coven is finally complete!'

'Maddie,' Cassandra scolded her, 'this isn't about you. It's about them.'

Madeline pouted. 'It's about us. All of us. And so what if I'm excited about finally getting our four?' She elaborated for Mia and Dino's benefit. 'We need four to make a strong coven of witches. That's where the big power is. But it's only ever been the two of us, your mother and I. Well, since Anton and Phillip, anyway.'

'My uncles?' Mia furrowed her brow. She had never met her uncles, but she recognised their names from the rare occasions that her mother or aunt spoke of them.

'Yes. We were a coven,' Cassandra confirmed. 'But that was a long time ago.'

'What happened to them?' Mia asked.

'Those two useless fools!' Madeline scoffed. Her red hair bobbed wildly as she turned her attention back and forth between Mia and Cassandra. 'They are poor excuses for witches. Pitiful men . . .'

Cassandra cut her off abruptly. 'Can we please not talk about them today? This is supposed to be a happy day.'

'A happy day?' Dino snapped curtly. It was strange to hear his voice after such an extended silence. 'How is this is happy day? Our lives are over and you're sending us away to live with some old nut-job.'

Cassandra and Madeline shared a quick glance.

'We're not sending you away,' Cassandra reasoned. 'You've been blessed with a gift, and Wendolyn will help you to develop it. You'll only be here during the summer. You'll be back home in time for school.'

'Oh, wonderful,' Dino scowled.

'And she's not a nut-job,' Madeline said, glaring at him, a little less tolerant than his mother. 'She's opening up her home to you, and I hope you will show her some respect.'

'Madeline,' Cassandra stepped in diplomatically, 'have a little patience. He's going through a hard time.'

Madeline rolled her eyes.

'And, Dino,' Cassandra added, 'we're only a short drive away if you want to come home. But with your . . . *new abilities*,' she chose her words carefully, 'I think it's important for you to be here. Wendolyn will guide you, and soon the pain will subside,' she assured him.

'Why aren't I in any pain?' Mia wondered out loud.

Dino narrowed his eyes resentfully.

'Because your power is not the same as your brother's,' Cassandra explained.

'Oh.' She chewed on her thumbnail. 'So, what is *my* power?'

Cassandra and Madeline laughed. They ignored her question and continued chatting among themselves.

Mia looked at Dino, and for the first time during the car journey, he looked back at her. She sucked in her breath sharply. He was her brother, but all of a sudden she didn't recognise him – not as she had previously known him, anyway. His eyes were like bottomless pits and his stare was intrusive, as though he were stealing all of her thoughts before she had even had them.

Can you hear me? she asked silently, testing him.

He didn't respond, but he continued to stare at her. The anger in his eyes was unnerving.

Mia turned away from him, but she could feel his gaze still upon her. *Stop it!* she wailed inside her head. Swiftly she lifted her hand and covered his eyes, breaking the stare. She smiled in spite of herself as Dino returned his focus to the back of his mother's head.

As they drove along the vague track snaking through the meadow, their view of the castle became clearer. It was exquisite. The building looked as though it had been standing for centuries – and it had. Yet for all the solidity of its old stone walls it seemed somehow insubstantial, as if masked by a veil of secrecy and wonder.

'Wendolyn lives here?' Mia murmured in awe.

'Yep!' Madeline nodded. 'That's why she takes in young witches. She's got so much space, and you're cut off from civilisation out here. I think you need that when you're trying to control new power.'

'Is she royalty or something?' Mia enquired.

'No!' Madeline laughed musically. 'She's an elder witch. They tend to dwell in old buildings.'

'Plus,' Cassandra joined in, 'this is a *glass* castle. It's quite common for practising witches to shadow their homes. It's sort of an illusion – it makes them invisible to regular civilians. As translucent as glass.'

'Early powers can be rather temperamental,' Madeline mused. 'So it's good to have a place where you can grow, away from the prying eyes of the powerless.'

They reached the end of the road and rolled to a stop in the castle's courtyard. Cassandra turned off the engine and unbuckled her seatbelt. With a deep breath, she swivelled around in her seat to face her children.

'I'm very proud of you,' she said, her blue eyes glassy with tears.

Madeline clumsily nudged her sister aside. 'You're going to have the best time!'

All of a sudden, Mia was filled with a sense of foreboding. Her mother and aunt's words of encouragement had actually had the opposite effect on her. She didn't want to get out of the car. She had never been away from home before – not for more than a few days, anyhow. And with all of the changes thrust upon her, the last place she wanted to be was in a glass castle, cut off from the rest of the world. Alone.

'Will you visit?' she asked meekly.

'Probably not,' Cassandra said simply. 'Now is the time for you to stand on your own two feet. My presence would hinder you. I can't help you with this, and neither can Aunt Maddie.'

The colour drained from Mia's cheeks. Automatically she gripped the back of her aunt's chair.

'Don't worry,' Madeline said brightly. 'Dino will be here with you. He'll take care of you. Won't you, Dino?'

He stared straight ahead, obstinately disregarding their comments.

12

Madeline shrugged, unconcerned. 'Don't worry, baby,' she said to Mia, 'you'll be fine.' She stretched into the back seat and playfully pinched her niece's cheeks.

'OK. It's time,' Cassandra announced. She opened the car door and stepped out gracefully. Madeline followed her lead.

Only Mia and Dino remained in the car, one afraid and the other petulantly stubborn.

Madeline skipped up to the castle, her long, flowery skirt flowing and her eyes enchanted and childlike. Cassandra busied herself with unloading the bags from the car.

Mia looked at Dino. 'Come on,' she said quietly. 'We should get out.'

Without another word they accepted their fate and left the security of the car. The simple act was the first step on a path that would subsequently change their lives for ever. Neither was prepared, but destiny had picked them and it was out of their hands.

Madeline banged her fist against the arched mahogany door, her wrist jangling with its freight of chunky, multicoloured bracelets. 'Wennie!' she yelled.

'Don't shout like that,' Cassandra reprimanded her, in typical older sister fashion.

'Wennie!' Madeline screamed again, more stridently than ever.

The second call seemed to work, because at last the castle door heaved open and an older lady stepped out into the courtyard. She wore a full-length purple dress over her rounded frame, and her long, white hair was twisted into a braid that tumbled over her left shoulder.

'Girls!' the lady greeted her guests with a cheery smile. 'Don't you look well!'

Madeline virtually jumped into the lady's arms. 'I know! I look fantastic, don't I? Would you believe I'm thirty-six? I don't look a day over *twenty*-six,' she boasted shamelessly.

Dino snorted. 'You wish,' he muttered under his breath.

ne shot him a frosty glower.

Cassandra cleared her throat loudly, keen to skim over the squabbling. 'Wendolyn, it's so wonderful to see you. It's been far too long.'

The lady took Cassandra's hand and rubbed it affectionately.

Cassandra beckoned to Mia and Dino. 'This is Wendolyn,' she said courteously. 'She has kindly invited you into her home for the summer. Wendolyn, these are my two beautiful children, Dino and Mia Bicks.'

'Notice,' Madeline interrupted, 'Bicks. They have *our* family name, not their father's.'

Mia smiled nervously while Dino stared steadily at the older woman.

'Dino,' Madeline chuckled flippantly, 'stop staring at everyone! It's rude.'

Dino looked down to the ground, affronted by his aunt's remark. In all honesty, he wished he could stop staring, but it was beyond his control.

'Oh, nonsense!' Wendolyn jumped to the boy's defence. 'He's just not used to his power yet. It can be very difficult at first.'

Mia watched the scene inquisitively. She couldn't help but wonder what exactly her brother's power was. Or what her own power was, for that matter.

'You'll soon find out,' Wendolyn said in a knowing voice. She winked at Mia.

Mia froze. *She can hear my thoughts.*

'Only when I want to,' Wendolyn replied good-humouredly. The aged skin on her face framed remarkably youthful eyes that swirled with a mixture of blue and hazel.

Madeline appeared to be delighted by the whole exchange. She clapped her hands in glee. 'Wendolyn is a Reader. She has the ability to read thoughts. You can't get anything past her!' she chortled. 'Believe me!'

'And Lord knows you tried,' Cassandra smirked.

The three women smiled as though they were sharing a private joke.

'Now it's time for the new generation to take their turn,' Wendolyn said warmly.

Mia suddenly felt as if Wendolyn were commanding her, summoning her and her brother towards her.

Mia took an involuntary step forward, but Dino didn't budge.

'Come here, boy,' Wendolyn called to him. Her words, although blunt, sounded safe and compassionate.

But Dino didn't move.

Madeline rolled her eyes. 'Cassie, tell him,' she said in a tight voice.

'I have no control over him,' Cassandra replied impassively. The statement was probably truer than any parent would wish to admit.

'He's your son!' Madeline pointed out, her voice hushed discreetly.

Wendolyn held up her hand to silence them, and like naughty schoolchildren they shrank back.

'You're going to be very powerful, Dino,' Wendolyn said in a voice that seemed to reverberate around the peaceful meadow. 'You're blocking me. You know that, don't you?'

Dino didn't reply, but he wore a sudden air of complacency.

'I can't read your thoughts,' Wendolyn went on. 'You're blocking me.'

'What?' Madeline gawped. 'How has he done that? He's only had his powers for a few days!' There was a distinct note a jealously in her tone.

Wendolyn smiled kindly. 'Come along, boy. It's time to go inside.'

This time Dino submitted. But his look of arrogance was replaced with a brooding grimace.

In dazed uncertainty, Mia lifted her rucksack from the courtyard floor and slung it over her shoulder. She watched as Dino did the same. When she caught his eye, he glared at her as though somehow all of this was her fault.

Deep down, Mia knew that Dino blamed her. After all, she had been the one to light the candle and read out the words on the basement wall. But to live through this, knowing that she was to blame, was shattering, so she banished the thought immediately.

Above them a jackdaw crowed raucously. Mia looked up and saw its ebony wings shimmering blue as it soared overhead. As if by miraculous coincidence, a feather fell from the bird, tumbling through the sky like a piece of black silk. It slowly floated to the ground, landing at Mia's feet. She picked it up and studied it, admiring its sleekness.

'A jackdaw feather,' Cassandra noted insightfully. 'They say that's lucky.'

Mia clung to the feather, taking a strange sense of comfort from it as she waved goodbye to her mother and aunt.

Wendolyn led the way down a long, dimly lit corridor. The carpet below was a dull red and the hardwood walls were patterned with intricate carvings, telling a story that Mia knew she could not yet read. At the far end of the corridor Wendolyn pushed open a heavy door.

'Come in,' she authorised her two guests. 'Take a seat.'

Mia and Dino followed her into the room. It was a small library, the walls lined with hundreds of dusty leather-bound books. There was no window in the room, so Wendolyn set to work lighting a myriad of long black candles which projected from the walls in ornate brass candlesticks.

Mia took a seat in a green velvet armchair. In the quiet of the room she heard the wooden structure creak as it took her weight. Dino sat down in a similar chair beside her, and

Wendolyn strategically took a seat opposite them. Between them was a low-set apothecary table on which was already arranged a tea tray with a white china teapot and matching teacups.

'Welcome to my home,' Wendolyn said humbly. 'It's a pleasure to finally meet you as young adults. I remember you only as babies in your mother's arms.'

Dino's expression remained stony. 'Well, that must have been a long time ago.'

'It was,' Wendolyn replied, unaffected by his icy tone.

'Thank you for having us,' Mia added, trying to balance out her brother's insolence.

She suddenly felt Dino's eyes on her. To avoid his stare, she looked around the room, absorbing every detail of the extraordinary decor. Her gaze landed on a striking oil painting set inside an elaborate gold frame. It was a double portrait of a finely dressed man and woman, both looking intensely out from their painted world.

'Who are they?' Mia asked.

Wendolyn joined her gaze. 'The man is William Wix. He was once lord of this castle. The woman at his side is his wife – me!'

'It's beautiful,' Mia complimented.

'Yes,' Wendolyn agreed. 'William, my husband, was the founder of the Glass Castle. He envisioned a place where young witches could be nurtured, rather than discriminated against and spurned.'

The idea made Mia uncomfortable. 'So, he wanted a safe place for witches to . . . hide?'

'Not hide,' Wendolyn corrected. 'More like a place for adolescents to develop their powers freely and without prejudice. Without guidance it's not uncommon for new witches to turn to the dark arts. You see, powers are simply an expression of emotion. When your emotions are wild, so are your powers. William understood that.'

'Is he here?' Mia asked. Dino touched her arm, urging her to stop. He had obviously picked up on something that she had not.

'No,' Wendolyn replied amenably. 'William passed away some time ago.'

'I'm sorry,' Mia said quietly.

Wendolyn chuckled lightly, but there was a definite sadness in her eyes. 'It was a long time ago,' she said. 'Almost eighty years ago, in fact.'

'Eighty years?' Mia frowned in confusion. Surely she had misheard. 'Eighty?' she repeated.

'Almost.' Wendolyn nodded her head.

Mia rolled the notion around in her head. If Wendolyn's husband had passed away that long ago, she wondered, how old did that make Wendolyn? In the painting they were easily in their thirties, so that meant that Wendolyn must be . . .

She scrunched up her nose; mathematics had never been her strong point.

Wendolyn smiled but carried on. 'This castle is William's legacy, and I intend to maintain it for many years.'

'Do you take in *lots* of people?' Mia enquired. She guessed that it would be naive of her to assume that she and Dino were the only ones.

'Some years more than others. At the moment we have around fifteen Arcana and four Hunters. Would you care for some tea?' Wendolyn didn't wait for a response. She lifted the white teapot and poured the contents into the three waiting cups.

Mia sat up a little straighter in her chair. 'What's an Arcana?' She paused. 'And a Hunter?'

Wendolyn raised the teacups individually and circled each one three times in a clockwise direction. 'An Arcana is what you are. In other words, a pacifist witch who lives as a civilian.' She handed Mia a teacup. 'Your powers are con-

18

nected to nature and are used placidly. A Hunter, however, is a witch bred as a warrior. They too source their power from nature, but it is of, let's say, a darker strain. They need these extra powers to aid them in combat.'

'Combat whom?' Dino asked, suddenly breaking his sullen silence.

'Usually other Hunters or malevolent witches.'

Mia chewed on her bottom lip nervously. 'Are Hunters . . . human?'

'Yes. All witches are born human. But Hunters are raised differently. As I mentioned, they are bred as warriors, and are not taught to respond to human emotion as you or I would.'

Mia flinched. 'Will they attack us?'

Wendolyn's kind eyes were unreadable. 'You would be wise to be wary of them,' she said smoothly. 'But they shouldn't be of any bother to you. In truth, you'll rarely see them. The Hunters reside in a different wing from the Arcana, so your paths will seldom cross. Occasionally I will need to call you all together, but even then they keep their distance.'

A wave of misgiving flooded over Mia. She shuddered involuntarily. Feeling particularly tense, she took a sip of her tea. It didn't taste like the sort of tea she was used to.

'What is this?' she asked, wrinkling her nose in distaste

'Tea,' Wendolyn told her.

'From a teabag?' Mia stared down at the pale orange liquid stewing in her cup. Quizzically, she fished out one of the small tea leaves that floated on the surface. The little brown dot clung to her finger while she examined it.

'It's witches' brew,' Wendolyn explained. 'Tea extracted from plants. Let's see, it's made up of fennel, rowan berries, mugwort, elderflower . . .' she listed a long catalogue of plants, counting them off on her fingers. 'It's known to enhance psychic powers and bestow protection on those performing magical works.'

'No, thank you,' Dino said briskly, slamming the delicate teacup down on the apothecary table.

Wendolyn smiled at him strangely.

Mia took another sip. On her second try it wasn't so bad. Different, but not awful. She picked a tiny rogue leaf from her tongue and surreptitiously wiped it off on Dino's T-shirt.

He glared at her.

'Try some,' she said, offering her cup to him. 'It's nice. Like a cup of . . . flowers.'

'Sounds delicious,' he remarked sarcastically. 'No, thanks. I'm not in the market for any more psychic powers.'

'Well, I am,' Mia retorted.

Wendolyn laughed in a jolly fashion. 'Oh, you don't need tea to give you power, my dear. I can see power exuding from you even as we speak.'

Mia tightened her grip around the teacup. 'Really?'

Wendolyn studied her for a long moment. 'You are a daughter of nature.'

Mia frowned. 'So . . . ?'

Wendolyn smiled affectionately. 'It'll come to you when you're ready,' she said cryptically.

I'm ready now, Mia thought irritably. 'Am I psychic?' she asked out loud.

'No. Be patient. You'll use your powers when the time is right. And as for you,' she turned her focus to Dino, 'you will learn to shut them off. After all, that's why you're both here – to learn.'

Mia took her final sip of tea, hoping to gain something from it. In actual fact, she doubted that she had any powers at all. She certainly didn't feel any different.

'Are you finished?' Wendolyn asked, gesturing towards the teacup.

'Yes. Thank you.' Mia handed her the empty cup. And much to her surprise, Wendolyn looked intently down into it, examining the gathering of leaves at the bottom.

'Hmm . . .' Wendolyn muttered incoherently to herself.

'What does it say?' Mia asked anxiously.

Dino shook his head with a dry laugh. 'It doesn't say anything. It's just a pile of leaves!'

'What does it say?' Mia repeated, ignoring her brother's obnoxious outburst.

Wendolyn placed the cup down on to the table. 'I'll tell you when you're more able to deal with it.'

Mia's voice went up an octave. 'What does that mean?'

'Nothing to worry about,' Wendolyn assured her. 'But if I told you now, I don't think that you'd understand.'

Mia looked fearfully at Dino, hoping for some form of comfort.

'OK,' he said evenly. 'Read my fortune.' It was a challenge more than a request. He lifted his untouched tea and knocked it back in one gulp, then thrust the empty cup into Wendolyn's hand.

Without batting an eyelid, she peered down into the depths of the cup.

Mia held her breath while they waited. The room was silent other than the quiet crackle of a burning candle and the slight rasp of Dino's breathing.

'You've got an interesting path ahead of you, Dino,' Wendolyn said at last. 'And you're going to have to make some difficult choices.'

'What kind of choices?' Dino demanded.

'It's not my right to say,' she reasoned tactfully.

'But it's your right to keep me here?' he shot back.

Wendolyn stood up slowly. 'You're free to leave whenever you please.' She eyed the door meaningfully.

Dino let out a cold chuckle – the sound of a man defeated.

'Well, then,' Wendolyn said brightly, her breezy voice lifting the tension. 'Shall I show you to your bedchamber?'

Dino slapped his hand to his head. 'Please don't tell me we're sharing.'

'Yes, you'll be sharing,' Wendolyn confirmed.

Mia felt a degree of relief. With everything that was going on at the moment, the last thing she wanted was to feel even more isolated and alone. At least now she'd have the company of a familiar face.

'Please,' Dino said, his surly tone suddenly dissolving into desperation. 'Please, I'm begging you. I can't share a room with *her.*'

Mia's jaw dropped open. 'That's a horrible thing to say!'

Dino spoke only to Wendolyn. 'I'm begging you,' he said, his hands clasped together pleadingly. 'You don't understand.'

She began to blow out the candles. 'I do understand,' she said sensitively. 'I'm afraid there is nothing I can do.'

'What do you mean?' Dino exclaimed. 'This is your place! Surely there's somewhere else you can put me?'

Wendolyn opened the library door and ushered them back out into the long, narrow corridor. 'I'm afraid not,' she said.

Fuming, Dino ran his hands through his dark-brown hair.

Mia watched the display with a mixture of anger and sorrow. Why was the idea of sharing a room so loathsome? Of course it was a little unfortunate, but they'd shared rooms in the past. As she trailed her hands along the indented carvings on the wall, she realised that his blame and resentment towards her had evolved into pure hatred.

They walked on through the dark corridor until they reached a wide staircase furnished with the same dull-red carpet and a grand, mahogany banister. As Mia took the first step, a small brown sparrow fluttered past her. She gasped.

'Everything OK?' Wendolyn enquired, pausing her ascent on the staircase.

Mia looked around her for the bird, but it had vanished from sight. 'There was a sparrow,' she explained, mystified.

'Ah,' Wendolyn smiled. 'That'll be the tea showing you a little glimpse into the future. Keep an eye out for sparrows;

they must have some significance.' She continued walking, the others following her mechanically.

At the top of the staircase, Wendolyn brought them to a tall oak door. 'This will be your bedchamber,' she told them. 'You're free to explore the grounds, but be cautious. Do not venture too near to the forest – it's Hunter territory.'

Dino looked at Mia, his dark eyes almost venomous. At that moment she noticed just how dark they were, especially in comparison to the pale grey of her own eyes. Looking at him now, she supposed they probably didn't look much like brother and sister at all. Well, aside from their brown hair, and perhaps their smiles – although Mia hadn't seen Dino smile in a while, so it was difficult to judge. She turned away from him. She didn't want to look at him any more. The emptiness in his eyes was alien. She could barely recognise him. In fact, something in the pit of her stomach told her that he was no longer her brother.

2

How the Birds Fly

Dino and Mia's bedchamber proved to be just as impressive as the rest of the castle. It was a spacious room with two four-poster beds situated in opposite corners. Both beds were covered by a canopy made out of embroidered gold curtains.

After emptying the contents of his rucksack on the carpet, Dino flopped back on to one of the beds and closed his eyes. Although it was still daylight outside, he managed to fall asleep – or at least, he pretended to.

Mia sat up on her own bed and drew the curtains across. There, sheltered inside in the confines, she felt as though she had disappeared into her own private little haven, away from the rest of the world. And away from all that had happened that day.

When the minutes had turned into hours, she began to get restless. A growing sense of inquisitiveness began to out-weigh her anxiety, and she made the decision to leave the safety of the room. She pulled apart the heavy, gold curtains and crawled out from the bed.

Across the room, Dino's bed curtains were drawn.

'Dino?' Mia called in a small voice.

She heard him sigh impatiently. 'What?'

'I'm going to explore,' she told him. 'Do you want to come with me?' At this point she didn't actually know if she wanted him with her or not. She wasn't sure how much more of his obnoxious behaviour she could take.

'No,' he said bluntly. The decision was made for her.

But despite his brash attitude, there was still a small – or large – part of her that feared wandering around the castle alone. The thought of crossing paths with a Hunter sent a chill down her spine.

'I could wait for you if you want,' she suggested.

'No!' he shouted. 'Go!'

Mia winced. They had had arguments in the past, some worse than others, but this was in a whole new league. By the tone of his voice, his feelings towards her were unmistakably hateful.

'Fine,' Mia muttered. 'I guess I'll see you later then.'

'I'll look forward to it,' Dino replied, his words dripping with sarcasm.

Mia stormed out of the room, purposely slamming the door behind her. At least, if nothing else, his comment had fuelled her with a much needed burst of adrenaline, which came in useful when she found herself alone in the dark corridor. Boldly, she scanned her surroundings. The ceilings were so high that they almost disappeared into the shadows, and the long narrow corridor seemed endless, eventually getting lost in an abyss of darkness. All of a sudden she wasn't feeling quite so plucky any more.

It seemed sensible to follow the path that she already knew, so she made her way to the staircase and crept down it. The floorboards creaked as she descended the steps, and the ghostly noise echoed hauntingly in the hollow building. Each moment felt like an eternity, but finally she made it to the bottom of the stairs. By this point her heart was racing, so she picked up her speed and ran down the corridor towards the main door.

Bursting out through the door, Mia found herself back in the courtyard. It seemed completely different now as she stood there alone, in the same spot that she had stood with her mother and aunt just hours earlier. It suddenly felt like the loneliest place in the world. The very thought made her want to cry. But she held the tears back, breathing deeply and steadily.

In a flurry, a small sparrow shot past her. Mia looked twice, wondering if she was seeing things again. But this time it was really there. It circled the courtyard and then darted through a hedge archway. Remembering what Wendolyn had told her, Mia tentatively followed the little bird. She broke into a trot to keep up with it, passing under the hedge and emerging out on to immaculately maintained grounds.

Mia was momentarily taken aback by the breathtaking scenery. In the pale-blue sky, the sun shone behind a faint haze of cloud, illuminating the rolling green landscape as far as the eye could see. Directly in front of her were elegant, well-tended gardens, laid out geometrically with hedge mazes and neatly arranged flower beds. Beyond the gardens was a broad grassy embankment leading down to a pine forest. Mist clung to the outskirts of the forest, so that only the tips of the trees could be seen.

Still in pursuit of the sparrow, Mia stepped out on to the grass. She tracked the bird to an immaculately pruned hedge which appeared to be encircling a small patch of land. The bird hovered above the area and then fluttered away into the sky.

Somewhat warily, Mia approached a gap in the hedge and peeked inside.

She gasped at the sight of a girl lying on her back on a circular section of grass.

'Sorry,' Mia excused herself quickly. 'Are you OK?' she asked as an afterthought.

The girl, startled by the unexpected voice that had disrupted the tranquil garden, let out a shrill scream. She scrambled to her feet and clutched at her heart melodramatically.

'Sorry,' Mia said again, holding her hands up in surrender.

26

'Are you . . . a vision?' the girl whispered, edging closer to Mia. Her blonde hair was tied up with a shoelace.

Mia thought about it for a second. 'No,' she said. 'I don't think so.'

The girl relaxed slightly. 'So, you're real?' she asked, sounding a little disappointed.

Mia frowned. 'Yes.'

'Oh.' The girl smiled sheepishly. 'I was hoping that you were a vision. No offence.'

Mia nodded as though she understood. But she didn't.

'Yeah,' the girl continued, 'it's confusing sometimes. I'm trying to tap into my power. I've been here a whole week and I'm not getting anywhere.' She slumped back down to the ground with a huff. 'I think I'm trying too hard.' She idly rolled up the bottoms of her oversized denim dungarees, which she wore loosely over a bright-orange top.

'I know how you feel.' Mia consoled sympathetically. 'I'm having some trouble in that department, too.'

'Well, I guess that's some comfort. At least I'm not the only one,' the girl said and giggled. 'Everyone else's powers are so active that they can't control them, and then there's people like us who can't even get ours started!'

Mia sat down on the grass. 'I'm not even sure I have a power.'

'Oh, God! That hadn't crossed my mind!' the girl laughed good-naturedly.

'Sorry,' Mia smiled. 'I'm sure that's not the case for you.'

'Nor you,' she replied amiably. 'I'm Kizzy, by the way. Kizzy Mortimer.'

'Nice to meet you. I'm Mia Bicks.' She wasn't being insincere – it really was nice to meet her. Kizzy seemed to be around the same age as Mia, and, most importantly, she was friendly. And Mia could definitely do with a friend.

Kizzy carried on, 'I'm a Seer. I should be able to see visions of the future. But the visions just aren't coming to me yet.'

Mia furrowed her brow. How could a person know of their power without ever having experienced it? She thought of her vision of the sparrow brought on by the tea, and wondered if perhaps she too might be a Seer.

'How do you know what you are?' she asked, absent-mindedly knotting her fingers through the grass.

Kizzy shrugged. 'I just . . . know.'

'I don't know what I am,' Mia admitted.

'That's odd,' Kizzy scratched her head. 'Has no one ever told you?'

'No. Should they have?'

Kizzy pondered it. 'No, I guess they prefer you to work it out on your own. Sadists! But sometimes powers are genetic,' she added helpfully. 'Both my parents are Seers.'

'I don't know what my mother's power is,' Mia confessed, suddenly wondering why she had not asked. 'And I never knew my father. But my brother's here, too, and he seems to have an active power.'

Kizzy's blue eyes lit up excitedly. 'What can he do?'

'Hmm . . .' Mia deliberated. 'From what I can gather, he gets headaches and stares.'

'Wow,' Kizzy smiled wryly. 'Don't mess with him! Hey,' she teased, 'maybe he's a Hunter.' She paused. 'Wait – you're not a Hunter, are you?' She seemed to be suspiciously studying Mia's eyes.

'Of course not!' Mia exclaimed.

'Good. Neither am I.'

'Do I really look like a Hunter?' Mia asked, somewhat traumatised by the prospect of resembling a monster.

Kizzy chuckled in amusement. 'Hunters can look more or less like regular people. The only real difference is their mentality. Haven't you ever seen one?'

Mia shuddered. 'No. And I don't want to.'

But Kizzy didn't seem to hear the last part because she

abruptly sprang to her feet. 'Come on!' she said, grasping Mia's hand and hoisting her up.

'Where are we going?'

Kizzy smiled mischievously. 'Hunting. Excuse the pun.'

'Whoa, whoa, whoa!' Mia wriggled free of Kizzy's grasp. 'I don't want to go looking for Hunters! I want to avoid them!'

'But if you've never seen one, how will you know what to avoid?' Kizzy pointed out innocently.

Mia grimaced. 'Well, I'll just avoid everyone.'

Kizzy rolled her eyes. 'Follow me,' she said, skipping out from the confines of the hedge.

Mia brushed the grass from her hands and mulled her options over. Despite her protests, she was sort of curious to get a glimpse of a Hunter – it was beginning to feel like forbidden fruit. And she was definitely glad to have someone to talk to; Kizzy was a far cry from Dino right now. All things considered, she had to admit that she was tempted to follow Kizzy. So, with some reservation, she stepped through the hedge wall.

Kizzy was waiting on the other side.

'I thought that you'd be way ahead of me by now,' Mia remarked shrewdly.

'No way! I'd never go alone. I don't have a death wish!'

'That's reassuring,' Mia muttered.

The two girls paced across the gardens and across the lawn.

'Where exactly are we going?' Mia asked, trying to hide her building trepidation.

'The forest,' Kizzy told her.

Mia's eyes drifted down to the edge of the forest. It was nearer now, and the mist shrouding it appeared even thicker, almost impenetrable.

The closer they got to its boundaries, the less confidence Kizzy exuded. Now Mia took the lead, walking gallantly ahead. To her right, she noticed a graveyard which was fringed with a row of wind chimes ringing musically in the light breeze.

'What's that?' Mia asked. 'I mean, I know it's a graveyard, but why here?'

Kizzy seemed indifferent and merely shrugged.

Strangely enough, the nearer Mia got to the forest, the more courageous she felt. The opposite could be said of Kizzy

'Maybe we shouldn't actually go into the forest,' Kizzy reasoned timidly. 'I mean, we know they're in there; we don't need to *see* them.'

'We're here now,' Mia replied confidently. 'We might as well go in.'

'But we're intruding on their territory. They won't like that.'

'They won't catch us,' Mia insisted, surprisingly sure of herself. 'Do they live in the forest?' In her imagination, the Hunters had become something like half-naked savages living out in the wild.

'No,' Kizzy chuckled quietly. 'But I think they train there pretty much all day. Hidden among the trees . . .' she trailed off, frightened by her own words.

Instinctively, the girls came to a standstill at the beginning of the mist. Mia strained her eyes, trying to peer through it. Admittedly, she couldn't see much further than the first few trees, but there was no sign of movement so she edged forward. In the blink of an eye, the mist had swallowed her whole.

'Mia!' Kizzy cried in a stage whisper. 'Stop!'

But it was too late. Something was pulling Mia in. She was like a tiny magnet being drawn forward by an invisible force. Somewhere in the depths of her mind she knew she should stop, but the pull was far too strong. She heard the crunch of leaves behind her. She couldn't turn her head, but she knew that Kizzy had been pulled in, too.

The girls trudged on like zombies, marching through the

smoky mist. As they were drawn deeper into the shadowed maze of pine trees, the daylight turned to dusk and the tuneful chirping of birds was replaced by the occasional sinister caw of a crow.

'Kizzy,' Mia murmured, barely able to speak. 'I can't stop.'

'Neither can I!' Kizzy cried. The pounding of her feet continued in a slow, steady rhythm.

Stop, stop, stop! Mia commanded herself silently. But her legs kept plodding on, deeper and deeper into the forest.

'We need to break stride,' Kizzy told her hurriedly.

'How?'

'By stopping!' Kizzy replied unhelpfully.

'I can't!' Mia wailed. It was hopeless.

Just as she was about to accept her doom, she was blessed by a stroke of luck. Straight ahead of her, Mia noticed a rotted tree root protruding from the ground. Impulsively she jammed her foot underneath it, losing her balance and toppling forward. She landed with a thud on a bed of crisp leaves.

'Help!' Kizzy squealed as she marched robotically past her friend.

Quickly, Mia grabbed hold of her ankle, tugging Kizzy down to the ground.

Kizzy tripped and fell to the forest floor.

'Are you OK?' Mia asked in a hushed voice.

Kizzy sat upright and rubbed her grazed hands. 'Yeah. You?'

They looked at each other, unsure whether to laugh or cry.

'I think so,' Mia replied. 'We need to get out of here.' She quickly clambered to her feet.

Huddled together, the two girls raced through the forest, back in the direction they had come from. But in the confusing web of trees, finding their way out wasn't quite so simple.

And that wasn't their only problem. A sudden sense of

instinct nagged at Mia to stop running. 'Wait!' she said, grasping Kizzy's arm to hold her still.

'What is it?' Kizzy panted frantically. 'We have to keep going!'

'Shush!' Mia held her breath. 'What's that noise?'

They clung on to each other as the distinct sound of footsteps approached.

Kizzy's eyes grew wide with terror. 'What should we do?'

Mia held her index finger to her lips.

And then, sure enough, two dark figures weaved through the trees, combing the area like predatory animals hunting their prey. There was no doubt about it: they were Hunters.

Pressed flat up against a tree trunk, Mia watched them with a combination of fear and respect. They were brawny young men in their late teens and could easily have been taken for normal 'civilians'. But they weren't normal – they were Hunters. Everything about them was innately predatory. The way in which they moved, so sleek and precise, was as though every step had been calculated to the finest detail. And their powerful bodies, taut and strong, seemed like they had been sculpted into the perfect soldier. Even their hair and clothes were dark, blending them into the shadows, almost as if they were shadows themselves.

'They've sensed us,' Kizzy whimpered in a nearly inaudible voice.

And she was right. The two Hunters were on a trail, tracking the intruders. In seconds they were just a stone's throw away.

Mia felt as though her heart had stopped beating. She was so close to them that she could practically smell them. One of them turned his head slowly towards her; he seemed to be absorbing the air, almost as if he were tasting it. His eyes were rabidly intent and a sullen green – the colour of the pine forest. Mia pressed herself even closer to the tree trunk. With a sharp jab, something pricked her thigh. It was the jackdaw feather that she had found earlier that day; she had tucked it into her pocket for safekeeping.

In a reckless motion, she drew the feather from her pocket and aimed it like a dart. With a swift throw, she sent it spearing through the air, landing several metres away from where she and Kizzy were cowering. The feather rustled the dry leaves as it collided with the floor.

The Hunters spun around to trace the noise.

'Run!' Mia clasped Kizzy's arm and set off through the trees, sprinting as fast as her legs would carry her. She knew that the diversion wouldn't last long and the Hunters would be close behind them. She guessed that it was only a matter of time before they caught them, but she kept running anyway. She ran until she thought her legs would drop off. And just when she thought she couldn't run any farther, they broke through the trees and were once again engulfed by the blinding mist.

'Keep going!' Kizzy yelled. With one last spurt they broke out into the bright light of day and raced up to the graveyard, dropping to the ground in relief.

Wheezing for breath, the girls slumped behind a large gravestone.

Mia never thought she could ever have felt so glad to be in a graveyard. But then this wasn't an ordinary graveyard. Well, it wasn't like any graveyard that Mia had seen before, anyway. Instead of the usual array of shiny, elaborate head-stones, it merely boasted chunky slabs of rock with names etched into them.

'Do you think we're safe?' she asked breathlessly.

Kizzy peeped out from behind the gravestone. Everything seemed quiet. Only the gentle sound of wind chimes floated through the air.

'I think so,' she said at last. 'Those were Hunters, by the way.'

Mia gave her a look. 'Yeah. I figured.'

'Lotan and Colt,' Kizzy went on. 'They're the leaders of the Hunter coven and you just threw a feather at them!'

Mia laughed.

'Hey,' Kizzy added, 'how did you get the feather to fly like that, anyway?'

Mia shrugged. 'Guess I was lucky,' she mused, remembering what her mother had said about the jackdaw feather bringing luck.

'Very lucky,' Kizzy agreed. Strands of her blonde hair had fallen loose from her shoelace tie. She was looking somewhat dishevelled from the run.

Mia looked comparatively unaltered. Her dark hair tumbled down in loose waves and, aside from a slight pinkish blush to her cheeks, it would have been hard to tell that she had been fazed at all.

'Is that what they're called?' she asked, intrigued by the Hunters. 'Lotan and Colt?'

'Yep.'

'Which one is which?'

Kizzy contemplated how to distinguish them. 'Colt was the one with darker hair.'

'Colt,' Mia repeated his name, sounding it out on her tongue. He had been the one whose green eyes she had glimpsed. The one whose eyes had smouldered with wrathful supremacy. Somehow Mia knew that he was the one to fear.

Dino lay motionless in the blissful tranquillity of the bedchamber. He was undeniably relieved that Mia had gone out, for the simple reason that it gave him a brief spell of peace. A precious time span during which he could escape the deafening emotions of others that burrowed their way into his head, screaming like baying beasts. That was what it felt like – feral creatures screaming and clawing at his brain. And he couldn't escape it, no matter what he did. The only rest was the few treasured moments that he had to himself. Completely alone.

That was why he felt so desperate to distance himself from Mia. For some reason, her emotions were the loudest. Perhaps it was because she was linked so closely to him. Or perhaps it was because she was going through such an emotionally heightened time. Either way, every subtle shift in mood that she experienced would shriek in his head like nails on a blackboard. He felt like his brain was going to explode from the immense pressure pounding down upon it.

Dino knew that he had hurt her feelings – he literally heard the sound of her sadness. And he imagined that she probably thought he blamed her for all of this. Perhaps he did. But predominantly he wanted to be away from her because the searing sound of her emotions was unbearable.

There was a knock on the bedroom door.

Dino groaned inwardly.

The knock came again, louder this time.

'Come in,' Dino said reluctantly.

The door creaked open. Hidden behind the drapes of the four-poster bed, Dino couldn't see who had entered the room. But he knew that it was Wendolyn.

'Hello, boy,' she said.

'Hello,' he replied in a short voice. He squeezed his eyes shut in an attempt to block out the sound of her sympathy. But it was a futile wish. The noise instantly branded itself on to his brain. A couple of days ago he could never have imagined that sympathy could be recognisable from a sound. But it was. It was as clear as if someone had said the actual word. Every emotion had its own sound. Fear, happiness, sadness, love – they were all uniquely identifiable. The only similarity was that they were all excruciatingly deafening, intense, and fierce.

'How are you feeling?' Wendolyn asked, though her question was spoken only out of politeness, for she already knew the answer.

'Peachy,' he said hotly. 'Thanks for asking.' He smirked, as though he were secretly congratulating himself on something.

'It gets better,' Wendolyn assured sagely. She kept a respectful distance from the bed where Dino was still concealed behind the gold-embroidered curtains.

'When?' he demanded. Hidden in his curt tone was a glimmer of vulnerability.

'When you're ready.'

Dino laughed scornfully. 'I'm ready!'

Tentatively, Wendolyn stepped closer to the bed. 'I will help you.'

'I want it gone. I want it out of me,' Dino hissed through clenched teeth.

'It's a gift,' Wendolyn reminded him gently. 'And it's who you are.'

'It's a curse,' Dino corrected her sharply. 'And you have no idea who I am.'

Wendolyn didn't respond.

'I don't want this,' Dino exclaimed, his voice softening somewhat.

With slow caution, Wendolyn drew apart the bed drapes. She observed Dino where he lay, his hands knotted into his hair and beads of perspiration glistening on his brow. Every muscle and vein in his arms was visible, tensed and taut under the vigour with which his hands were clenching his scalp.

'Try to embrace it,' Wendolyn advised soothingly.

'I can't,' he groaned.

'You are a Sententia,' she told him. 'You have the ability to hear human emotion. It's a wonderful, precious thing, and if nurtured correctly it will grow into a phenomenal power.'

'I'm not a Sententia,' Dino spat out the word. 'I'm a human.'

'The power would not have come to you if you were truly unable to cope with it.'

'It was an *accident*! It was Mia who read the words out . . . This is *her* fate. And she isn't even suffering from it!' he scowled grudgingly.

'And you wish her to suffer?' Wendolyn asked in an even voice. It was more of a statement than a question.

Dino became rigid. 'No,' he admitted. 'But why me? Why me and not her?'

'Perhaps,' Wendolyn said wisely, 'you should stop pitying yourself and accept that this is not a sinister doom meted out on you, but rather that it's just who you are. And who you have always been. The sooner you stop fighting it, the less you will have to endure.'

Even if he'd wanted to, Dino couldn't have understood her. How could he accept that such a brutal pain was simply a part of his genetic make-up? He was damned and, as far as he was concerned, there was no other explanation.

'Try to allow it,' Wendolyn implored him.

The comment only enraged Dino further. 'I don't *want* to allow it!'

'The more you defy it, the longer the pain will persist.'

'I can't!' he cried. 'I can't bear it!' His body began to tremble violently. Short strands of hair fell forward and stuck to his clammy brow. 'Please, leave,' he requested in a strangled voice.

'Very well,' Wendolyn submitted calmly. She was aware of his condition and knew that he meant no disrespect. 'If you are feeling up to it, I've asked the others to meet in the drawing room later. I'd like to talk to you all together.'

Fearfully Dino imagined the intensity of a room full of emotions.

'I understand,' Wendolyn said supportively. She had managed to read his thoughts. 'But if you change your mind, we'll be meeting at dusk.'

Annoyed by her uninvited intrusion, Dino focused on blocking her from entering his mind. He wasn't entirely sure how he was able to do such a thing, but somehow he was confident that he had successfully accomplished it. It was as though he was able to raise a mental guard, a wall of sorts. The ability seemed to come naturally to him.

'Clever!' Wendolyn congratulated him; she was impressed rather than bothered.

Dino closed his eyes.

'Remember, the drawing room at dusk,' Wendolyn added, before gliding out of the room and leaving Dino to the peacefulness of solitude once more.

3

Buttons and Daggers

As dusk set in, the residents of the castle congregated in the drawing room. Like the library the room was hung with elaborately framed portraits whose pale watchful faces were illuminated by flickering candles that were mounted into the mahogany-panelled walls. The only real difference was that the drawing room was considerably larger, and the hundreds of dusty volumes were replaced by vast leaded windows facing out on to the courtyard.

Mia and Kizzy strolled in and took a seat on an unoccupied sofa. There were ten or so other teenagers already seated, clustered together in little groups.

Wendolyn stood at the head of the room, quietly observing the gathering of people.

'Help yourselves to tea and biscuits,' she said, gesturing towards a lavishly laden table.

Mia and Kizzy peered over at the table.

'I'll get us some,' Kizzy offered. She hopped up from the sofa and skipped across the room towards the table, the bottoms of her oversized dungarees trailing along the carpet behind her.

Once she was alone, Mia scanned the groups of people in search of her brother. Dejectedly she quickly realised he wasn't there. She wondered if he even knew about the meeting. After all, she hadn't seen him since storming out of the bedchamber earlier that day.

'Are you OK?' Kizzy asked, reappearing with two china teacups with a couple of biscuits balanced precariously in their saucers. 'You look a little spacey.'

Mia was jolted back to reality. 'It's nothing. I was just kind of hoping that my brother would be here,' she explained.

Kizzy gave her a sympathetic look and handed her a teacup, filled to the brim with the murky orange witches' brew. The abundant liquid sloshed over the edge of the cup, pooling in the delicate saucer.

Mia took a sip to reduce the volume. The strange taste was not so potent now that she was familiar with it.

'So what's the story with your brother?' Kizzy mused, plopping down on to the sofa.

'I don't know. He doesn't want to be here.'

'How come?'

'I suppose he's just having a hard time coming to terms with all of this,' Mia speculated. 'Plus, he blames me.'

'Blames you for what?'

'For turning him into a witch.'

Kizzy snorted. 'That's insane! You didn't turn him into a witch. If he's looking to blame anyone, he should do as everyone else does and blame the parents!' she joked.

Mia took another sip of tea. 'Don't worry – I'm sure he blames them, too. He'd blame you if he got half the chance.'

Kizzy laughed, her eyes shimmering like sapphires.

'Anyway,' Mia shrugged. 'I don't think I'm speaking to him at the moment, so it's probably a good thing he didn't show up.' The words were easy to say, but not so easy to mean.

The sound of Wendolyn's voice put an end to their conversation. 'Thank you all for coming,' she said graciously. With her white hair pulled back, she stood staunchly before the room, naturally commanding attention. 'Take a look around. These are your brothers and sisters. United as Arcana.'

Mia felt a pang of sorrow as she looked around the room.

While the others regarded each other with a sort of tribal pride, she saw only strangers. She wished to see a brother, too – her *real* brother.

Suddenly, Kizzy choked loudly on a mouthful of tea. 'I just had a vision!' she whispered into Mia's ear, once again snapping her out of her reverie.

'From the tea?' Mia looked down at Kizzy's empty cup.

'Maybe. Or maybe it was my fabulous natural power.' She feigned a conceited smirk.

Mia smiled light-heartedly. 'What did you see?' she asked.

'A boy. Dark hair, dark eyes. I think he might have been a Hunter.'

'Is he here?' Mia enquired in a hushed voice.

Kizzy quickly glanced around the room. 'No,' she confirmed. 'I wonder what it means. I hope it's not a warning.' She dramatised an over-the-top gulp.

From the corner of her eye, Mia caught a glimpse of silver. But when she looked again, it was gone.

'Oh, my God,' she gasped, her breath catching in her throat. 'I think I just saw a dagger!'

'A Hunter and a dagger. Talk about bad omens,' Kizzy remarked wryly.

Mia groaned quietly. 'We should never have gone into the forest.'

'Maybe it's just a caution, telling us to stay away – you know, from now on, I mean.'

'I was planning on doing that anyway,' Mia replied dryly. 'In fact, I am hereby proclaiming that this afternoon was the first and last time that I'll ever be anywhere near a Hunter.' She grinned in satisfaction.

Kizzy eyed her dubiously. 'What if you accidentally cross paths?'

'Nope,' Mia shook her head obstinately. 'I'll run.'

Wendolyn was speaking again. 'You are all here for the same reason: because you are gifted. I want to spend the

41

coming months helping you become who you are capable of being: strong, fine witches . . .'

Her sentence was cut short by the drawing-room door bursting open. A cold gust of air blew into the room and the flames of the candles flickered tremulously. Some wavered in their struggle to stay alight, while others were extinguished instantly. Then the four Hunters marched in, dark and dangerous. In the vanguard were the two older boys whom Mia and Kizzy had seen in the forest – Lotan and Colt.

'You were saying . . . ?' Kizzy muttered quietly.

Mia froze.

'Welcome,' Wendolyn greeted the new arrivals.

The Hunters nodded in response. They stood motionless in the deep shadows at the back of the room. The atmosphere became rigid.

Mia clasped her hands together, her eyes purposefully locked on Wendolyn. She was painfully aware of how close the Hunters were. They were more or less directly behind her.

As Wendolyn returned to her discussion, Kizzy leaned towards Mia. 'Do you think they recognise us from the forest?' she whispered.

Mia bit her lip. 'Maybe they didn't see us,' she offered weakly.

'What if they picked up our scent?'

'Can they do that?' Mia asked.

'Sure. They're Hunters. That's what they do.'

'Well, then, they probably *do* recognise us.'

'Mia!' Kizzy pinched her arm. 'Don't say that! You'll give me nightmares!'

Mia smiled in jest.

'Hey,' Kizzy went on, 'I wonder if one of them is the boy I saw in my vision.'

'Did you look?'

'No way! I'm not looking at them!' Kizzy spluttered.

Mia wasn't entirely sure why she chose to do so, but in a reflex action she craned her neck to get a look at the Hunters. It was only for a brief instant, but she saw them. There they stood, sturdy and impossibly still. All four expressionless faces fixed unwaveringly on Wendolyn.

A sudden breeze brushed over Mia's cheek, tousling her hair. Very slowly, Colt turned his head and looked back at her. There were those eyes again: dark green, the colour of the pine forest. His stare was vacant, yet threatening at the same time. And a subtle twitch in his nose told Mia that she had indeed been recognised.

Her heart leapt into her throat. She hastily returned her focus to Wendolyn, ruing the fact that she had looked away from her in the first place.

'Colt,' Mia mumbled to Kizzy. 'He spotted me.'

Kizzy lowered her voice. 'Are you sure?'

'Yes.'

From the front of the room, Wendolyn addressed the Hunters. 'Lotan, could you please bring forward the Athame?'

Lotan, the leader of the Hunter coven, stepped out of the shadows and approached Wendolyn. He walked with remarkable bearing, his stride heavy yet graceful.

Mia and Kizzy shrank back into the sofa, hoping to go unnoticed. In an attempt to be inconspicuous, Kizzy inadvertently knocked her empty teacup, causing it to clatter loudly against its china saucer. Both girls cringed.

But Lotan didn't even give them a second glance. He handed Wendolyn a small, silver dagger and then retreated to the back of the room.

Wendolyn raised the dagger and displayed it to her guests.

'That's what I saw in my vision!' Mia blurted out in amazement.

'This is an Athame,' Wendolyn declared. 'One of the

43

witches' most sacred tools. The Athame is a ceremonial knife, passed down from generation upon generation of powerful witches. It directs magical energy in a way that is personal for each witch.' She ran her fingers over the grooves in the blade. 'Magical inscriptions engraved into it engage unseen helpers and channel the strongest of powers. As you can see, it is attached to a chain. This is because it's a pacifist's tool and is worn as a charm during rituals – it can *never* be used as a weapon. One day most of you will come into contact with, or even use, an Athame, which is why I felt it necessary to explain to you its purposes. However, for now, it's far too powerful for undeveloped abilities like your own.'

Another arrival burst into the drawing room, interrupting Wendolyn once more.

'Welcome,' Wendolyn said, her eyes full of warmth.

Mia and Kizzy turned towards the door. With a nonchalant air, Dino swaggered in.

'That's him!' Kizzy cried. 'That's the Hunter I saw in my vision.'

'That's my brother!' Mia laughed, pleasantly surprised to see him.

Dino walked into the room with a remarkably self-assured stride. He slumped casually into a seat beside a boy with sandy blond hair. The boy, who had been previously sitting alone, glanced at Dino, then quickly looked away.

Mia watched Dino for a moment. He seemed powerful – just as powerful as any Hunter. But to her disappointment, it didn't feel as though she was looking at her brother; he was more like just another stranger.

An hour later Wendolyn brought the meeting to a close and hung the Athame from one of the wall-mounted brass candle-sticks. One by one people began to leave. But not Dino. Even when Wendolyn suggested he join the rest of her students for a meal in the dining room, Dino declined. He wasn't hungry. He remained casually slumped in an armchair as the room slowly emptied.

Mia walked past him. They looked at one another briefly, but said nothing.

Soon the room was completely empty apart from Dino and the sandy-haired boy who sat beside him.

'What's your name?' the boy asked.

Dino petulantly rolled his eyes. Couldn't this boy tell that he didn't want to chat?

'No name,' Dino replied brusquely. He didn't dare look at the boy for fear that he would connect with the intensity of the stranger's emotions.

The boy blinked at him through round, honey-coloured eyes. 'Oh, right. S . . . sorry,' he muttered self-consciously. He stood up to leave, accidentally dropping his notebook in the kafuffle.

Oh, man! Dino thought irritably, but also a little guiltily. He picked up the boy's notebook and handed it back to him.

'Listen,' he said with a reluctant sigh, 'I didn't mean any offence. I'm just not looking for a buddy. OK?'

'Yeah. No pr . . . problem,' he stammered nervously, clearly embarrassed by the whole exchange.

Dino raked his hands through his hair. *Great. Now I feel bad!* he thought tetchily. 'Well, now I can't be a jerk to you,' he said, frankly disappointed by the revelation.

The boy furrowed his brow in bewilderment. 'Huh?'

'You know,' Dino snuck a glance at him. 'Because . . . you know.'

'Because I have a stammer?' the boy finished the sentence for him.

Suddenly Dino felt like the worst person in the world. 'Well, yeah,' he replied honestly.

'Just b . . . because I have a stammer doesn't make me any less of a man than you are,' he snapped defensively. 'You think you're not a j . . . jerk? Well, I've got news for you – you are. A jerk, I mean,' he added, just in case it wasn't clear.

Dino held up his hands in defeat. 'You're right. I'm sorry,' he apologised, and not just because of his small-mindedness, but because this boy was genuine. He liked him. 'My name's Dino,' he relented.

'I'm Benny Blue,' the boy replied. He offered his hand for Dino to shake.

'So, Blue, what wonderful power have you been cursed with?' Dino asked snidely.

'I'm a Conjurer,' Blue told him.

'Oh, yeah?' Dino became marginally interested. Being a Conjurer sounded a lot better than his own power. 'What exactly can you conjure?'

'Um . . .' Blue sat back down in his seat. 'I think s . . . some Conjurers can make anything they want.'

Dino's dark eyes glinted at the world of possibility. 'You've hit the jackpot, then!'

Blue smiled uncertainly. 'I'm still kind of working on my power. It's been a y . . . year.'

Dino let out a low whistle. 'A whole year? You must be pretty good. Show me what you can do.'

'OK,' Blue said tensely. He dug through his jeans pocket and pulled out a translucent vial packed with what appeared to be grains of dirt.

'What's that?' Dino asked, his eyes on the tube-like vial.

'It's ciron thistle extract.' Blue sprinkled some of the granules into his palm and closed his hand to make a fist.

Dino observed him with curiosity.

Blue mumbled something under his breath and tapped his fist with his other hand. Then he cautiously opened his fingers and displayed his palm to Dino.

Dino peered at the contents. 'It's a button,' he said, impressed but confused. 'Cool.'

'Thank you.' Blue shoved the vial and the little brown button into his jeans pocket.

'Wait!' Dino stopped him. 'Don't put it away yet. What else can you make?' For the first time, he was actually seeing the benefits of being a witch. He was envious of not having the power himself, but at least it was entertaining to watch.

Blue reluctantly brought out the vial again. Half-heartedly he repeated the procedure and then opened up his hand to show the finished result.

'A button,' Dino noted.

'It's a different colour,' Blue told him.

Dino squinted his eyes. 'Is it?'

'Yes. This one's m . . . more of a reddish-brown. The other was a much d . . . darker shade.'

'Oh. Right.' Dino cleared his throat. 'So, what else?' He decided to be a little more specific. 'Can you make a bar of chocolate or something?' He had been craving a sugar fix all day, and Wendolyn's nutritious biscuits weren't quite satisfying his taste buds.

'Maybe one day,' Blue said impassively.

'OK. So, what exactly can you make?'

Blue looked down to the carpet. 'Buttons.'

'You only conjure buttons?'

'Y . . . yes.'

In any other circumstances, Dino would have burst out laughing. But deep in his mind, the sound of Blue's shame and disappointment echoed noisily.

'Hey,' Dino said brightly, 'that's still cool. I don't know anyone else who can make a button out of thin air. And everybody needs buttons, right?'

'It's, um, it's not thin air. It's ciron thistle,' Blue corrected.

'Yeah, sure. Whatever.'

'Thanks,' Blue smiled bashfully. 'So, what about you? What's your p . . . power?'

'I can hear people's emotions.' That was the first time he had actually said it out loud. It was strange to finally admit it.

'A Sententia?'

'I think that's what the kids are calling it, yes.' Dino shot him a wry smile. 'You're pretty clued up on this magic thing, huh?'

Blue shrugged. 'I was here all of last summer. I've read a lot of books.'

Dino pictured the library and its walls lined with dusty, aged books. Reading them was definitely not on his list of fun things to do. 'Is that how boring life gets around here?'

Blue laughed quietly. 'No. There're plenty of other things to do.'

'Like what?' Dino pressed.

'I've seen some of the other guys take dirt bikes out. They play lots of sports around the grounds. I don't really know what, though,' he confessed.

Now that sounded more like Dino's idea of fun. 'Don't you join in with them?'

Blue shook his head. 'No. They don't w . . . want me to.'

'Why not?' Dino couldn't help but feel a little angry at the idea that Blue was being excluded.

'I don't really f . . . fit in with those guys.'

'Well, then, neither do I,' Dino said loyally. Suddenly he realised that the sympathy he was experiencing was in fact his own sympathy, as opposed to someone else's that had forced its way inside his mind. He could still pick up on Blue's emotions, which were tapping away at his subconscious. But it wasn't quite as painful as it had been before. In fact, in contrast to Dino's own feelings, Blue's were combatively quiet.

'You OK?' Blue asked, noticing Dino's bemused expression.

He exhaled loudly. 'I hope so.'

After supper, as night settled over the Glass Castle, Mia and Kizzy wandered through the gardens, their path lit by a chain of solar lanterns.

'Do you think they'll come after us?' Kizzy asked absent-mindedly.

Mia sat down on a garden bench. 'Maybe not,' she said, instantly knowing that Kizzy was referring to the Hunters. 'Not if we keep out of their way.'

'With pleasure!' Kizzy laughed. She joined Mia on the bench, gazing up at the stars. 'Besides,' she added, 'twice in one day is more than enough!'

Mia shuddered at the thought of Colt's penetrative eyes. All evening she had been haunted by the memory. Never before had she seen a look of such hunger and dominance. It was chilling.

'Whoa!' Kizzy suddenly gasped. 'How did you get that?'

Mia frowned. 'Get what?'

Kizzy blinked at her. 'I think I just had a vision,' she murmured. 'I saw the Athame around your neck.'

'The dagger?'

'Yes. The one that Wendolyn showed us,' Kizzy told her.

The girls looked uncertainly at one another.

'Strange,' Mia commented. 'I suppose that means I'll be using the Athame at some point in the future. But I'm guessing it'll be a long way into the future, seeing as though I don't even have a power yet.'

'Or maybe . . .' Kizzy paused. 'Maybe it was advice.'

'How do you mean?'

'Well,' Kizzy elaborated, 'maybe the Athame is the key to tapping into your power.'

A feeling of uneasiness washed over Mia. 'Maybe,' she agreed. 'But Wendolyn made it perfectly clear that we aren't ready to use it.'

Kizzy was silent for a moment. 'You're probably right.'

'But . . .' Mia held up her index finger, deliberating it further. 'But, the Athame is used for channelling powers, right? And maybe that's precisely what I need to do – channel my powers.' All of a sudden the thought of using the dagger became seductively tempting.

Kizzy peered up to the sky. 'Well,' she reasoned, 'I did see you wearing it. Surely that means you're capable of controlling it?'

'It does imply that . . .'

Kizzy picked at the snagged wood on the bench. 'And,' she said, a little nervously, 'I must have had the vision for a reason.'

'A reason,' Mia repeated. 'Or a hint,' she said, as though the two words were one and the same.

'So, where exactly are we going with this? You want to find the Athame?'

The corner of Mia's mouth curled upwards into a smile. 'There'd be no harm in looking for it. Wendolyn had it in the drawing room. We could walk past, and if it's still there, then . . . who knows?'

'Sure,' Kizzy agreed. 'It's probably not even there anyway . . .'

Mia knew they were goading each other just like before when they had entered the forest. Nonetheless she sprung up from the bench. 'Let's go.' Her eyes were energised at the prospect of the plan. She needed to know what her power was.

Kizzy joined her and the girls walked swiftly back towards the castle.

They crossed the dark courtyard and heaved open the sturdy castle door. Fortunately, the corridor was quiet and deserted, so they were able to skulk along it unnoticed. At the drawing room, they pushed the door ajar and peeked inside. The grand room lay dim and empty, with only a handful of the candles now flickering with a warm orange glow.

'Creepy,' Kizzy remarked. Her eyes drifted over the lifelike oil paintings hanging on the shadowed walls.

Mia tiptoed to the head of the room where Wendolyn had stood hours earlier. Immediately she caught sight of the Athame, which was draped over a wall-mounted brass candlestick. She stood before it, so close that the blazing candle flame reflected in her eyes like fire on ice.

The razor-sharp blade glinted, beckoning her. Mia obliged, edging forwards until she was near enough to make out every inscription and symbolic mark that had been engraved on to it.

'Kizzy,' Mia whispered, transfixed by the Athame. 'It's here. What should I do?'

Kizzy trotted over and inspected the dagger, full of awe.

Tentatively, Mia reached out and touched the smooth blade. It sent a wave of electricity through her fingertip. She recoiled in shock.

'Did it hurt?' Kizzy asked, looking down at Mia's hand.

'No,' Mia responded in a somewhat detached voice. 'It felt . . . good.' Unthinking, she lifted the Athame's chain up over the candlestick.

Kizzy's mouth went dry. She watched the scene with tense trepidation. Merely by holding the Athame in her hands, Mia had somehow transformed into a powerful being, radiating a magnificent strength.

'I love it,' Mia whispered. 'I feel as though it belongs to me.'

Kizzy giggled nervously. 'OK, let's not get carried away . . .'

'I'm going to put it on,' Mia told her. Without waiting for a response, she twisted her hair to the side and slipped the chain over her head, letting it drop around her neck. The Athame rested against her chest, its blade cold through her thin cotton top.

'Now what?' Kizzy asked in a choked voice. 'Do you feel any different?'

Mia nodded her head slowly. She did feel different, but suddenly she didn't feel quite so powerful any more. Nor did she feel as though the Athame belonged to her. In fact, she felt extraordinarily weak – as though *she* now belonged to *it*.

'Mia?' Kizzy's face clouded with concern.

'I need to take it off,' Mia rasped, suddenly gripped by the sensation of suffocation. It was as though the air was being squeezed out of her lungs. 'I need to . . .' The words caught in her throat.

She tried to lift her hands, but she was too weak even for that. The Athame burdened her, draining the life from her. It was far too strong for her.

Kizzy grabbed the chain from Mia's neck, but a spark shot out from the Athame and sent her hurtling across the room. She collided into the wall with such immense force that the impact cracked the mahogany wood. Slumping to the floor, Kizzy lay unconscious on the dull-red carpet.

Mia staggered backwards, gasping for air. The Athame clamped tighter to her, burning through the material of her top and attaching itself to her skin. As its essence flowed through her, it erupted into a flood of emotion – a flow too intense for a human to handle. Mia's head whirled with emotion and her eyes overflowed with anguished tears. It was as if all the pain, all the fear and all the power of the witches who had ever handled the dagger were being transmitted to her in a single, searing moment.

The Athame had taken control of her, overpowering her and absorbing her life force. She felt herself begin to lose consciousness. As her vision started to speckle and blur, she glimpsed the distorted sight of the drawing room door opening.

At an unnaturally swift speed, Colt was upon her. He clasped the Athame from her chest and raised his free hand, directing his palm towards Mia. An inexplicable gust of air exploded through the room, propelling Mia backwards and snapping the chain from around her neck. Her head clipped sharply against a brass candlestick, and she dropped to the floor with a thud.

Colt clenched the Athame in his fist, the broken chain dangling down like the tail of a mouse caught in a cat's jaw.

He let out a vicious growl. 'Fool!' he spat.

Mia cowered on the floor, a trickle of ruby-red blood dripping down from her temple.

Lotan appeared on the scene, stalking across the room to Colt's side. He took the Athame from Colt and slid it into a sheath on his belt. Lotan's eyes were vacant, but even in the darkness Colt's eyes flamed with an impossible rage.

'Argh!' Colt roared. He gripped his head with both hands, as though he were battling a ferocious demon inside his mind. His fingers became entangled with strands of his raven-black hair. 'I can't stop it,' he seethed. 'I'll kill her.'

Lotan said nothing. He simply stood and watched patiently. The new glint in his eyes showed that he was anticipating a bloodbath. And that he would relish in it.

Mia looked up at them in horror. Her face was ashen, striped with tears and a solitary trickle of blood. She had been freed from the Athame's hold only to come face to face with an equally dangerous threat: Hunters.

She glanced at Kizzy, who lay motionless on the other side of the room.

Then Lotan spoke for the first time. 'Give in to it,' he said to Colt in a low, fluid voice.

Until that moment, Colt had been resisting his wrath, but

on Lotan's command he dropped his hands from his head. Raising his left hand, he turned his palm to face Mia. He no longer struggled but slipped into a serene trancelike state.

And then Mia felt a coil of air close in around her throat, seizing her as though it were a solid mass, as though it was an invisible snake. Somehow Colt was manipulating the air to strangle her.

Their eyes locked intensely as he relentlessly wrung the life out of her.

4

Come to Me

Consumed by fury, Colt held his hand steadily, his palm facing Mia. He unremittingly commanded the air to close in around her throat, tighter and tighter. Mia coughed and wheezed, clawing at the invisible snake, but her attempts were futile. There was no turning back now. He would kill her.

And then something collided into him, snapping him out of his trance and sending him crashing into the furniture.

Thoroughly disoriented, Colt pushed his attacker off of him.

It was Dino.

Before Lotan could descend on him, Dino scrambled over to Mia and hauled her upright.

She staggered and gasped hungrily for air. Colt's hold on her had been broken, but her throat burned in the aftermath.

In a split second Colt was back on his feet. He swiftly sliced his hand through the air and a strong breeze blasted through the room, knocking both Dino and Mia to the floor.

Lotan circled them, his eyes narrowing vengefully. He was like a lion ready to pounce.

Colt looked on, hesitantly. 'Lotan!' he barked. 'Not here!'

Lotan continued to slowly circle his quarry. But his eyes flickered to Colt. The boys seemed to be communicating silently.

And then in a flash, Lotan lunged at Mia. But he didn't

harm her – he simply licked the trail of blood from her temple and then darted out of the room. Colt was hot on his heels and in the blink of an eye they were both gone.

Mia and Dino looked at one another in horror.

Mia hastily wiped her face. 'What was that?' she stuttered. Her voice was hoarse and scratchy.

Dino eyed the smear of blood on her face. 'I don't know. They're disgusting. Probably best not to think about it.' He collapsed back on to the floor with a rough breath. 'Are you OK?' he asked, looking up at the dark ceiling.

'I'm alive,' she answered loosely. 'Thanks for that.' She smiled.

Dino tried to hide his own smile. 'You're welcome.' He sat up and shook out his arms. 'But that was a one-off,' he added with a scowl.

Mia leaned over and hugged him.

Although Dino didn't reciprocate the hug, he didn't pull away either. He sat, staring at the wall, and letting her rest her head on his shoulder.

'Besides,' he added quietly, 'Cassandra and Madeline would never let me hear the end of it if something happened to you.'

Dino had started calling his mother by her first name a long time ago. It had begun as a rebellious act, but then it had just sort of stuck. In truth, he didn't want to call her 'Mother'. Why should he, when he didn't feel like her child? In fact, he didn't feel as though he were a part of the family at all. He wondered sometimes if they resented him for being male. It wasn't as though his mother and aunt were out-and-out feminists or anything, but they weren't the most trusting of women. Somewhere along the line, men had become the enemy.

And sometimes, when Madeline was feeling particularly sour or when Dino was indulging in an especially bad-tempered mood, she would not spare him from telling him what a disappointment he was. She would rant on about how saddened his mother had been to find out that she was having a boy, and then how happy they both were when Mia was finally born.

To this, Dino would curtly reply, 'You're a poisonous old hag. You're so bitter that no man can stand you. You've driven away every man in your life – your boyfriends, my uncles . . .'

'How dare you!' Madeline would scream, flapping her arms around feverishly.

But her protests would not stop Dino. 'And you even drove away your own sister's husband – my father!'

'Your father was a vile man!' Madeline would scream. 'And you should thank us for driving him away.'

'*Thank you*?' Dino would splutter. 'I resent you for it. If it wasn't for you, my father would still be here. But instead I'm alone in this hellhole with you three witches!' Little did he know at the time just how accurate his statement was.

'I wish your father had taken you with him! I for one would be glad to see the back of you!' Madeline retorted before storming off in a whirlwind of anger, hurt and bitterness. But never more than an hour would pass before the guilt set in. She would appear at his bedroom door with a plate of cookies and a please-forgive-me expression. Of course, they would make amends and all would be forgotten – until the next time.

Dino accepted the way things were. And he supposed he was fond of his aunt in some ways. And his mother, too, for that matter. It wasn't a question of not liking them – more that he was just distanced from them.

The irony of it all was that Dino's detachment from his mother had stemmed from his belief that she did not love him. But as soon as his powers began to come to light, he was suddenly able to feel the true extent of her love for him. Or, more accurately, he *heard* it. It turned out that her love was quite insurmountable – which was a surprise to say the least. And as luck would have it, of all of the painful sounds drilling through his head, love was the mildest.

All things considered, he supposed that he loved her, too. But then there was Mia, and that was a different situation entirely. He had adored Mia from the day that she was born. Everyone did. And as soon as Dino had been able to, he would carry Mia around, introducing her to all of the wonderful things in the world that she was too young to discover for herself, like flowers, insects, and thunderstorms, and the wide blue sky.

However, as they grew older, he rebelled against her, too. She became just another female with whom he was forced to live. But deep down, he'd never stopped adoring her. He simply couldn't.

And now, almost completely grown, her eyes were still those same innocent grey eyes that had looked up at her first thunderstorm with curious fear. Dino hoped that she would always retain those childlike eyes, even if they lived on a woman's face.

In the dim light of the drawing room, Dino untangled himself from the hug and looked down upon her eyes for a second. Yes, they were still the same.

'Kizzy,' Mia mumbled, dazed, as she recalled her friend's presence. Shakily, she rose to her feet and hobbled across the room to where Kizzy lay.

Mia crouched down and tapped her face gently. 'Kizzy,' she said in a clear, crisp voice.

Dino knelt beside Kizzy and shook her.

'Be careful!' Mia scolded him.

But Kizzy blearily opened her eyes. She glanced around, somewhat confused. 'What happened?'

'I think you hit your head,' Mia told her, glimpsing up to the crack in the wall that illustrated just how hard the blow had been.

'Ow!' Kizzy moaned as she rubbed at her bruised scalp. 'The Athame,' she murmured indistinctly.

'Everything's fine,' Mia assured her, not wishing to delve straight into the details.

Kizzy's eyes fell upon Dino. 'Is this your brother?' she drowsily asked Mia.

Dino edged away self-consciously. He could sense the girl's wariness of him. But for some reason it wasn't screaming quite so stridently any more. It was now merely an awareness.

'Yes,' Mia replied significantly. 'He's my brother.'

That night Mia crawled into bed. But she was uncomfortably aware that it wasn't her bed. The sheets felt new and stiff – not like the soft, worn sheets she was used to at home. She wondered if the lavish bedchamber would ever feel like home.

Resting her head on the duck-feather pillow, she peered out through a gap in her bed curtains. Dino paced around the room rigidly. His hands were balled into fists and his breathing was ragged.

'What's the matter?' she asked quietly.

'For God's sake!' he snapped. 'Don't pity me! It's a horrible sound.'

Mia couldn't begin to comprehend the severity of what he was saying. In fact, she had absolutely no idea what he was going through.

Dino's pain had lessened greatly throughout the day. But now, alone in the room with Mia, he had lost his control over it and it devoured him once more.

In a rage, he picked up a lamp and threw it across the room, tearing the plug from its socket. The glass bulb shattered upon impact with the floor.

Mia gasped. 'Have you lost your mind?'

'No!' he shouted. 'I've gained yours!'

Mia sat up in bed, the blankets pulled up around her. 'What?'

He pressed his knuckles to his mouth. 'Your mind is . . . deafening.'

'You can hear my thoughts?' She suddenly felt very exposed.

'No,' he said in frustration. 'I can hear your *feelings*.'

Mia frowned. 'How do you mean?'

'There's no other way to explain it!' he exclaimed. 'You feel happy, I hear it. You feel sad, I hear it. You feel scared, I hear it. It's like the annoyance of having to talk to you without the luxury of escape!'

'Wow. So that's your power?'

'It's not a power,' Dino groused. 'There are no benefits to it.'

'I'm sure there . . .'

'Shut up, Mia!' he interrupted her curtly. 'Just shut up.'

Mia closed the gap in the bed curtains and pulled the covers up over her head. Much to her bother's dismay, she could feel a lump forming in her throat. 'Turn the light off,' she snapped crossly.

Beneath the thin white bed sheets, she noted the bedroom lights dimming. She lay there for a while in the darkness, listening to the sound of Dino pacing back and forth, and then eventually retreat to his bed. She heard the drapes being drawn and that was the last thing she remembered before falling asleep.

But her sleep was not a restful one. Images of Hunters haunted her dreams, warping them into nightmares. She saw Colt's eyes blazing with wrath as he morphed into a grotesque, gnarled monster. And then his eyes grew larger and larger until eventually the deep-green colour blended and distorted into the forest. Mia watched herself step inside the bottomless pupil, which had now transformed into a tunnel leading through the forest. A portal leading into a merciless unknown land.

She felt the air close in around her throat, just as it had done in the drawing room. But this time it wasn't choking her – it simply settled on her neck like a dog's collar. She was being dragged by an invisible leash further along the tunnel.

And then she heard a strange whispering in her ear. The words were indistinguishable, but the voice was familiar. Where had she heard that menacing voice before? The whispers grew louder, more commanding. Gradually it became clear. It was Lotan.

'Come to me,' Lotan said firmly.

Mia opened her eyes with a jolt. The room was dark and silent, just as she remembered it. But now, her cotton pyjamas were drenched in sweat and her hands were clenched together so tightly that her fingernails had pierced the skin on her palms.

Automatically, she climbed out of bed and strode to the bedroom door. Somewhere in the back of her consciousness a voice screamed at her not to go. But it was out of her hands. She realised that the warning voice was her own, but it was eclipsed by the much stronger voice of Lotan. She was going; the only thing that she didn't know was where.

Barefoot, she pattered down the staircase and stepped out into the courtyard. The stones and gravel dug into her feet, but she hardly noticed. She carried on walking, beneath the hedge archway and out into the gardens. As she moved, her body felt weightless, almost as though it no longer belonged to her. It was like she was being carried. Or *pulled*.

In the dead of night everything about the gardens seemed different. No longer were they beautiful and inviting. Now, under the ebony sky, the neat topiary hedges looked like looming demons.

But they were of no concern to Mia; her fate was elsewhere. She continued marching on, closing in on the wall of mist that cloaked the pine trees. However, that night the mist wasn't the translucent grey that she had witnessed before. It was now an opaque purple – just like the strange smoke that had engorged the basement of her home.

As Mia descended the grassy embankment, a breeze swirled through her silken hair. It swept the strands back from her face, exposing her ethereal beauty – an ageless beauty that seemed to be exuded directly from her soul.

With each stride she took, the breeze seemed to play with her, toying with her hair and wrapping itself around her legs and arms.

When she reached the mist, Mia hesitated. The breeze subsided and the night abruptly felt unnaturally still. Everything was quiet.

But, although she heard no sound, there was still something calling to her.

Mia outstretched her arm, touching the purple mist with her fingertips. Seductively it took her hand, urging her in further. And she obliged, stepping into it until it swallowed her.

She walked mechanically until something dived in front of her path. Its deep-green eyes were visible even through the dense mist.

In alarm, Mia opened her mouth to scream. But the sound caught in her throat as Colt plummeted his hand through the mist, causing an immense ripple of air to catapult her backwards. She hit the ground with a smack and kept rolling, as though she had been thrown from a moving vehicle.

'Ow!' she groaned, her face pressed into the dewy grass.

'Mia!' another familiar voice called her name. 'What on earth are you doing out here?' It was Wendolyn, dressed in a nightgown and shawl, her white hair plaited to the side.

Mia blinked dazedly. *Out where?* she wondered. It took

her several seconds to realise that she was in fact outside. But for the life of her she couldn't understand why. The memory of walking out into the gardens was vague, but present nonetheless. What she couldn't fathom, however, was what had possibly motivated her to do such a thing. It was a complete mystery.

She looked down at her muddy bare feet, and then looked to the thick mist that shrouded the forest. Considering the distance between her and the mist, it was almost unfeasible that she had ever stepped into it. Could a blast of air have really thrown her so far away from it? A part of her wondered if she had been sleepwalking and imagined the whole thing.

'Mia!' Wendolyn said as she helped her to her feet. 'Why are you out here?' she repeated the question, now with a note of urgency.

'I don't know,' Mia stammered.

'Let me take you back inside,' Wendolyn offered. She gently but hastily guided Mia up the embankment and back towards the castle.

Seeming a little troubled, Wendolyn led Mia to the library and urged her to take a seat. Mia willingly cooperated.

'My dear,' Wendolyn said compassionately, 'what made you go outside? Were you heading for the forest?'

'I think so,' Mia admitted weakly.

'But you know that it's not safe,' the older woman said.

'Yes. I'm sorry.' There wasn't much more that she could say.

'Just like your mother!' Wendolyn chuckled with a trace of uneasiness. 'Always getting up to mischief!'

Mia frowned. 'My mother?' That didn't sound much like her mother at all. In fact, Cassandra was notoriously sensible and prudent. 'Don't you mean my aunt?'

'Oh, well, I suppose that Madeline was no saint, either!' Wendolyn smiled. 'But Madeline was more noncompliant whereas your mother . . . well, she was merely a free spirit in search of adventure.'

'I'm not looking for adventure,' Mia explained. 'I really don't know why I went to the forest.'

'Oh, I believe you,' Wendolyn reassured her. 'You'll have to excuse me; I was simply indulging in my memories.'

Mia smiled. 'Actually, it's interesting to find out what my mother was like at my age.'

'I see a lot of her character present in you,' Wendolyn divulged. 'And in your brother, too.'

'Really?'

'Very much so.' Wendolyn paused for a moment. 'Mia,' she said, 'you must not go out to the forest again.'

'I won't,' Mia replied, hoping that she would be able to keep her promise.

'You're unsure?'

'You read my thoughts?' Mia guessed.

Wendolyn chortled. 'No. Sometimes I don't need to.'

'Oh.' Mia blushed.

'The reason why I ask for you to stay away is for your own safety. Do you understand?'

Mia nodded her head.

'Now more than ever you must exert caution,' Wendolyn went on, her voice grave. 'You see, I've picked up on a presence around the forest boundaries. Hunters. A coven, I believe.'

The hairs on the back of Mia's neck bristled. 'Lotan and Colt?'

'No, no.' Wendolyn shook her head. 'Lotan and Colt are a part of the Glass Castle just as much as the Arcana. In fact, the forest is their domain. What I've picked up on is activity just beyond *our* forestland.'

'More Hunters?' Mia exclaimed in dismay.

'Perhaps. Their presence is imprecise.'

'Why are they here?'

'I can't be sure,' Wendolyn mused. 'Try not to fret. They'll be no bother to you. They're simply unwelcome guests. I imagine they're here out of curiosity more than anything. But while the threat is at large, you must be extra vigilant.'

'Do you think they'll leave?' Mia asked.

'Eventually, I'm sure. Once I've located them, I will find a way to exile them.' She smiled at Mia. 'Try not to worry,' she said again. 'They're not here for you.'

5

The Language of the Rain

Over the next few days the rain began. And it didn't stop. It lashed down constantly in a barrage of bulging raindrops. It was as though someone had pulled the plug from the sky and there was no way of resealing it.

As it happened, the miserable weather was an apt reflection of Mia's mood. No longer did she possess the naive hope that her power would eventually come to her. Now, she was surer than ever that a mistake had been made. And to top things off, she and Dino had drifted even further apart. Their argument in the bedchamber days before had sparked a chain of quarrels, which gradually escalated to the point of their scarcely speaking at all.

Mia sighed as she ambled into the drawing room. Imprisoned by the rain, the Arcana had come to depend on the drawing room as a port in the storm, so to speak.

Keen to avoid socialising, Mia awkwardly dragged a hefty armchair over to the window, deliberately closing herself off from the rest of the room. She curled up on the chair and watched the rain as it blanketed the courtyard. Cosily wrapped in her soft cream jumper and a pair of jeans, she gazed up at the black rain clouds, amazed by how such swollen, heavy things could float so effortlessly in the moody sky.

The drawing-room door burst open and Kizzy trudged in. Her canary-yellow raincoat was fastened to the top and rainwater from her blonde hair dripped steadily on to the carpet. She grabbed an unoccupied armchair and hauled it to the window, arranging it beside Mia.

'You call this summer?' she remarked huffily, clambering into the chair.

'Hmm,' Mia agreed distantly.

Kizzy unbuttoned her raincoat and wriggled out of it. 'Still no luck with the power?'

'Nope.'

'Have you talked to Wendolyn?' Kizzy asked.

'Yep.'

'And?'

Mia shrugged. 'She says to look inside my heart.'

Kizzy rolled her eyes. 'I hate it when people say that. It doesn't even make any sense!'

'Tell me about it.' Mia forced a weak smile. All things considered, she didn't feel much like talking. Not to Wendolyn, not to Kizzy, not to anyone.

Blissfully oblivious, Kizzy shook the water from her coat and then discarded it on to the floor. 'Is there anything I can do to cheer you up?' she asked thoughtfully.

Mia's smile was genuine this time. 'No, I'm fine,' she replied. 'How's your Seer ability coming along?' She pried her attention away from the window. Even if her own power was nonexistent, it didn't mean that she couldn't be happy for her friend.

'It's OK. So-so,' Kizzy said, purposely downplaying her success. The truth was, Kizzy's power had accelerated quickly. Her control was growing stronger, and her visions were noticeably sharper and more precise. In fact, she'd been seeing more than she could have anticipated – including some unnerving images, many of which she felt she should warn Mia of. But something held her back.

*

Across the room, two other new friends sat together deliberating their own skills. Dino and Blue . . . and a tower of buttons.

Blue stretched out his fingers. 'One more t . . . try,' he decided. Evidently on edge, he sprinkled a dusting of ciron thistle into the palm of his hand. He clamped his fingers down over it and tapped the closed fist.

'Well?' Dino asked, feigning hope.

Blue cursed at the little brown button that nestled in his palm. 'This must be the h . . . hundredth one t . . . today,' he muttered dejectedly.

'Nah.' Dino subtly kicked a pile of buttons beneath the sofa. 'There hasn't been that many,' he lied.

Blue stared despondently at the button in his hand. His honey-coloured eyes were bleak.

'Don't worry about it. Who cares?' Dino said brazenly. He picked up a deck of cards and began skilfully shuffling them. 'Wanna play Switch?'

Blue looked down at the button once more, then threw it in frustration. It became apparent to him that he must have lobbed it harder than he had intended, because it soared across the room and hit a boy in the back of the head.

'Hey! Who did that?' the boy yelled, scanning the room for his assailant. Then he noticed the button lying dormant on the floor. 'Oh, right!' he cackled loudly. 'Button boy! Hey, loser!' he shouted to Blue. 'Keep your buttons to yourself!'

Blue bowed his head in shame.

But Dino's reaction was quite different. He slammed the deck of cards down against the coffee table. 'You better watch your mouth, Patterson!' he threatened the boorish boy.

'Oh, yeah? What are you gonna do about it?' the boy retorted.

Dino spluttered with rage. He leapt from his seat and thundered across the room.

Unsurprisingly, the loudmouth boy began to lose some of

his bravado. 'Hey, relax,' he said anxiously. 'It was just a joke.'

All of a sudden, everyone in the room fell silent, their eyes fixed on Dino with a mixture of alarm and excitement. Hastily, Mia sprung to her feet, rushing to her brother's side.

'Dino! Calm down!' she ordered, grasping his arm before he could reach his rival.

Dino glanced at her briefly and shook free from her hold.

Soon Blue and Kizzy were both on the scene, too.

'Forget h . . . him,' Blue urged.

Dino grimaced. Why were they all jumping on him like this? *I'm not the one in the wrong*, he thought petulantly.

Mia renewed her clasp on his arm. 'Look,' she said, 'you've made your point.' Her eyes drifted to the boy who was now cowered behind a chair, half-heartedly trying to retain some of his masculinity by occasionally puffing out his chest.

'Aaron Patterson,' Kizzy grumbled under her breath. 'He's such a moron. I say hit him!'

'Kizzy!' Mia exclaimed.

'Sorry,' she grinned puckishly.

Dino relaxed slightly. Until then, he hadn't even realised how taut his shoulders had been.

Aaron cleared his throat. 'I was only having a bit of fun. It was a joke,' he excused himself feebly.

'A joke?' Dino scowled. 'Didn't seem like a joke to me.' He reluctantly allowed Mia to drag him back to his seat, where he slumped irritably. Gradually the rest of the room lost interest in the fracas and the former indistinct drone of chatter resumed.

'I should have hit him,' Dino muttered tersely.

'Why?' Mia questioned. 'So you can prove what a big man you are?'

'No,' he glared at her. 'So I can prove what a big man he *isn't*.'

Blue laughed quietly at the statement.

The response brought a smug smile to Dino's lips. 'That Patterson's an idiot,' he remarked complacently, more to Blue than anyone else.

But Dino wasn't the only one whose attention was on Blue. Kizzy appeared to be observing him as though she recognised him from somewhere. 'You're Benny Blue,' she said at last. 'The Conjurer, right?'

Blue nodded his head.

'Wendolyn mentioned there was a Conjurer here. It's nice to finally meet you,' Kizzy held out her hand amiably. 'My name's Kizzy.'

'I know,' Blue admitted shyly. He shook her hand.

Nonchalantly, Dino propped his elbow up on the arm of the chair and rested his head on his fist. 'Blue, this is my sister, Mia,' he said with obvious disinterest.

'Hi, Blue,' Mia acknowledged him, but her eyes were still on Dino.

'Drop it, Mia,' Dino grumbled under his breath.

She raised her eyebrows at him.

'You know what?' Dino suddenly snapped at her, dropping his arm down sharply. 'You can stop thinking your feelings of disapproval. Because I can hear them loud and clear. And it's annoying.'

'Stop telling me what to think and feel!' she cried. 'Get out of my head!'

'Get out of mine!' Dino shouted back.

Mia folded her arms crossly. 'It's not my fault that you're . . .'

'Seriously!' Dino bellowed at her. 'Get away from me!'

Mia bit her tongue to stop herself from verbally opening fire on him – it was either that or bursting into tears. She held her dignity and simply turned and walked calmly away.

'Mia!' Kizzy called after her.

'I'm OK,' Mia insisted as Kizzy trotted up to her. 'I just need to take a walk.'

'I'll come with you,' Kizzy offered. 'I'll grab my coat.' She glanced over to the window where her raincoat lay sprawled out on the floor, still drenched from her last outing.

Although company would have probably been wise, Mia just wanted to be alone. 'No,' she said. 'I'm fine, honestly.'

Kizzy furrowed her brow uncertainly. 'Are you sure?'

'Yep.' Mia nodded and faked a cheery smile.

Although Kizzy wasn't fooled, she surrendered and waved goodbye as Mia paced out of the room.

Mia left the shelter of the castle and carelessly wandered out into the pouring rain. Within a matter of seconds she was thoroughly drenched. Her delicate cream jumper was instantly saturated and it clung uneasily to her skin, weighed down by the overload of water. Her chocolate-brown hair hung in thick darkened tresses, dripping down her back.

But none of this seemed to discourage her. She walked swiftly across the abandoned courtyard and through the hedge archway. She hadn't been back to the forest since her late-night encounter with Wendolyn, and she didn't intend ever going back, either. She just needed to get out of the castle for a while, even if that meant roaming around the gardens in the rain.

As she weaved in and out of the flower beds, she began to notice how grim everything seemed. The neat rows of dainty pink flowers drooped sadly in the flooded soil, struggling to stand tall as the rain hammered down on them. High above, the murky sky swirled and churned.

Mia suddenly realised how desperately she wanted to leave the Glass Castle. She wanted to go home. Besides, what reason was there for her to be there? As far as she was concerned, she had no power. And even if she was wrong, her power was inactive anyway, so what was the difference?

The pattering sound of rain echoed all around her, louder

and more defined than she had ever heard before. It was almost as though it was raining just for her, and speaking to her in a secret language that she felt obliged to understand. In fact, she felt as though she should have been able to understand it, but for some reason couldn't.

Of course I can't understand it! she reminded herself with a little laugh. *It's just rain. It's not speaking to me.*

Still lost in her own thoughts, Mia reached the embankment that signified the end of the gardens. The forest was in sight now, vast and brooding in the dismal weather. Wary of straying too far away from Arcana territory, Mia stopped walking and sat down on the ridge of the embankment. What had once been parched soil with dry grass yellowed by the sun was now soggy mud that stained her jumper and jeans.

Mia pushed her wet hair back from her face and wiped the dripping rain from her eyes. But it was pointless, because the rain continued to pour, trickling down her cheeks like tears. And that was exactly what it felt like – all of the tears that she wanted to cry but was unable to. It was as though the rain was crying for her, releasing all of the pent-up emotion that had been bottled inside. In some ways, feeling the water on her face gave her a much needed sense of freedom, and she didn't want it to stop.

She gazed around the land. Beyond the embankment, the forest stood staunchly behind its silvery mist. A natural curiosity held her focus to it. She was at a safe enough distance to really study it, and she couldn't resist indulging in the temptation of doing so. After all, the forest held such mystery – it was impossible not to be intrigued by it. But the longer she watched it, the more uncomfortable it made her. Suddenly she felt extremely exposed, as though she was no longer simply watching, but was, in fact, being watched.

Mia glanced around, intimidated by the thought of eyes

upon her. There was no one around; she was alone. Although perhaps that wasn't a good thing.

When she looked back to the forest, the rain before her eyes seemed to distort her vision. It was as though the flow of rainfall was different somehow. And as it progressively worsened, she could barely see her own hand in front of her face. Now, the rain was no longer falling straight down, but rather it was dropping diagonally and in zigzag patterns, as though it had been caught in a ferocious whirlwind.

A familiar breeze caressed her wet hair. Mia stiffened instinctively. A Hunter was near.

Scrambling to her feet, she started to run, but blinded by the wild rain she could not make out her path. There was no time to get her bearings so she kept on running, silently praying that she was on course for the castle.

With some relief she noticed the waterlogged flower beds beneath her feet as she unwittingly trampled on them. At least now she knew that she was heading in the right direction. But her relief was premature, because with an unexpected smack she collided into something solid. For a moment she wondered if she'd run into one of the hedges. However, it quickly became clear that it wasn't, because whatever it was grabbed her, its fingers pressing into her arms. Through the barrier of rain, Mia glimpsed a pair of deep-green eyes looking down upon her. It was Colt.

Terrified and disoriented, Mia kicked out at him until her foot impacted with his shin. Colt didn't seem particularly affected, but nevertheless he submissively relinquished his hold on her. Almost *too* submissively.

Seeing her chance for escape, Mia turned and sprinted away from him. As she dashed across the sodden grass, she could sense him behind her, somehow walking yet matching her speed effortlessly.

Then, out of nowhere, Mia felt her foot skid across the

slick, muddy ground. She fell on to her back with a thud and slid downwards. It dawned on her that she was plummeting down the sloping embankment, unable to stop. Her hands groped frantically for anything that might save her from her descent, but she could only seize clumps of grass, which pitifully broke away in her clutches. As she tumbled down the incline, her jumper rose up, exposing her bare skin to the toothed, rutted ground. Finally, she reached the bottom of the slope with a thump. She lay motionless for a moment, bruised and cut.

But it wasn't long before she was forced to move again. In a daze, she rolled over on to her side. The rain still clouded her vision, but she saw Colt pounce to the ground just inches from her face, as though he had jumped from a much greater height.

Refusing to surrender to him, Mia clambered to her feet and bolted off in the opposite direction. Even though her body ached from the brutal fall, she staggered on as fast as she could manage, out of breath and limping.

The gentle sound of wind chimes rustled somewhere to the right, and in dismay, Mia realised what she was running towards.

He's driving me into the forest! she deduced in alarm. Perhaps all along, Colt had been the sheepdog, herding the defence-less lamb into its pen. And just like a lamb, she truly was defenceless.

Panting for breath, Mia knew that she had two choices: either to succumb to the forest or not to. She picked the latter. Following the sound of wind chimes, she changed direction and raced towards the graveyard.

The wind chimes grew louder and louder until she was directly beneath them. With a yelp, she crashed into a tall slab of stone. The hard gravestone knocked her to the ground and she slumped against it, exhausted and petrified.

All of a sudden the rain calmed and returned to its usual

flow, falling downwards as nature had intended and granting her an unaltered view.

But what she saw made her wish for the distortion of before. Colt stood above her, blocking her path and cornering her against the gravestone.

He smiled.

This time there was no escape.

6

Spangles' Grave

As the rain pounded down, Mia crouched on the ground, her arms shielding her face and her body pressing up against the rock gravestone. She squeezed her eyes shut, preparing for Colt's onslaught.

'Spangles won't like that,' Colt said in a smooth, even voice.

Mia cautiously opened her eyes. 'What?' she asked in a shaky stutter.

'Spangles.' Colt pointed to the gravestone. 'I'm sure he wouldn't think much of your crawling all over his grave like that.' He raised an eyebrow, seemingly a little bored. His ebony hair was stuck flat down from the rain, but remarkably he didn't flinch as the overspill trickled on to his face.

Reluctant to take her eyes off him, Mia quickly glanced at the headstone behind her. Sure enough, the word 'Spangles' had been etched into the stone in large, italic writing.

Mia turned her attention back to Colt. 'What are you going to do to me?' she asked in a tiny voice.

He shrugged offhandedly.

Mia's hands flew to her throat. Was it her imagination, or could she feel the air closing in on her again?

'Stop!' she gasped.

Colt looked at her with a bemused expression. 'I'm not doing anything.'

She drew in several deep breaths. Perhaps it had been her mind playing tricks on her after all.

Colt frowned. 'How very dramatic,' he muttered under his breath.

'But, before . . .' Mia trailed off. She blinked fearfully up at him, remembering those eyes which had locked with hers as he'd tried to choke the life out of her just days before.

'The drawing room,' Colt acknowledged. 'I suppose you would like an apology for that.'

Mia swallowed nervously. 'OK,' she stammered.

'It wasn't a question.' The corner of Colt's mouth twitched in amusement. 'Merely a statement.'

'OK,' Mia repeated, utterly baffled by the whole exchange.

'Oh, stop being silly!' he said abruptly. 'Are you really that desperate for an apology? That was a question, by the way.'

'Uh . . .' Mia was knocked for six. She didn't care about an apology – she was simply confused by the interaction. Her terrifying attacker was suddenly talking to her so casually, as if they were old friends.

'No.' He shook his head stubbornly, raindrops spilling from the drenched strands of hair. 'I won't apologise. I refuse. But I will admit that I could have exercised more restraint. Happy?'

Mia held her palms skyward. 'Um . . . yes?'

'Why are you asking me?' Colt demanded.

'Because I have absolutely no idea what to say to you!' Mia blurted out.

Colt mumbled irritably to himself. Then, with a submissive sigh, he said, 'The night you stole the Athame . . . I am willing to admit that perhaps I should have contained my temper. I'm sure I tried, but it's quite complex. Once it starts . . . Anyway, I feel that's apology enough. Shall we move on?'

'Move on to what?' Mia gulped. She could feel the cold, wet gravestone through her saturated jumper; try as she might, she couldn't move back any farther. Maybe she could run, but she guessed that she wouldn't get very far.

Colt let out a throaty chuckle. 'Relax. I'm not here to harm you. I want to ask something of you.'

Mia's mind raced. What could he possibly want to ask her? Was he blackmailing her? Did he want her to do his sordid biddings? 'I won't kill,' she declared drastically, feeling particularly proud of her fearless display of nobility.

Colt slapped his hand to his head. 'Oh, good Lord,' he muttered. 'Don't be so ridiculous!'

'Then what do you want from me?' she demanded, beginning to feel a fraction braver. She tried her best to look powerful and confident – although it was rather difficult with rain dribbling in and out of her mouth as she spoke. 'I am powerful,' she bragged. 'Yes, very powerful . . . Actually, I'm the most powerful witch of all time. And I am not to be tested.'

Colt wrinkled his nose in distaste. 'Anyway,' he went on, completely ignoring her, 'I want you to stop the rain. I suppose I should say please. It's not in my nature to do so, but I understand that your kind love it. So puh-lease. How did that sound? Believable?'

Mia gawped at him. 'What are you talking about?'

'Please. Puh-lease. That's the correct word, isn't it?'

'Yes, please is the right word,' she said distractedly. 'But I don't understand why you're saying it to me. I can't stop the rain. It's just a . . . thing.'

Colt folded his arms. 'Why are you being difficult? I said please, didn't I? Is this still about the incident with the Athame?'

'No.' Mia looked at him as though he were insane. 'This is about me not being able to control the weather.' For a moment, she wondered if maybe he had actually believed her proclamation about being all powerful. *Am I really that convincing a liar?* she mused, secretly impressed by the idea.

'I see. You insist on being stubborn. So I suppose we all must continue to suffer.' His dark-green eyes bore into her, patronisingly disappointed by her supposedly rebellious behaviour.

Mia threw up her hands. 'I'm sorry, but I really can't stop the rain,' she stated firmly.

'Yes, you can.'

'No, I can't.'

'Yes, you *can*.'

Mia narrowed her eyes. 'No, I can't.'

'Yes – you – can,' Colt insisted, enunciating each word perfectly.

The back-and-forth debate was driving Mia crazy. 'No, I can't!' she screamed. 'How do you expect me to stop the rain? It's beyond my control!'

'You're doing it. You can stop it.'

'Doing what? I'm not doing anything,' Mia protested.

Impatiently, Colt clicked his tongue on the roof of his mouth. 'You're making it rain,' he told her.

'And how exactly would I manage that?' she challenged.

'I'm not a mind reader!' Colt exclaimed. 'How am I supposed to know what puts you females in your foul moods?'

'I'm not in a bad mood,' Mia argued defensively.

Colt eyed her with an infuriatingly dubious expression.

'And even if I *were* in a bad mood,' Mia carried on, 'I'm certainly not making it rain. It's just nature.'

'No, it's you.'

'Stop saying that! I wouldn't have the faintest idea how to make weather like this!' She cupped her hands together, catching the bombardment of droplets in her palms.

Colt smirked. 'I thought you were the most powerful witch of all time,' he mimicked her, mockingly.

'I am,' Mia retorted. 'But I can't make rain. I'm not . . .' She racked her brain for an appropriate example. '. . . I'm not Rain Man,' she said at last.

'Rain Man didn't create rain,' Colt corrected her. 'It was just his nickname.'

'Oh. Well, anyway, this isn't my doing.' Mia looked up to the gloomy, purple sky.

'Yes, it is.'

'Stop it!' Mia wailed. He was relentless!

'It looks like you. It smells like you. How else can I put this? It *is* you.'

She stared blankly at him. 'Huh?'

'You're everywhere,' he elaborated, although without much clarity. 'You're a Tempestus, yes?'

'What's a Temptestus?'

Exasperated, Colt rubbed at his temples. 'Oh, for God's sake,' he muttered, 'not a Temptestus. A Tempestus. That's what you are.'

Mia was visibly dumbfounded.

'This is just pathetic. Do I have to spoon-feed everything to you?' Colt grumbled.

'OK,' Mia replied sheepishly.

'That wasn't an offer,' Colt snapped. 'You're a Tempestus. You have the ability to manipulate the elements. You do know what the elements are, don't you?' he checked, half jokingly.

'Um . . .' she pondered it. 'Atoms?'

'No, no, no,' Colt cut her off intolerantly. 'The elements: earth, air, fire and water. Are you familiar with those words?'

Mia scowled at him. 'Yes.'

'Good. You command them.'

Mia fell silent. On the one hand, she was elated at the prospect that she may have actually found her power. On the other hand, how could she trust what Colt was saying? He was a Hunter, after all. And up until a few minutes ago, she was under the impression that they were mortal enemies. Besides, how could he possibly know?

She decided to verbalise her misgivings. 'How can I trust you? How do you even know this about me?'

Colt laughed brashly. 'Darling,' he droned, somewhat intimately, 'I don't want your trust. It makes no difference to me whether you believe me or not. But, to answer your question, I recognise you as a Tempestus because I'm one, too.'

Mia was momentarily taken aback. 'Well, then, maybe you're the one making the rain. Have you ever considered that?'

In a show of absolute frustration, Colt knotted his fingers through his soaked hair. 'I'm not. You are. Now be a good girl and stop it, because it's highly annoying.' He paused, and then added archly, 'As are you.'

Mia contemplated the thought dreamily. 'I'm a Tempestus,' she murmured in a euphoric tone.

'Yes. And a fabulous one at that . . . I'm being sarcastic, of course.'

'What can I do?' Mia asked, suddenly enthralled.

'Not much, by the looks of things.' Colt tapped his foot against the waterlogged ground. 'Making it rain seems to be your forte,' he added dryly.

'No, I mean, what will I be able to do? What can a Tempestus do?'

'You'll figure it out,' Colt said with clear indifference.

'No!' Mia cried. 'That's all anyone ever says! Please teach me. Puh-lease,' she imitated his previous use of the word.

Although he tried to resist it, Colt cracked a smile. Reluctantly he ran his hands over his face. 'OK,' he said finally, 'I won't teach you, but I will give you a demonstration.'

Mia's slate-grey eyes lit up like twinkling stars. Miraculously, the more enthused she became, the more the rain subsided.

True to his word, Colt raised his hand and swiftly turned his palm skyward. All the while his eyes remained locked on Mia.

She gasped as a forceful rush of air lifted her to a standing position. Disoriented, she clutched on to Spangles' gravestone, steadying herself. It was as though the air had literally picked her up off the ground. In fact, she supposed that was exactly what it had done. She gazed around the graveyard in disbelief.

Quickly, Colt drew his outstretched hand into his body. 'Look at me,' he ordered, and a gust of air firmly tilted her face back towards him.

'That's incredible,' Mia breathed.

'*I'm* incredible,' Colt amended boastfully.

'Did you distort the rain?' Mia asked, all of a sudden piecing together the bizarre rainstorm that had driven her to the graveyard.

'Yes.'

'Why?'

'Because I wanted you to stay still. I thought if I blurred your vision it would hold you in one place.'

Mia's lips pressed together into a pretty smile. 'But it didn't.'

'No, it did not.'

'Why didn't you just tell me that you wanted to talk?' she asked.

Colt grinned. 'Because I was having fun.'

Mia rolled her eyes. 'Glad my terror was so entertaining for you,' she said wryly. 'How did you do it, anyway?'

'Watch,' he instructed. Smoothly, he raised his index finger and spun it in a fluid, circular motion. The light dusting of rain between them spun like a tornado and then plunged to the ground with a splash.

'Am I able to do these things, too?' Mia pressed.

'Perhaps,' he responded aloofly. 'But you'll never attain my standard of excellence.'

Mia focused on a puddle of rainwater. She directed her palm towards it, awaiting a reaction. Nothing happened.

Colt chuckled. 'You're absurd!' he said brightly.

Mia frowned. 'Can you tell me how you do it?' she asked, desperate for him to divulge his secrets.

Colt glanced up to the sky, where a gleaming ray of sun had broken through the grim storm clouds.

'I'm not one for thank-yous,' he said frankly. 'But I'm glad the rain is over. I'm done with you now.' In the blink of an eye he was gone.

Mia stood alone in the flooded graveyard. She shivered in her wet clothes, but glorious sunshine glistened in her eyes.

As the sun set over the forest, it illuminated the land with a dusty-pink blush, which would soon disappear in the twilight hour.

Dino wandered around the gardens in search of Mia. He wasn't planning on apologising to her, mostly because he didn't feel that he'd done anything wrong, but she'd been absent all day and he felt obliged to at least make an attempt at finding her.

He walked past a couple of Arcana boys who were sitting on the grass laughing about something. When the boys noticed Dino, their laughter died away. Dino could feel, and hear, their wariness towards him. He glanced back at them briefly and vaguely recognised them from the drawing room. Evidently they had witnessed his aggressive outburst earlier that day.

Dino rubbed his head in a familiar circular motion, although he didn't know why he bothered – it did nothing for the discomfort inside his mind. But at least the placebo effect provided him with a small degree of relief.

Keen to distance himself from the boys, Dino carried on walking. He cut straight through the gardens and kept going until he reached the sloping embankment. There he stood, looking down upon the maze of pine trees.

Dino gazed absent-mindedly at the ground beneath his feet. The waterlogged mud had dried out somewhat, and the grass now seemed quite inviting with its dewy green blades and the occasional scattering of dainty flowers.

He stamped his foot down on a tiny yellow buttercup, crushing it like a merciless giant. For a moment he felt sick. Sick at the realisation of how much pleasure he had taken from exerting his dominance over the helpless flower. It was almost wicked.

In fact, lately there were a number of things that Dino had done that had unnerved him. Of course, he would be the first to admit that he had a nasty streak, but recently his volatile temperament was becoming quite sinister. His unpleasant behaviour seemed to be becoming more frequent and increasingly remorseless. It was as though a demon had been awakened inside of him and was now gradually consuming him.

He shuddered at the disturbing thought. *Don't be ridiculous*, he reprimanded himself. *You're not a demon. You're just you.*

He moved his foot from the flower and bent down towards it. Tentatively he plucked the little crushed buttercup and released it into the breeze as a sort of recompense.

As the buttercup tumbled through the air, off on its journey, a hand swooped out and snatched it from its course with the speed and agility of a viper striking its prey.

Startled, Dino spun around. He hadn't heard anyone approach. But there, just a foot away from him, stood a man.

The man was older than Dino, although it was hard to tell exactly how much older he was because his strange hollow face was both haggard and robust at the same time. He stood as still as if he were made from stone, and by the looks of his pallid skin he almost could have been made from stone. The man pinched the buttercup between his thumb and forefinger, squashing it into a yellow pulp.

'I know you,' Dino said uncertainly.

'Perhaps you've seen me around,' the man replied in an acid tone. His mouth was coiled into a smile, but his eyes were emotionless and vacant. 'My name is Tol.' When he spoke his name, his tongue flickered out like a serpent's.

Dino swallowed nervously but retained his composure on the outside.

'Nothing to say?' Tol noted in a low, hissing tone.

'I'm not interested in introductions,' Dino retorted bluntly. 'You don't need to know my name.'

Tol sneered. 'I already know your name, Dino.'

Dino stiffened. He eyed the man suspiciously. The stranger's face was unlike any Dino had ever seen. His complexion was sickly and sallow against his dark hair and clothes. His empty eyes were sunken and shadowed, and his hair, although slick, appeared coarse like animal fur. In fact, there was something about this man that seemed inhuman. Yes, he was human in his basic anatomy, but it was as though he was somehow devoid of a life force. He was a shell.

'It's an honour to meet you,' Tol went on.

Dino grimaced. 'What? Are you drunk?' He concentrated his mind to gauge the man's emotion. It was joy. But a *warped* sense of joy. Dino didn't like it in his head; it felt toxic and spoilt.

'What do you sense?' Tol demanded, his dark eyes still dead.

'I sense that you need to get back to the nut house before they start wondering where you are.'

Tol growled like a ferocious dog. Despite his bravado, Dino shrank back.

Then, abruptly, Tol began to cackle. 'Come into my mind,' he offered menacingly. 'Have a look around. When you're invited, you can truly experience the full potential of your gift.'

Dino glared at him. 'No, thanks.'

Tol slowly closed his eyes. The veins on his eyelids were purple and bulging. 'Do it,' he urged.

Dino licked his lips anxiously. Perversely, he actually wanted to explore the man's mind. He had never been invited to do such a thing before – previously he had only been forced to hear snatches like the sound of a radio tuning in and out.

Why not? he wondered a little sadistically. *Why not see what I'm capable of?*

So, with a deep breath, he permitted himself to channel into Tol's mind. It was simple – all he had to do was allow it. Once their minds had synced together, the sensation hit Dino like a ton of bricks. He wasn't just hearing the man's emotions – he was *feeling* them, too. He felt Tol's repulsive joy as if it were his own. And, more significantly, he could feel Tol's supremacy and immense power, now flowing through him also simply by using his mind as a vessel. Dino trembled. He had never experienced such strength and might. It was phenomenal.

And then, in a flash, Tol opened his eyes and broke the connection.

Dino dropped to the ground, exhausted.

'So, I was right,' Tol sneered. 'You are a Sententia.'

Dino staggered shakily to his feet.

'You felt my power,' Tol deduced. 'And you want it.'

'No.' Dino recoiled at the assumption.

'Don't you crave power? The power I have? I can show you how to get it.'

Dino shook his head. 'I don't want it,' he stuttered.

Tol ran his tongue along his serrated teeth. 'A Sententia's power goes far beyond mere empathy. I can teach you how to not only hear the emotions of others, but to also manipulate their emotions to your will. Come with me.' He extended his gnarled hand.

Dino tensed. 'No.'

Tol beckoned him closer with his hooked finger.

In mortified revulsion, Dino looked down at the man's jagged, rotten fingernail. 'I'm not going anywhere with you. Ever.'

'You're wrong,' Tol disagreed. 'Sooner or later, I will have you. You belong in my coven.'

Speechless and sickened, Dino turned and ran full pelt back towards the castle.

Tol didn't attempt to pursue him; he simply watched with a cruel smile on his lips.

Dino didn't stop running until he'd reached his bedchamber. He burst into the room and slammed the door shut behind him, pulling the deadbolt across. When he caught sight of his hands, he noticed that they were quaking. The thought of Tol made his skin crawl.

He jumped when Mia poked her head out from behind her gold bed curtains.

'Where have you been?' she asked.

He let out a sharp breath. 'Where have you been?' he returned the question snappily. 'I've been out looking for you all day.' That was an exaggeration, but he hoped that his irritation would disguise his fear.

'What's wrong?' Mia asked perceptively. She climbed out from her bed and swept over to him. 'You're shaking,' she told him, taking his hands in hers.

Dino pulled his hands away and linked them behind his head.

'What's wrong with you?' she repeated. Her eyes started to cloud with concern.

Dino side-stepped past her and sat down on the edge of his bed. He slumped his head into his hands.

'I don't want to be evil,' he mumbled quietly.

Mia walked over to where he sat and stood before him faithfully. 'You're not evil.'

'Aren't I?' he challenged curtly.

She placed her hands on her hips. 'You're not evil. Obnoxious, yes. But not evil.'

Dino peered at her through the gaps between his fingers. 'Aren't I?' he asked again, his voice becoming softer and surprisingly vulnerable.

Mia sighed. She took a seat beside him on the bed. 'You could never be evil,' she assured him, draping her arm over his shoulders.

Dino dropped his hands into his lap. He wasn't so sure of that any more. 'I don't know *what* I am,' he admitted.

'Well, I do,' Mia replied firmly. 'You're my brother. Warts and all!' she added with a sweet smile.

Dino reached up and clutched her fingers as they rested on his shoulder. 'Mia,' he said gently, 'I hope you never get your power. It takes hold of you. I wish this had never happened to me.'

Mia fell silent. She had been so excited at the prospect of telling him of her encounter with Colt. But now it didn't seem like such a good idea.

So she simply smiled and said, 'It'll get easier.'

Dino laughed rigidly. 'What makes you so sure?'

'Call it a gut instinct. I've got a feeling that things are about to change.'

7

Allies and Enemies

Mia woke up at the break of dawn, still reeling from her run-in with Colt the previous day. He had seemed convinced that she was a Tempestus, but the idea of being able to manipulate the elements as he had done seemed utterly preposterous. However, the possibility fascinated her nonetheless.

Mia lay in her bed, far too awake for such an early hour. Her eyes were wide open and her mind was painfully alert. All she could think about was what Colt had told her – or, more to the point, what he had *shown* her. She hungered for the ability to do those things herself. His words seemed to echo in her head. Had she really created the rain? Colt certainly seemed to think so. Now the only question that remained was how.

That was the final straw. She couldn't stay in bed for another second. She had to get outside.

Noiselessly, Mia crawled out of bed. Moving as stealthily as she could, she slipped into a pair of jeans and a plum-coloured fitted T-shirt. Dino didn't stir. He continued to slumber soundly behind the thick gold bed curtains.

Mia quickly pulled her hair up into a ponytail and carefully skulked to the bedroom door. She crept out of the room as though she were embarking on a covert operation.

The stairwell was unlit and the grand mahogany banister threw an ominous shadow across the steps. It looked like a giant spider's web, and Mia was the unsuspecting fly.

When she reached the bottom of the stairs, she peered along the corridor. Considering the immense size of the castle, she had barely explored even a fraction of it. Wendolyn had set clear boundaries as to where the Arcana were permitted to be. But the mere thought of what lay beyond their designated area was provocatively alluring.

Hastily expelling the temptation from her mind, Mia returned to her mission and tiptoed outside.

The morning sun was just rising and the air was crisp and fresh. Everything was quiet, apart from the tranquil sound of the birds chirping their morning song. It was a magical time of day: not quite night, but not quite morning. While the rest of the castle slept unawares, Mia strolled into the gardens. She felt like she was the only person in the whole world. The world belonged to her.

She inhaled deeply, welcoming the new day. As she wandered around the flower beds, she saw them in a new light. Today they were alive – as alive as she was. In fact, everything around the gardens seemed to breathe and flourish in a glorious state of undisturbed beauty.

And then she saw him. Another form of unspoilt nature, astonishingly beautiful in a way that she had never known before.

It was Colt.

He lay on his back beneath a weeping willow tree. His hands were raised above his heart, palms facing skyward. Just inches above his hands, pink blossom petals hovered and danced in a gentle, rhythmic motion.

Mia observed the scene in admiration. She had never witnessed anyone so at one, so at peace. And to see him, whom she had feared enormously, lie so docile and connected to the earth – it was quite extraordinary.

A soft breeze embraced his skin and tousled his dark hair across his brow. His eyes were closed and his body was incredibly still; it was as if he were a painting.

Everything about him drew Mia to him. She couldn't resist stepping closer. She had to be closer.

'You know,' Colt said, his abrupt voice startling her, 'a lesser fool than I would kill you now.'

Mia froze. 'I'm sorry. I didn't mean to disturb you.'

Colt carried on, oblivious to her apology – or disregarding it at any rate. 'You'd be wise to not approach a Hunter, no matter how compelling. Some will lure you in this way, looking for a kill.' His eyes remained closed as he spoke, the blossom still playing above his hands.

'Is that what you were doing?' Mia asked. She knew she should be nervous, but for some reason she wasn't.

'No,' Colt replied. 'I'm meditating. Or, at least, I *was* meditating.' He opened his eyes and the pink blossom petals sprinkled down over his body. Tilting his head towards her, he shot her an icy glare. 'Well?' he said snappily.

'Well, what?'

'What do you want?' Colt demanded, surprised and annoyed that Mia had not yet left.

Much to Colt's irritation, she sat down on the grass.

'Why are you sitting down?' he exclaimed, baffled. 'Go away!'

'Maybe we could talk?' Mia suggested coyly. She hadn't expected to bump into him, but now that she had, it seemed like an opportunity had presented itself. After all, Colt appeared to be the only one willing to help her gain knowledge of her powers. He wasn't exactly eager, but at least he wasn't morally obligated to withhold information.

'I don't like to talk,' he replied bluntly. Still lying on the grass, he eyed her suspiciously.

'Then I'll talk,' Mia suggested.

'I don't like you to talk, either.'

'It wasn't a question,' Mia said daringly.

Colt groaned. 'Why me?' he uttered scornfully.

'It's about your powers,' she explained. 'Actually, it's about *my* powers.'

Colt didn't respond.

'I need your help,' Mia told him. She shuffled closer until she was beside him, peering down at his face.

Colt recoiled sharply. 'Too close!' he barked.

Mia shuffled back. 'Can you help me?'

'No.'

'Why not?' she pushed.

'Because I don't want to.'

'Please,' Mia clasped her hands together earnestly.

Now Colt sat upright. He looked at her, thoroughly mystified. 'Have you got a death wish? I could snap your neck without even laying a finger on you. It would be easy – and fun. And do you know how much remorse I would feel?'

'Some?' Mia guessed hopefully.

'None,' he corrected.

'Well,' Mia held her ground, 'maybe I think it's worth the risk.'

Colt pressed his fingers to his eyelids and muttered something under his breath. 'Fine,' he growled. 'One question.' His sullen green eyes locked on her intensely.

'OK,' she granted. 'Go ahead.'

Colt slapped his hand to his head. 'No! You can ask *me* one question!'

'Oh. Right.' She began to ponder it. If she only had one question, it would have to be a good one.

'But first of all,' Colt added, 'take your hair down.'

Mia ran her fingers along her ponytail. 'Why?'

Flinching in discomfort, Colt subtly covered his mouth and nose. 'There's a cut on your neck,' he told her.

Mia touched her throat. She was aware that she had suffered a few scrapes as a result of her fall the day before. 'And?' she pressed, confused.

'I can see it. And smell it. It's . . . rousing.'

'What – are you a vampire or something?' Mia laughed, although the sound of it was a little tense.

'No, of course not. But I like the taste of blood.'

With that unnerving reality check, Mia untied her ponytail and let her dark, silken hair cascade down like a waterfall.

Colt clenched his teeth. 'That's worse!' he said hastily.

'Why?' Mia patted at her hair, unsure whether to leave it loose or pull it back up.

Colt pressed his hand more firmly over his mouth and nose. 'Because I can smell your scent! Get back! Get back!'

Mia scrambled several feet away from him. 'How's this?' she asked in a raised voice. She sat cross-legged on a patch of grass, her hair tumbling over her shoulders.

Cautiously, Colt dropped his hand down to the ground. 'Better,' he confirmed, adjusting to the aroma in the air. 'It's somewhat diluted.'

Mia stared at him for a moment. 'What did it smell like?' she asked before she could stop herself.

Colt grimaced. 'It smelled like you.'

Mia frowned. 'And that's a bad thing?' She was evidently insulted by his comment.

Absent-mindedly, Colt trailed his index finger along his lips. 'I'm not sure.' He deliberated for a moment. 'Sometimes I thrive off it. Sometimes I despise it.'

Mia shifted nervously. 'Do you often smell me?'

'Yes.'

The thought sickened her. 'How?'

'You're everywhere.'

'How did I get everywhere?'

Colt let out a tired sigh. 'Well, most memorably, we had three days of your bothersome rain.' He scrunched up his nose at the memory. 'Every drop was you. But I believe I first picked up your scent in the forest.'

With everything that had happened lately, Mia had almost

forgotten about her very first encounter with Colt, when she and Kizzy had been drawn into the forest. 'So you did know I was there,' she realised quietly.

'Of course I knew you were there! I'm a supreme Hunter, and you are just a child!'

'Hey!' Mia protested. 'You don't look that much older than me!'

'I don't mean it in that context,' Colt snapped. 'You see, this is exactly what I mean – naivety,' he groused to himself. 'I've been alive for eighteen years. But I've also been a witch for eighteen years. You, however, were born only yesterday as a witch.'

'I wasn't born yesterday,' Mia argued, smiling to herself at how comical it sounded to use that phrase literally.

'Fine. A week ago, then,' Colt said dispassionately. 'What's the difference? You don't even know how to use your power yet!'

Mia folded her arms stubbornly. 'That's why I'm here. If you're so fantastic, why don't you show me how it's done?'

'I am fantastic,' Colt agreed casually. 'I'm unparalleled.'

'And you're your own biggest fan,' Mia remarked under her breath.

'It seems to me that *you're* my biggest fan,' he retorted with a snide smile. 'Anyway, as I said – one question.'

Mia gazed up to the sky, contemplating the perfect question. She needed to include everything that she wanted to know in one statement.

'I'm waiting,' Colt reminded her.

'I'm thinking,' Mia shot back.

'Then I should warn you that I'm also imposing a time limit.'

'Of course you are,' Mia grumbled, hardly surprised by the revelation.

'Ten seconds,' Colt announced.

'That's not fair!' she objected.

'No, darling, what's not fair is your clinging on to me like a limpet.'

Mia glowered at him. 'It doesn't matter, anyway. I have my question.'

'I'm on the edge of my seat,' Colt said dryly.

'My question is,' she declared meaningfully, 'how do I control the air?'

'That's very vague,' Colt pointed out.

'But it's what I want to know.'

'Well, it's subjective,' Colt reasoned. 'What works for me may not work for you.'

'I understand. I still want to know,' Mia hurried him along, banking on the hope that what worked for him would indeed work for her, too.

'You need to be in tune with nature, to the point where you *are* nature. Think with your soul, not with your head. Will it so. Watch.' He raised his palm to her and sent a light breeze through her hair, purposefully pushing the strands back and exposing her throat. His eyes drifted to the graze on her neck. 'Just a peek,' he told her with a devilish wink. Then he drew his hand back towards his chest, commanding the breeze to flick her hair back to its original position.

Mia inhaled the air deeply. Her lips parted as she exhaled. Out of the corner of her eye, she spotted Colt staring attentively at her mouth. It made her incredibly self-conscious.

'Stop looking at me!' she scolded him.

'No.'

'You're making me lose concentration,' she accused.

'That's the problem,' Colt responded huffily. 'You're thinking too much. It's not about concentration. It's simply about doing. About being.'

Mia ignored him and raised her hand in front of her. The cool air dusted her skin, but nothing out of the ordinary happened.

Move, she commanded silently, focusing on a scattering of pink blossoms.

'Stop thinking!' Colt demanded irritably.

'I can't help it!'

'You're not getting anywhere! Cast your mind back to how you did it in the forest,' he suggested.

'OK,' Mia said calmly. Then she paused. 'What did I do in the forest?'

Colt rolled his eyes. 'You threw a jackdaw feather. That's how I knew that you were a Tempestus. You directed a breeze to carry the feather.'

'I did?'

'Of course you did!' he cried. 'Did you never think to question how a wispy feather could fly like a steel arrow?'

'I thought it was a lucky feather,' she justified weakly.

Colt fell backwards laughing. 'That's pitiful! And by the way, there's no such thing as luck.'

Mia pouted. 'Well, I still don't know how I did it.'

'You did it because you needed to,' he explained, composing himself and sitting back upright. 'You feared us and you wanted the feather to distract us. Am I correct?'

'Yes,' she admitted.

'Use that fear. Use that need. Become it.'

'Will you help me?' Mia asked meekly.

'No.'

'But, we'll speak again?' she pressed.

'I hope not.' Colt smiled slightly. Then all of a sudden he tensed, like an animal under attack. 'Lotan,' he murmured. 'Lotan is near,' he told Mia. 'Go!' His eyes were filled with sudden urgency.

Mia rose to her feet.

'Go faster!' Colt hissed. And with a swift raise of his hand, he enveloped her in a forceful gust of air, propelling her backwards.

She landed several metres away, her fall cushioned by a

cluster of leaves. Dazed, Mia sat up among the foliage, but when she looked back to the willow tree Colt was gone.

Mia returned to the castle with a spring in her step. It was still early, but she guessed that the others would be up and about by now. She trotted along the corridor and peeked around the drawing-room door. Sure enough, several Arcana were dotted around the room, polishing off plates of buttered toast. Mia spotted Dino, Kizzy and Blue congregated in the far corner of the room.

Dino, look at me, Mia thought. And to her surprise, he did. Kizzy and Blue turned, too.

From the doorway, Mia beckoned them to her.

The little group rose from their seats and quietly made their exit. They followed Mia along the narrow corridor until they reached the library. Mia hustled them inside the unoccupied room and closed the door behind them.

In the windowless library, the musty smell of books and centuries of candle smoke lingered in the air. Mia quickly lit a candle to illuminate the dim room. Then she turned to face the others, her face aglow in the candlelight.

'I'm a Tempestos,' she announced proudly.

Dino frowned, puzzled. 'You're asbestos?'

'No,' Mia said, rolling her eyes at him. 'A Tempestos.'

Blue cleared his throat uneasily. 'Actually, I . . . I think the word is, Tempest*us*.'

Mia waved her hand aloofly. 'Same thing. Anyway, I'm one.'

Kizzy clasped her hands together enthusiastically. 'Congratulations!'

Mia beamed. 'I can influence the elements! Can you believe it?'

'How did you figure it out?' Kizzy asked.

'Someone told me,' she replied evasively. For some reason,

she felt reluctant to divulge any information about her inter-
actions with Colt. She feared that her alliance with a Hunter
would be a taboo issue.

But Kizzy didn't give up that easily. '*Who* told you?' she
pressed.

'Some guy,' Mia said casually. 'But that's not important.
The important thing is, I'm a Tempestos!'

'Tempest*us*,' Blue corrected her again quietly.

Tol! Dino suddenly thought, reminded of the sinister man
he had encountered the night before. 'Who was the guy?' he
demanded.

'Just a guy,' Mia answered, silently wishing for him to
drop the subject.

'Older?' Dino pushed.

Mia thought back to her conversation with Colt. He had
told her that he was eighteen, which made him two years
her senior. 'A little older,' she confirmed at last.

Dino felt his stomach knot. Instantly he concluded that Tol
had found Mia and offered her the promise of power, just as
he had done with Dino. And Mia had fallen for it.

'Did he tell you his name?' Dino asked her.

Mia glared at him, wondering why he was so fixated on
this. 'What does it matter what his name was?'

'It matters,' he stated. 'Some strange guy appears out of
nowhere and tells you that you've got a fantastic power. You
don't think that's a little odd?'

Mia blanked him out. 'Can you imagine,' she gushed to
Kizzy and Blue. 'I can control the elements! Me!'

'Wow!' Kizzy cheered. 'Show us something.'

Mia shifted her weight from left to right. 'Well,' she fiddled
with a thread on her top, 'I can't exactly do it yet. But I'm
working on it. And the guy I met, I think he's going to help
me,' she explained.

'Are you insane?' Dino spluttered. 'I hate to burst your
naive little bubble, but this freak is scamming you. He's

making you believe that you have a power and that he can help you, but it's all a con to trap you!'

'That's not it at all!' Mia protested.

'Don't be a fool,' Dino muttered coldly.

'Perhaps I am a fool. A fool to think that my brother would be pleased for me.'

Dino shook his head solemnly. 'If you are so blind to think that this man has got your best interests . . .'

'Maybe you're jealous because you want to be the only one with a power,' she challenged, cutting him off sharply. 'In fact, you said it yourself, didn't you? You hope I never get a power,' she recounted his words with shrewd accuracy.

Dino narrowed his eyes. 'Suit yourself. Act like a reckless little girl if you want. But don't come crying to me when it all blows up in your face. If you insist on being an idiot, then you're on your own.'

Mia held his gaze unfalteringly. 'I'm not on my own,' she responded frostily. 'I don't need you.' She turned to Kizzy. 'Let's get out of here.'

Kizzy looked awkwardly between the siblings, trying to remain neutral. But of course her loyalty had to be with Mia.

'Sorry, Blue,' Mia added politely.

He smiled weakly at her. 'C . . . congratulations on . . . on . . .' He glanced at Dino's stony face, hesitant to take sides.

'Thanks,' Mia replied. Without another word, she and Kizzy left the boys alone in the library.

Dino looked sceptically at Blue. 'Why did you encourage her? You really think she's this asbestos thing?'

'Tempestus. Maybe,' Blue told him, diplomatically.

'No way.'

'What makes you s . . . so sure she's n . . . not?'

'Because it's all too convenient, if you ask me,' Dino mused. 'She met a guy and he told her what she wanted to hear.'

'Possibly,' Blue agreed. 'But maybe he t . . . told her the

t . . . truth. What reason would someone in the Glass Castle have to l . . . lie to her? What would they have to gain?'

'Exactly!' Dino concurred, as though Blue had made a point rather than asked a question. 'And I know just the culprit.'

'Who?' Blue's honey-coloured eyes rounded in bewilderment. Despite being dubious, he was nonetheless keen to hear Dino's paranoid ramblings.

'Something happened last night,' Dino clarified, 'when I was out looking for Mia.'

Blue's cynical confusion altered to intrigue.

Dino carried on, 'This foul, shifty-looking guy showed up out of nowhere, telling me about my power and asking me to join him.'

'What?' Blue furrowed his brow. 'Who?'

'He called himself Tol.' As Dino spoke the man's name, the flame of a nearby candle flickered agitatedly.

The boys eyed it, unnerved by its movement.

Then Blue spoke. 'I've been at the Glass Castle for a y . . . year, and I've never met anyone called T . . . tol. What did he look like?'

Dino grimaced. 'Like a monster. He could have been a Hunter, but even less human than the Hunters around here. He wanted me to join his coven. And I'm willing to bet that it wouldn't be me who would benefit from that little merger.'

Blue glanced around the dark room, as though suddenly even the books were potential spies. 'What did he want you for?'

Dino shrugged. 'I don't know. Recruiting, maybe?'

'Did you tell Wendolyn?'

'No,' Dino confessed. 'I was all the way out at the forest boundaries, and I'm not looking for a lecture. Know what I mean?'

Blue held his hands up impassively. 'And now you think this g . . . guy is after Mia?'

'I know it,' Dino insisted. 'But he'll have to go through me first.'

Something about his final words was more ill-omened than even he could have comprehended.

The rest of the day passed by uneventfully, until at last the sun disappeared and night-time set in. Mia and Kizzy spent most of the evening lounging around Mia's bedchamber, chatting and swapping stories.

Kizzy hopped up on to Mia's bed. 'And now,' she was saying, 'I can almost will a vision to come to me. They're so clear and distinct, it's like they're real.'

'Are they similar to the visions we get from the tea?' Mia enquired curiously. She sat on the bed opposite Kizzy, her legs tucked underneath her.

'Sort of,' Kizzy explained. 'But they're much clearer, and sometimes I can watch them for almost an entire minute. It isn't just a glimpse any more – it's the whole picture.'

'That sounds amazing,' Mia breathed in awe. 'What kind of things have you seen?'

'Um . . .' Kizzy pondered over it. 'Yesterday morning I saw a fox, and then in the evening I saw the fox run through the garden.'

'Cool! Have you seen any warning signs?' Mia asked, half in jest.

Kizzy looked away. 'Some,' she replied, gazing up at the carved canopy of the four-poster bed.

'Really?' Mia's slate-grey eyes lit up like shimmering silver. 'What have you seen?'

'I don't know. Nothing major.'

Mia paused. 'Is something wrong?' she asked intuitively.

'Is there something you don't want to tell me about the visions?'

Kizzy returned her focus to Mia. 'It's nothing. I don't want to worry you.'

'Worry *me*?' Mia frowned. 'Why would they worry me?'

Kizzy bit her lip. Perhaps she had already said too much.

'Oh, my God!' Mia gasped. 'Are the visions about me?'

'I don't know. Maybe one of them *might* have involved you . . .'

'What was it?' Mia pressed.

'I don't want to frighten you.' Kizzy chewed on her thumbnail. It was obvious that she regretted starting on the topic in the first place.

'I'm already frightened!' Mia exclaimed. 'Please, you have to tell me. Besides, don't you get these visions for a reason? Maybe you're *supposed* to warn me.'

'And then perhaps you could avoid it,' Kizzy added, brightening at the prospect.

'Well, yeah, here's hoping!'

'Are you sure you want to know? No matter how bad it is? Not that it's *that* bad,' Kizzy was beginning to babble now. 'In fact, it's practically nothing. Nothing to worry about, at least.'

'Go on,' Mia agreed, bracing herself. 'Tell me.'

Somewhat reluctantly, Kizzy surrendered. 'OK.' She drew in a deep breath. 'You remember the Hunter, Colt?'

'Yes,' Mia responded, trying to sound indifferent. She certainly hadn't expected Kizzy to bring up Colt.

'Well,' Kizzy continued as she toyed with a strand of blonde hair, twirling it around her index finger, 'I saw him . . . with you.'

Instantly Mia began to relax. That wasn't so bad.

'And,' Kizzy went on, 'he was holding a . . . uh . . . knife.'

'A knife?' Mia mulled it over. 'Maybe I bump into him

when he's carrying a knife. It happens. Not that I'm expecting to bump into him or anything,' she put in hastily.

'Sure,' Kizzy agreed. 'But . . . uh . . . he was holding the knife over you, and you were, um . . . what's the word?'

'Happy?' Mia offered.

'No, not happy. More like . . . dead.'

'Dead!' Mia cried. 'You said it was nothing to worry about!'

'Because I didn't want to worry you! That's what people say when they don't want people to worry!'

Mia clutched at her heart. 'I'm dead?' she murmured.

'Not yet,' Kizzy smiled supportively. 'I mean, not *ever*,' she corrected herself quickly.

'Are you sure it was me?'

'Look,' Kizzy said, dodging the question tactically, 'it doesn't mean anything. It was probably just a warning, to scare us away from the forest. It'll be fine.'

'That's easy for you to say,' Mia objected. 'You're not dead!'

'Neither are you,' Kizzy reasoned.

Mia flopped backwards on to her bed and buried her face into a pillow.

'There, there,' Kizzy consoled her rather unhelpfully. She patted her friend on the head. 'You've had a good life.'

Mia let out a distressed wail.

There was a loud knock on the bedroom door.

The girls gasped and looked at one another wide-eyed.

'Colt,' Mia whispered. She sat bolt upright and clung on to Kizzy for dear life.

The girls held their breath as the heavy door creaked open.

The sound of Wendolyn's motherly voice floated into the bedroom.

'Girls,' the older woman sang out jovially, 'time for bed. Kizzy, dear, off to your own room, please.'

Kizzy shrugged helplessly at Mia. 'Bye,' she mouthed.

Mia gave a look of dismay as she watched her friend depart from the bedchamber.

Wendolyn, however, hovered in the doorway. 'Mia,' she said in a smooth, gentle voice, 'where is your brother?'

'I don't know,' Mia answered. The truth was she had spent the day deliberately avoiding Dino. 'I saw him this morning, but he hasn't been back to the room this evening.' She didn't bother telling Wendolyn that she and Dino were at loggerheads, and that the reason why he wasn't there most likely had to do with the fact that Mia was there.

Wendolyn's sage, lined face crumpled into a perturbed expression. 'I see,' she said slowly.

Mia wondered for a moment if Wendolyn had read her thoughts. She abruptly changed the subject. 'Wendolyn,' she ventured, 'I've been meaning to ask – did you find the Hunter coven? I mean, the intruders that you told me about last week?'

Wendolyn shook her head. 'No. But it's been some time since I last sensed them, so perhaps they have moved on.'

'Good,' Mia responded quietly. That was one less thing to fret about.

Wendolyn smiled kindly. 'No need for alarm,' she assured her. She turned to leave the room. 'Would you like me to switch off the light?' she asked.

'Yes, please,' Mia replied. She crawled under the sheets and drew the gold curtains around the bed. The light in the bedchamber disappeared and the door clicked shut.

It didn't take long for Mia to drift off to sleep – after all, she had had an unusually early start. She slept soundly for at least an hour or so before the bedroom door creaked open once again.

A dark figure strode into the room, as light-footed as if he was gliding on air. He hesitated, breathing in fervently and licking his lips. Moving silently, he approached Mia's bed and slowly eased the curtains apart.

There she slept, so peacefully. Her pretty face so serenely beautiful and innocent.

For several long seconds Colt stood over her, watching her curiously. He tilted his head, seemingly uncertain. But that uncertainty soon vanished, and in one fluid motion he withdrew a dagger from the sheath on his belt.

A moonbeam came through the open window, catching the blade with a deadly glint. And then, Colt struck.

8

Blood of the Coven

Colt stood over Mia as she slept. He gripped the dagger in his hand, his knuckles white from the force of his grasp. Then swiftly he brought the blade down, piercing the flesh and dragging its point along the delicate skin of an arm.

But it was not Mia's skin that he had severed; it was his own.

A trickle of crimson blood dripped from the incision on his forearm. Without wasting a second, he pressed the wound to Mia's lips.

Instantly her eyes shot open. She struggled, frantically trying to push Colt's arm away, but he held it to her mouth unwaveringly. In the darkness of the bedchamber, his eyes locked on hers with a strange brightness. His forest-green eyes paled and glistened like ice.

'Drink!' he told her in a husky voice.

Mia's protests were muffled beneath his arm. She pursed her lips, refusing to ingest his blood. Impulsively she dug her fingernails into the wound on his arm.

Colt winced. 'Trust me,' he said through gritted teeth.

But trusting him was an unthinkable request. He was her assailant – how could she trust him? Desperately, she fought to resist, yet much to her dismay she began to taste the coppery tang of blood.

Colt let out a sigh of relief as he felt the exchange take place.

At first, Mia retched and lashed out at him, but steadily she slipped into a numb, trancelike state. Within moments she was willingly feeding off his blood, rapt in a hypnotic compulsion. Gradually she withdrew her nails from the wound and repositioned her fingers to his skin, clinging to his arm as though she were attaching herself to him.

Colt closed his eyes, strangely enjoying the sensation. 'That's enough,' he said at last.

His words were wasted. By now, all of Mia's rational, lucid mind had been overshadowed. The ritual had taken hold of her, turning her into an animal, thriving off the feed.

'That's enough!' Colt commanded again, this time with a hostile growl. His body began to feel limp and his head whirled. He too was beginning to lose himself to the ritual.

Mia gripped his arm tighter, unable to break the rhythm of the action.

With a strangled groan, Colt focused on summoning the core of his strength. He rigidly raised his free hand and charged a gust of air to throw him backwards. The speed and vigour of the air sent him hurtling away from Mia. His head cracked sharply against one of the oak pillars on the four-poster bed. Dazed, he shook off the blow and began licking the incision on his arm, aiding its recovery.

Mia collapsed on to her bed, motionless. It was as though breaking the connection with Colt had taken away her life force. She lay perfectly still, with blood smeared over her lips and a stray droplet dibbling down her chin.

Colt took a deep breath, regaining his serenity. Once he was sufficiently composed, he returned to Mia. He perched on the edge of her bed and licked the rogue trickle of blood from her face.

The bizarre act awoke her from her unconsciousness. In a haze, her eyes fluttered open. It took several seconds to adapt to the strange scene. The first thing she saw was Colt, sitting faithfully at her bedside. Disoriented, she reached out to him, and in a misguided search for comfort she coiled her fingers around the material of his black T-shirt. Their eyes met in a moment of union.

Instinctively Colt flinched. 'Don't do that,' he scolded her briskly, prying her hand from his T-shirt.

The jolt brought Mia back to reality. All of a sudden she felt sober again and a wave of panic flooded over her. 'What did you do to me?' she choked, pushing Colt away and swiping at him as hard as she could.

Colt effortlessly dodged each swing of her flailing arms. He smiled, distinctly pleased with himself.

'Answer me!' Mia yelled, short of breath. 'What did you do to me?'

'I thought you'd at least thank me,' Colt replied evenly. 'I don't get a lot of thanks in my line of work, and I feel I deserve it at times.'

Mia gawped at him. 'Perhaps you misunderstand the meaning of the word!' she spluttered. The aftertaste of blood was still rife in her mouth.

Colt chuckled whimsically.

Mortified, Mia wiped at her mouth. 'You're sick!' she spat. 'You're . . . warped!'

'Don't be dramatic, dear.'

'Dramatic!' Mia exclaimed. 'You're evil! You're a vile monster!'

'I'm flattered,' Colt smirked complacently.

Mia struck out at him again, but smoothly he ducked aside.

'Is this how you repay me for saving your life?' Colt asked with a snide smile.

'Yeah, right!' Mia shouted at him. 'You're not saving my life – you're trying to turn me into one of your kind!' she speculated irately.

'Ha!' Colt laughed loudly. 'Darling, you could never be one of my kind.'

'Then why did you make me drink your blood?' Mia

demanded. Simply saying it aloud sickened her to the pit of her stomach.

'Certainly not to change you into *my kind*,' Colt scoffed, placing extra emphasis on the final words. The idea of 'his kind' was evidently amusing to him. His eyes, now restored to their usual pine green, twinkled playfully.

'So why did you do it?' Mia scrunched up her nose, visibly nauseated by the revolting memory. 'It's disgusting!'

Colt gave her a wry smile. 'I didn't hear you complaining at the time,' he teased her crudely. 'In fact, you seemed to quite enjoy it.'

Mia flung her hand forward and successfully clipped him on the nose. 'You put me under a spell!' she accused.

Colt grinned and rubbed the affected area on his nose. 'Did I?' he challenged. 'Or maybe you just liked it. It's a good thing I managed to separate myself from you when I did,' he added cryptically.

'Why?' she asked fearfully. 'What would have happened?'

'I suppose we'll never know. But I must admit, I was beginning to enjoy myself, too. It's quite a pleasurable experience.'

Mia looked utterly horrified.

'Well, it is,' Colt justified unashamedly. 'It's powerful. The trade of one's life force. What greater exhilaration could there be? The only disgusting part about it is the appalling humane selflessness on my part.'

'S . . . selflessness?' Mia stuttered at the absurdity.

'Believe me,' he said, shuddering melodramatically. 'I tried to justify what I was doing as something that served my own ends. But I fear I must accept it as a selfless deed. My last, I hope. Although,' he added as an afterthought, 'the process did prove to be rather gratifying for me. So I suppose it wasn't *all* bad.'

'How did this benefit me?' Mia whispered, somewhat scared to ask.

'Think of my blood as the antidote,' he explained vaguely.

'The antidote to what?' Mia cowered under her bedcovers, leaving only her ashen face on show.

'Enticement.'

'Which is?' she pressed.

Colt rolled his eyes. 'Have you learned nothing since you've been at the Glass Castle?'

'Nobody will tell me anything!'

'There's a library full of books!' Colt exclaimed. 'I suggest you open one once in a while.'

Mia blinked up at him from her cocoon of bedding.

'Enticement,' Colt went on, 'is a form a possession. If a Hunter manages to sample your blood, then effectively he will have a hold on you. He can call out to you, whenever and wherever he chooses, and you will go to him.'

'Was a Hunter trying to take my blood?' Mia asked, drawing the bed sheets even further up.

Colt laughed. 'A Hunter already *has* your blood.'

'What?' Mia gasped. 'You?'

Colt pinched the bridge of his nose in frustration. 'No. Lotan. The night you took the Athame, your head was bleeding . . .'

'Yes,' Mia interrupted, 'because you threw me against the candlestick.'

'Yes, I did,' he replied guiltlessly. 'Lotan advanced upon you and tasted your blood. Do you remember?'

Mia nodded her head.

'Well, that was all he needed,' Colt told her. 'One small taste and you are his. He can call on you at any given time and you must come to him. Eventually, he will lure you in and kill you.'

'Kill me?' Mia whimpered.

'Not always,' Colt revised, his voice softening a little. 'Sometimes he'll settle for torture . . . But I imagine that's probably worse.'

Mia felt her stomach flip. 'He did call me!' she suddenly realised, recalling the night that she had been awoken by the sound of Lotan's voice beckoning her to him. She had walked in a stupor towards the forest, but something inside the mist had thrown her back, snapping her out of the trance . . .

'You!' Mia murmured, gazing up at Colt. 'Last week . . .'

'Clever girl,' he smiled patronisingly.

'Lotan called for me, but you stopped me before I walked into the forest.' Her stony eyes glistened with gratitude.

However, Colt's expression hardened. 'Don't get too excited,' he scowled. 'It wasn't a chivalrous act.'

'Why did you save me?' she asked tenderly.

'I didn't save you!' he snapped, affronted by the remark. 'I saved Lotan. I knew that his plan was to kill you. But Wendolyn was near, and she wouldn't have been pleased.'

Mia sat up in bed with the covers still tucked around her. 'But that was a week ago,' she pointed out. 'Why hasn't Lotan tried again?'

'Because, up until recently, I'd convinced him that you were no bother to us. Little did I know!' Colt joked, in an oddly light-hearted fashion.

'Up until recently? What changed?'

'Turns out that you are a bother!'

Mia frowned. 'I haven't seen Lotan since the night with the Athame. How can I have bothered him when I haven't even seen him?'

'You've seen me,' Colt explained. 'You're on my skin and he sensed you. You have a very distinctive scent.'

'So you keep telling me,' Mia muttered under her breath.

'Yes. It's . . . annoying.'

'And Lotan doesn't like it,' she guessed.

Colt shrugged. 'He probably liked the scent. I'm sure they all do. It's captivating in some ways. But he doesn't want you near us. And he especially doesn't want you near *me*. I'm far too valuable.'

Now it was Mia's turn to roll her eyes. 'I bet you are,' she said sarcastically.

Colt grinned. 'I am.'

'So, can I stop him?' Mia asked, steering the conversation back to Lotan.

Colt extended his arm, displaying the wound. 'Done,' he confirmed.

With some reservation, Mia peered at the cut. A look of revulsion formed on her face. She could see the imprints of teeth marks around the lesion. Had she really been so fervent?

Colt continued, 'To break the enticement hold, you need to drain the blood of your possessor. In other words, you need to slaughter him. Alternatively, you can feed off the blood of his coven. An eye for an eye, of sorts. It levels out the playing field.'

Grudgingly, Mia began to piece the information together. 'And you're part of his coven?'

'Yes. Myself, Lotan, Roc and Siren.'

'In other words, by drinking your blood, I'm now immune to Lotan's enticement?'

'Yes.'

Mia swallowed nervously. 'Are you sure?'

'Of course I'm sure!'

There was a long pause while Colt's admission truly sank in.

Eventually Mia spoke again. 'Why did you do it?' she asked in a small voice.

'I don't know.' Colt absent-mindedly licked at the wound on his arm. 'I'm extremely ashamed of myself. I suppose I wanted to give you a fighting chance. After all, it was I who sought you to end the rain. Perhaps in doing so, I led you to believe that you were permitted to approach me.' He frowned. 'Which you're not, by the way.'

'Then go,' she retorted in a shaky voice.

'Besides,' Colt added with a cocky sneer, 'I like to think that if anyone gets to kill you, it'll be me.'

'Maybe I'll kill *you*,' Mia shot back, feigning a slightly unconvincing display of courage.

The corner of Colt's mouth curved upwards slowly. 'I doubt that very much. But I can honestly say that I'd love to see you try.'

His words sent a chill down Mia's spine.

'And on that very exciting note,' Colt announced brightly, 'I will leave you. Sweet dreams,' he added menacingly. In the blink of an eye, he vanished.

Mia lay in bed, her heart pounding wildly. Once she was certain that Colt was gone, she scrambled out of bed.

'Dino!' she cried, stumbling in the darkness.

She yanked his bed curtains apart, but her brother was still not there.

The call of an owl echoed in the hushed night sky. Somewhere below it, Dino paced along the grass embankment. He paused at the new sound and stood like a statue, his dark hair painted with a silvery moonlit streak.

It was late. He wasn't sure exactly how late, but it was safe to assume that the other residents would all be asleep. Not Dino, though. He hadn't even been back to his bedroom yet. Not since that morning. In fact, after his dispute with Mia, his mind was fixed on one thing: finding Tol. And it was a mission he did not intend to back out of.

'Tol!' he hollered into the emptiness of the night.

There was no response.

Dino cursed under his breath. He had been there for hours now, waiting in the same spot. The reality was that he had no idea where to find Tol, but he figured his best chance would be to return to the place of their first encounter. So that's where he waited, on the crest of the sloping embankment.

Rapidly losing hope, Dino scanned the blackened forest, searching the darkness for any sign of movement. But still there was nothing. It seemed as though a second encounter was not quite so easy to happen upon.

'Tol!' he shouted.

And then, the world began to stir. All around him, the leaves on the trees rustled. It was as though they were quaking, anticipating something terrible.

'Tol!' Dino bellowed again. His voice rasped with an aggression that even he was unfamiliar with.

At long last he got his response.

Before he saw or heard anything, he felt it. He felt the hot breath on the back of his neck, and he knew that the man was behind him. But this time Dino was prepared. He showed no fear or reaction at all. He simply turned until their eyes were level.

'What a surprise,' Tol hissed. 'You calling me. How very unexpected.' The repugnant man seemed even more grotesque the second time around. His beady eyes were void and soulless, and his face, though human, was the face of a serpent. Despite the sizeable distance between them, Tol's body language was uncomfortably intrusive.

'I called you,' Dino agreed audaciously, 'and you came.' He hoped that fact would assert his supremacy, but regrettably his Sententia ability showed him that Tol was not intimidated. Not in the slightest.

'To what do I owe the pleasure?' Tol inquired with a touch of venom in his tone.

'You know why I'm here,' Dino snarled.

'Is that so?' The man's voice dripped with predatory curiosity.

'My sister.'

'Your sister?' Tol was momentarily stunned. Then smoothly his expression returned to a malicious leer. 'What of her?'

'I know what you're doing,' Dino confronted him. 'Promising her power and tricking her into falling for your lies.' He was so adamantly convinced that Tol was Mia's mystery confidant that he had become blind to any other possible alternative.

'I have no use for her,' Tol scoffed. 'It's *you* I want, boy.'

'Then leave her alone,' Dino replied fiercely.

Tol bared his jagged teeth in a sinister smile.

'What can you offer me for her life?' he bargained.

Dino's mouth went dry. 'What do you want?' he returned. All of a sudden, he didn't feel quite so brave any more.

'You know what I want,' said Tol. He eyed Dino hungrily, his mouth watering at the very prospect.

'You want me,' Dino answered for him.

'I want you to join my coven.'

Dino stiffened. 'And do what?' he asked. He couldn't believe that he was actually considering this.

'And become the fourth Hunter. The final piece needed to complete our coven.' Tol's breathing started to accelerate in sheer excitement.

Dino backed away involuntarily. Of course, he had presumed that Tol was a Hunter and he already knew what the man wanted from him. But to hear it said so openly was bloodcurdling.

'I'm not a Hunter,' Dino told him defiantly.

'You were born to be a Hunter,' Tol argued. 'It's inside of you. I can see it building, desperate to break free.'

'The only thing building is my desire to rid the world of you,' Dino fired back. As much as he hated to admit it, Tol's remark had undoubtedly shaken him.

'It's your destiny,' Tol persevered. He began to claw at his own skin in expectancy. 'I am your destiny.'

115

'Oh, well, if that's the case then I suppose you should kill me now,' Dino jeered, ''cause that's not a destiny I want to fulfil.'

Tol carried on, unfazed, 'You're a Hunter. I can taste it in the air that surrounds you.' He closed his eyes to savour the aroma in the atmosphere.

Dino balled his hands into fists. 'I'm not a Hunter,' he repeated. But his self-belief was starting to falter.

'Not yet,' Tol admitted. 'But I can change you.' He salivated at the idea. 'All you have to do is give yourself willingly and I will take care of the rest.'

'No,' Dino said in a firm yet quiet voice.

'Then I'll take the girl,' Tol stated simply.

'No!' Dino exclaimed.

'I'm losing my patience,' Tol said, his face contorting into an inhuman snarl.

Dino opened his mouth to speak, but no words came out.

'The girl will die,' Tol declared finally, 'and you will watch.' He turned and began to walk away.

'Wait!' Dino stopped him.

Hidden from Dino's eyes, Tol smiled triumphantly. He spun around to face his prey.

'There must be another way,' Dino pleaded. No longer was he the bold, confident boy who had summoned Tol to him. Now he was broken and begging for mercy.

Tol mulled it over, dragging out his decision with agonising torment. At last, he spoke. 'There is no other way. It's you or her.'

Dino's heart plummeted. 'What will happen to me if I join your coven?'

Tol's snake eyes lit up in corrupt delight. 'I will unshackle you from your humanity and transform you into the greatest warrior that ever lived. Others will tremble before you while you destroy them. And you will thrive off doing so.'

'No,' Dino stammered.

'I have already seen it. It is written.'

'No,' Dino choked. 'No! There has to be another way. I'll find a way,' he stuttered. 'I can protect my sister from you.'

'Can you?' Tol baited him.

'Yes,' Dino spat, staring him down.

Tol directed his focus to a nearby tree, its trunk thicker than any other in sight. 'Watch me,' Tol barked. He raised his hand, and then, with an almighty tearing sound, the tree trunk cracked along its centre. The dense trunk shattered into two halves, which split and bowed away from each other.

Dino looked on in petrified awe.

'The girl will be first,' Tol warned hatefully. 'But I won't stop there. I'll take all of them. I'll work my way through them until you are left entirely alone. And by then you will *beg* me to take you.'

All of a sudden Dino felt short of breath. There was no way out. In the depths of his mind he heard the searing sound of Tol's glory.

'OK, OK,' Dino relented, holding his hands up in defeat. 'Just please, give me some time.'

'Time?'

'Just some time to think. You said I had to come willingly, right?'

'I will give you time,' Tol mused, allowing Dino a solitary lifeline. 'Time to think about my offer. On the condition that you tell no one of our deal. If you try to escape, or if you speak of our arrangement, then your time will be up. Do you accept my demands?'

Dino nodded his head in fearful understanding.

Tol went on, 'And you agree that you're willing to join my coven? Maybe not immediately, but you are willing to consider my offer?'

Dino nodded his head again, unable to speak.

'Then say it,' Tol urged. Although Tol continued to stand

at a distance from Dino, his presence was overwhelming, almost as though there was an invisible force field between them.

'I'll consider joining your coven,' Dino murmured, his voice quivering.

Tol let out a hollow, delirious cackle. 'Your words have unbound me,' he declared. And for the first time since their meeting, he stepped closer to Dino. So close that Dino could smell the rank odour of his rotting skin. 'You see, boy,' Tol said, now clutching Dino's face in a crooked hand, 'a long time ago, a witch's spell prevented me from approaching anyone like you. But there's always a loophole, and you just invited me in. I've waited many years to do this . . .'

'To do what?' Dino rasped in alarm. Tol held his face so tightly that it felt as though he was clamped in an iron vice.

'This,' Tol whispered. In one rapid motion, he trailed his serrated yellow fingernail along Dino's jaw line.

Dino winced as the skin split and blood dripped over on to Tol's hand.

Satisfied, Tol relinquished his grip and stood back. 'Now run away and think, boy. Because the next time you see me, it'll be on my terms.'

Stumbling over his own feet, Dino raced along the embankment, his heart beating at an impossible rate. He didn't dare look back, just in case Tol was in pursuit.

But Tol didn't attempt to follow him. Instead, he remained on the embankment, triumphantly licking the blood from his fingers.

9

Lies

Mia awoke in a bleary haze. The memories of her late-night visitor came back to her in a blur.

Was that a dream? she wondered, in a state of disbelief. But the spatters of dried blood staining her white bed sheets confirmed it to be true.

'Dino!' she called out.

From across the room, Dino groaned. 'What?' he responded groggily. His voice was muffled and slurred, not quite awake yet.

'Where were you last night?' Mia demanded.

Dino hesitated. When he spoke again, his tone was much more coherent, as though he too had been hit with an abrupt reminder of the previous night. 'Out,' he answered cagily.

Mia sat up in bed. 'Out? In the middle of the night?'

'Yes.'

What was he doing out so late at night? she mused, naturally suspicious.

Dino sensed her feelings of doubt. 'It's not a crime,' he snapped.

'I didn't say it was,' Mia retorted defensively. She listened to the scuffling sound of Dino getting out of bed. Moments later, the bedroom door creaked open and then slammed shut.

'Dino?' Mia peered out from behind her bed curtains.

He was gone.

Baffled by his prompt exit, Mia climbed out of bed and inspected the deserted room. It was hard to believe that he had actually left. He barely would have had time to get dressed.

Venturing over to his side of the room, she noticed that the curtains canopying his bed were ajar. Cautiously, she peeled them back and peeked inside. The bed was a complete mess. The sheets were twisted and tangled from what must have been an extremely restless night's sleep. Half-heartedly, Mia pulled the curtains apart and set to work making his bed. She figured he'd probably appreciate it. But as she straightened out the jumbled sheets, she spotted a large patch of dried blood on one of the pillowcases.

The sight was shocking. Instantly, Mia dropped the sheet she was holding and drew the bed curtains closed. For a moment she wasn't sure how to react. Why was there blood on his bedding? Had Colt been to see Dino, too? She had to talk to her brother.

In a fumble, Mia hurried to her wardrobe and yanked out a butter-coloured dress. She threw it on and quickly swept a brush through her hair before darting out of the bedchamber.

A few Arcana boys were loitering at the bottom of the stairwell. Mia raced past them without a word.

'Looking for me?' one of the boys commented sleazily. The others sniggered as though he had made a fantastically witty joke.

Mia grimaced. 'No,' she replied flatly. Paying them no attention, she methodically began flinging open the doors to the ground-floor rooms. 'I'm looking for my brother. Have you seen him?'

'What, you mean the psycho?' the loutish boy called out to her. 'Yeah, he passed us. We told him to keep walking!' The gathering of boys burst into hysterics like a pack of hyenas.

Mia glared at them. 'Is that so?' she challenged dubiously. 'Well, I'm betting you didn't say it loud enough for him to hear.'

They looked between one another, evidently maddened that she was testing their masculinity.

'We'd say it to his face,' one of the other boys spoke up. 'He thinks he's tough, but he's just a wannabe Hunter.'

'He is not!' Mia stared daggers at them. How dare they speak about her brother in this way!

'I'd take him on,' a heavy-set boy added, sneering brashly.

Mia looked at him through narrowed eyes. 'OK. I'll tell him to meet you in the courtyard in, say, ten minutes?'

The boy shifted uncomfortably. 'Nah. I'm busy.'

Mia smiled sweetly. 'I thought so.' Content with the outcome, she trotted away and returned to her search. She hated to hear people slander Dino like that. Especially when they didn't even know him. But she held him in such high esteem that her opinion would never be compromised, no matter what people said. She knew that, behind the belligerency, her brother had a good heart.

Eventually she found Dino in the drawing room. He was standing at the refreshment table, pouring himself a cup of witches' brew. Several other Arcana were dotted casually around.

'There's blood on your pillow!' Mia blurted out. A few of the Arcana turned to look at her.

'Shh! Keep your voice down,' Dino scolded, gripping her elbow and steering her towards an unoccupied corner.

'Why is there blood on your pillow?' Mia asked again, this time in a hushed voice. She half expected him to confess to having his own night visitor. And her number-one suspect was Colt.

'I cut myself,' Dino replied without batting an eyelid.

Mia eyed him cynically. 'Must have been a pretty severe cut. Your pillowcase was drenched.'

Dino tried to deflect the conversation. 'What are you doing snooping around in my side of the room?'

'How did you cut yourself?' Mia pressed, disregarding his counterattack.

'Shaving,' he embellished.

'Show me.'

Dino pulled down the collar of his polo shirt and tilted his head to expose his jaw line.

Mia cringed at the sight of the jagged gash that trailed along her brother's face. 'That's a strange kind of shaving cut. What were you using, a chainsaw?'

Dino flipped his collar back up. 'How would you know what a shaving cut looks like? It's not like you're an expert.' His expression was remarkably cool.

Mia wrinkled her nose. 'Does it hurt?' she asked, genuinely concerned.

'No,' he said with an offhanded shrug. Actually, it did hurt. It stung and burned, as though it had been infected with some sort of toxic residue from Tol's rotten fingernail.

Mia decided to give him one last chance to confide in her. 'Swear to me,' she said, searching his eyes for the truth. 'Swear to me that you got that cut from shaving.' At times like this, she wished that she had his power. It definitely would have come in handy.

Dino didn't respond. He raised an eyebrow at her, effectively ending their conversation.

'Fine,' Mia submitted. 'But if that's what happens when you shave, maybe you should think about growing a beard,' she uttered quietly. Something about this didn't feel right to her.

Their discussion was cut short as Kizzy and Blue strolled into the drawing room.

Dino called them over, glad to put an end to his sister's questioning.

'Blue,' Mia said abruptly, 'do you shave?'

Blue took a seat in an armchair and ran his hand along his face. Despite being the same age as Dino, Blue's skin had a more youthful appearance. 'Shave? Yes,' he said. 'Well, sometimes,' he added sheepishly. 'At least five times.'

Mia deliberated. 'And do you ever cut yourself?'

'Every time,' Blue grinned.

'Drop it, Mia,' Dino scowled.

She carried on regardless. 'Ever cut yourself this bad?' she asked, yanking Dino's collar down before he had a chance to pull away.

'Ooh,' Kizzy winced sympathetically. 'That looks sore.' Her blue eyes were wide with compassion.

'Yes, it does look bad,' Mia agreed. 'A little worse than your average shaving nick, wouldn't you say?'

In the split second that Mia's eyes were on Kizzy, Dino looked at Blue, signalling for him to play along.

Blue twitched nervously. 'Well, I . . . I've had s . . . some bad cuts.'

Mia frowned. 'That bad?'

Behind her back, Dino locked eyes with Blue.

'Yes,' Blue lied.

Kizzy and Mia shared a doubtful look. And, with a satisfied smile, Dino flopped into an armchair and took a swig of tea.

Mia studied him for a moment. 'Excuse me,' she said at last, 'I'm going to the library.'

'Bye.' Dino waved at her without bothering to look up.

Mia gestured for Kizzy to follow, and the girls made their exit.

Once they were out of the drawing room, Kizzy held up her hands quizzically. 'What was all that about?' she asked. 'Why was your brother acting so shady?'

'I have no idea!' Mia told her. 'Something weird is going on.'

The girls paced along the dark, winding corridor.

'No way was that a shaving cut,' Kizzy deduced. 'It looked more like he'd been clawed by a wild animal!'

'And since when does Dino drink witches' brew?' Mia pointed out. 'He's normally the most anti-vision person here!'

'I wonder what he's hoping to see,' Kizzy mused.

Mia pushed open the door to the library. 'Good question,' she muttered, mostly to herself.

As usual, the library was empty. Kizzy took a seat while Mia set to work scanning the wall-to-wall rows of books.

'What exactly are you looking for?' Kizzy asked.

'A book,' Mia responded distractedly.

'Oh!' Kizzy frowned. 'What are you going to do with it?'

Mia giggled. 'I'm going to read it!'

'You're going to read a book?' Kizzy regarded her sceptically.

'Yeah. Sure.'

Kizzy paused. 'All the way?'

Mia smiled sweetly. '*Some* of the way,' she corrected.

Kizzy chuckled. 'What do you want to read about?' She tucked her legs up on to the chair, observing her friend curiously.

'I want to find out about something called enticement.' Mia traced her hand along the wall of books, her fingers dipping periodically over their dusty spines.

'Enticement . . .' Kizzy tapped her chin thoughtfully. 'That's a Hunter thing, isn't it?'

Mia glanced at her. 'You've heard of it?'

'Yeah. I don't know all the facts, but I think it's got something to do with blood. If a Hunter takes your blood, he can get inside your head. Do you think that's what happened to Dino?'

'Maybe . . .' Mia said noncommittally.

'I don't think you should jump to conclusions,' Kizzy implored, diplomatically. 'Why do you think it's got anything to do with enticement?'

Mia returned her focus to the bookshelves. 'Maybe it's not enticement,' she agreed. 'But I wanted to check up on it for my own reasons – '

'Mia,' Kizzy cut her off, 'is this about what I said last night? Y'know, about my vision of Colt and the knife?'

For a second, Mia was taken aback. Until that moment, it hadn't occurred to her that Kizzy's vision had indeed come true – even though it had not panned out quite as Kizzy had predicted.

'Because', Kizzy went on, 'I really don't want you to worry about that. Forget Colt! He's just a scumbag Hunter. And I'm making it my personal mission to keep him as far away from you as possible.' She beamed at her noble declaration.

Mia laughed uncomfortably. She desperately wanted to talk to Kizzy about her meetings with Colt, but how could she when Kizzy despised him so much?

She cleared her throat. 'You don't think there might be some good in Colt?' she asked, once again trying to appear as noncommittal as possible.

Kizzy snorted. 'No way! He's a Hunter. They have no humanity, remember? They're pure evil!'

Mia cast her eyes to the floor. Suddenly, she felt an inexplicable sorrow in her heart. It was hard to fathom why exactly, but something about Kizzy's remark saddened her. She didn't want to think of Colt as evil. He wasn't evil.

'Hey, look!' Kizzy let out a whoop of delight. She hopped off her seat and skipped to a pile of books lying stacked on the apothecary table. Nimbly, she pulled a brown, leather-bound book from the centre of the pile. '*Hunters' Spells*,' she read aloud, handing the book to Mia.

Mia opened the old book and began flipping through the

musty pages. Eventually she settled on one page in particular. 'Found it,' she affirmed. 'Enticement and Entrapment,' she read out the subtitle.

'Well? What does it say?' Kizzy returned to her seat and studied Mia expectantly.

' "Hunters' enticement",' Mia continued to read from the yellowed page. ' "By ingesting the blood of his prey, the Hunter is able to perform an enticement ritual. If successfully accomplished, the Hunter can lure his victim by calling to them, enticing them to him . . ." Blah, blah, blah . . .' She skimmed over the next few paragraphs. ' "The only way to break the spell is by draining the blood of the possessor . . ." ' she trailed off.

'What does that mean?' Kizzy pressed.

All of a sudden Mia's throat went dry. Colt had lied to her. 'It means that if a Hunter takes your blood, the only way to stop the enticement is by killing that very Hunter. That's the only means of breaking the spell.' She closed the book and anxiously ran her hand through her hair. *He lied to me! He told me that the enticement could be broken through ingesting the blood of the coven.*

'Well, here's a thought,' Kizzy joked cheerfully. 'Don't let a Hunter take your blood in the first place!'

But Mia didn't smile. 'Kizzy, I've got to go do something.'

'What? You're not going to do anything stupid, are you?'

'No,' Mia promised. 'I just need some air.'

'Sure,' Kizzy nodded. 'Do you want company?'

'No, that's OK. I think I'm going to work on my power for a little while.'

'OK,' Kizzy said. 'I'll catch up with you at lunchtime.'

Mia smiled. She felt awful for lying to Kizzy, but she knew that if she was going to find Colt, she would have to go alone.

*

Outside on the grounds, things were comparatively quiet. It was still early so the Arcana were mostly indoors, and the Hunters had already begun their training in the forest. Well, that's what Mia was banking on anyway.

She stormed through the gardens, fearlessly heading for the abyss of pine trees. Some remote part of her knew that she would be putting herself in danger, but she was beyond caring.

Why would Colt lie to me? The question rolled over and over in her mind. *Or, more importantly, why did I think I could trust him?* She could have kicked herself for being such a fool. How could she have been so blind? He was a Hunter after all. A callous, heartless Hunter.

As Mia stumbled down the incline of the embankment, it dawned on her that maybe this had been Colt's intention all along. Maybe he had planned to gain her trust as part of a much greater ploy. She shuddered at the thought. What did he want from her?

Recklessly, she marched towards the mist. Nothing could stop her, not even common sense.

'Colt!' she screamed, plunging into the murky, grey mist.

Almost instantly she began to feel woozy. The mist slowly filtered into her mouth and nose, working its magic on her.

'Colt!' she called, a little less assertively this time.

As she walked on, she recognised that she was losing control and was being guided by the enchantment of the mist. It directed her stride, setting her on course like a moth to a flame.

She looked on in trepidation as the mist began to break. Unable to stop herself, she wandered onward into the looming pine trees. She knew it was her imagination, but she could have sworn that the trees curved and parted to grant her access.

Just as her foot crunched down upon the forest floor, she was grabbed from behind. A rough hand pressed firmly over her mouth, stifling her cries. Before she knew what was happening, she was lifted off her feet and hauled backwards.

Hidden among the web of trees, Mia clawed at the hand over her mouth. It was hard to tell who was behind her, because his arm held her securely, preventing her from moving. She could feel agitated breath on her neck, and the rhythm of a heartbeat against her shoulder blade.

'Just a quick question,' a voice hissed into her ear. 'Are you insane?'

'Ouch!' Mia moaned, biting at the hand that clasped her mouth. 'Get off!'

Colt loosened his grip, but his hand stayed slackly over her mouth. 'Don't come to the forest and call my name,' he scolded her sharply. 'What a foolish move.'

'Well, how else am I going to find you?' Mia protested. She reached up and tugged his hand away from her mouth entirely, but she didn't attempt to turn around.

'Simple answer: *don't* try and find me,' Colt berated her in a hushed voice. 'In fact, you're lucky I found you before you found me. You surely know that they can sense you as soon as you cross the perimeter?' His eyes flickered around apprehensively, as though he were expertly detecting every movement. 'If I hadn't got to you first, you'd probably be dead by now.'

'Well, in that case, I suppose calling out your name wasn't such a foolish move after all,' Mia retorted unflinchingly. She couldn't see Colt's face, but she felt him smile against the back of her head.

'My, my, little one, you are getting cocky,' he remarked sarcastically, his voice still lowered to a whisper.

'It seems to be a language you understand,' Mia snapped. She wriggled to free herself from him, but he refused to relinquish his hold.

'I'm already regretting asking this, but what do you want?' Colt said into her ear.

'I need to talk to you,' Mia ordered tersely.

'About?'

'Last night. What you did . . .'

Colt interrupted her hastily. 'Not here,' he murmured under his breath. 'Spangles.'

And before Mia had a chance to respond, she felt herself soar through the air and land with a heavy thud several metres clear of the mist. It was incredible. Only a matter of seconds ago, she had been inside the forest rendered helpless by Colt's grasp. Yet now she lay on the dewy grass at a remarkable distance from any of that. He had commanded the air to carry her as if she were nothing more than a weightless feather.

'Spangles,' she muttered in confusion, recalling Colt's final words. She sat herself upright, rubbing at the fresh graze on her elbow and racking her brain to decipher Colt's meaning.

'Spangles,' she said again. Slowly the penny began to drop.

Mia scrambled to her feet and set off towards the grave yard. She passed beneath the border of wind chimes and scanned the gravestones for the slab engraved with Spangles. It wasn't hard to find – it was one of the largest stones there. She sat on the grass beside it, idly running her hand along the soft moss that grew over the ground.

In a cloud of misgiving, she wondered if Colt would show up. Or if she even wanted him to.

What have I got myself into? she thought nervously.

Then, as if from out of nowhere, Colt surfaced, answering her unspoken question. 'Well, you've just gone and made things a damn sight worse for yourself. And me, too, I might add.'

Mia stood up to confront him face to face. 'You lied to me,' she stated. 'Why did you tell me that your blood would break Lotan's enticement?'

Colt glanced around to ensure that they were alone. 'It wasn't a lie,' he replied at last.

Mia folded her arms. 'It was a lie. I read up on it, and . . .'

'Oh, congratulations!' Colt sneered in amusement. 'You read a book!'

'Yes, I did. And I learned that the only way to break an enticement is to drain the blood of your possessor.'

Colt's sneer turned into a bemused smile. 'Oh, dear. It seems I celebrated too soon. You didn't read a book, you read *a page.*'

Mia scowled at him. 'Why did you lie?' she demanded.

Colt sighed and rubbed his brow. 'Your research, though thorough . . .' he paused to smirk sarcastically '. . . was imprecise. I suppose some things simply aren't documented. Yes, the standard procedure to break an enticement is to drain the blood of your assailant. However, blood of the coven is a common loophole for many ritualistic attacks.'

Mia hesitated, unsure if she should believe him or not.

'Although,' Colt went on, 'usually blood of the coven is not so easy to attain. You see, if a Hunter doesn't want you to drink his blood, then it's probably not going to happen. Not me, though – I'm just giving it away!' he added humorously. 'So, unless you can find a Hunter as generous as I am, you'd be better off going for the kill. To summarise, draining the blood of your possessor is indeed the most plausible escape.'

Warily, Mia looked him up and down. He stood with a blasé swagger, not quite smiling, but not quite frowning either. 'How can I be sure I can trust you?' she asked.

Colt laughed musically. 'You can't trust me! And don't ever allow yourself to feel as though you can.'

For some reason, what had been intended as a warning actually had the opposite effect on her. It somehow managed to reinforce her faith in him.

'So, it's true?' she said quietly. 'I'm no longer under Lotan's spell?'

'Shh!' He placed his index finger on his lips and winked at her.

'What about the mist?' Mia questioned him. 'How did it take a hold of me if I'm not being possessed?'

'The mist is a different entity entirely. To an Arcana, it's like breathing in a highly potent drug. It's a weapon in itself, designed to draw in an intruder. And you need to steer well clear of it, because you have already made yourself very conspicuous . . .'

Abruptly Colt stopped speaking. His eyes drifted southward from her face and his arrogant expression dissolved into a look of hunger.

Mia followed his gaze. 'Stop that!' she exclaimed, mortified. Her arms were still folded across her chest, where Colt's focus also rested.

'Cover it,' he said in a tight voice.

Blushing, Mia adjusted her arms to conceal her shapely body. 'You pig!' she cried.

Colt rolled his eyes impatiently. 'No, not that. Give me some credit. I'm surely a little subtler when I stare at your chest. I'm asking you to cover the graze on your elbow. It's bleeding.'

'Oh.' Mia inspected her elbow. He was right – it was bleeding. A smear of ruby-red blood glistened on the graze and a heavy drop drizzled down her arm like a solitary tear.

'I'm serious,' Colt said sternly. 'Cover it.' He backed away, his eyes never leaving her elbow.

Mia did her best to wipe the blood away, but it smeared across her arm like a smudge of red paint.

In a swift reflex action, Colt covered his mouth and nose.

'Oops,' Mia muttered. 'Sorry!' She licked her fingers and then dabbed at the blotted area. But this only seemed to aggravate Colt further. He bit down on his knuckles in an anguished struggle to distract himself. 'You're doing it on purpose!' he accused.

'I am not!'

'Then put your arm down!' Colt snapped. 'Stop displaying it, devil! You know I enjoy it so!'

Mia straightened out her arm so that he was no longer able to see the scrape. Contrary to Colt's allegation, she really hadn't been doing it on purpose.

'Is that better?' she asked.

Colt's mood altered somewhat. 'I suppose so,' he grumbled, letting out a tense breath. But despite his restored composure, his eyes didn't return to her face.

'Now what?' Mia groused, confused as to why his gaze was still lowered.

Colt grinned mischievously. 'Nothing,' he replied in a falsely charming voice. 'Perhaps I'm not as subtle as I thought I was.' He laughed to himself and reluctantly brought his eyes up to Mia's. 'Are we finished?'

As infuriated as she was by his boorish behaviour, Mia realised that she didn't want their conversation to be finished. In fact, it unnerved her to think about how much she enjoyed his company. She certainly didn't want to feel that way about him.

'Will the other Hunters come after me?' she asked openly. It was a genuine concern, but she couldn't deny that she was procrastinating.

All of a sudden Colt seemed almost serene. 'I'll do my best to stop them this time,' he assured her. 'But in return, you must stay away. I can't continue to protect you.'

'I'll stay away from the forest,' Mia agreed.

'And from me,' Colt added in an even tone. 'I'll do my part, and you'll be safe. But this must be the last time.' He stepped forward and placed his hand on Mia's shoulder, his fingers absent-mindedly coiled around a strand of her hair. 'I won't see you again.'

The thought of this being her last encounter with Colt sent a little twinge through her heart. 'But what about my powers?'

she pressed, in a feeble attempt to secure their alliance. 'Won't you help me?' She looked up into his eyes with the vulnerability of a lost child.

Colt returned her gaze, but shook his head remorsefully. 'No. You don't need me.'

'But I do!' Mia blurted out. They both knew that she was no longer speaking of her powers.

Colt removed his hand from her shoulder. 'They say moss grows on witches' graves,' he said distantly, his eyes cast down to the ground surrounding Spangles' grave. 'I don't know why, though.'

Mia swallowed a lump in her throat. 'Does it matter?' she wondered quietly.

'I suppose not,' he said in that same distant voice. 'But it incenses me. I'd like to know why moss will grow above my corpse. Wouldn't you?'

'Not really. I don't want to think about it.'

'Perhaps that's wise,' he smiled.

'I doubt it.'

Colt's eyes drifted back to her. 'Don't feel affection for me,' he cautioned gently.

'Why not?'

'Because I will never reciprocate.' At these final words, Colt jolted backwards violently.

Mia gawped as an arrow sped through the air and plunged deep into his chest.

Colt collapsed back on to the moss of Spangles' grave. Implanted into his chest was a slim, wooden arrow like a flagpole planted triumphantly into conquered territory.

10

Love's Sacrifice

Mia dropped to the ground, crouching at Colt's side as he writhed in pain. The slim arrow jutting out from his chest was rigid and unyielding.

And then a new sound cut through the tranquillity of the graveyard.

'Mia, run!' Kizzy's voice echoed stridently.

Everything seemed to be unfolding in such a blur that Mia barely registered what was happening.

'Mia!' Kizzy yelled again. 'Run!' She emerged into view several metres away, a wooden crossbow tucked under her arm.

'Kizzy!' Mia gasped. '*You* shot him!'

Colt let out an anguished growl. 'It's a poisoned tip,' he said through gritted teeth. In one swift, ferocious yank, he ripped the arrow from out of his body and tossed it aside.

'Mia, get away from him!' Kizzy cried. 'We need to get out of here!' She hovered at a safe distance from her immobilised victim.

'I can't leave him!' Mia called back, her voice cracking with emotion.

Guardedly, Kizzy edged closer, still clinging to the crossbow. 'He was trying to kill you,' she said frantically. 'Get away from him!'

'No,' Mia explained, 'he wasn't going to hurt me. He's my friend.' She was instantly racked with guilt. This was all her fault. If she'd been honest with Kizzy in the first place, none of this would be happening.

Kizzy gawped at her. 'He's your . . . what?'

'He's the one who's been helping me with my power,' Mia revealed hastily. She turned her attention back to Colt, who was lying wounded and in agony. His eyes seemed unfocused and beads of sweat glistened on his face.

'What was on the tip?' he rasped, woozily.

Kizzy took another cautious step forward. 'Rosewood sap and hancia extract,' she said in a shallow, fraught voice.

'I knew it,' Colt snarled, 'a poisoned tip. You did a ritual?' he spat venomously.

Kizzy's face was as white as a ghost's. 'Yes,' she confessed.

Mia furrowed her brow. 'A ritual? A ritual for what?'

'I saw him. After you left the library I had a vision: the two of you were in the graveyard and I thought he was going to kill you. So I . . .' she trailed off.

'So you thought you'd kill me first,' Colt finished with bitter resentment.

'I had to stop it,' Kizzy murmured. 'I'm sorry. I didn't know . . .'

Mia closed her eyes. 'There was no way you could have known,' she said as kindly as possible. 'What was the ritual exactly? Can it be reversed?'

'I . . . I think so,' Kizzy stuttered. 'I think there's a potion that acts as an antidote to the poison.'

Colt snorted. 'Oh, great! She *thinks*.'

Mia placed her hand on his brow, which sedated him somewhat. 'Kizzy,' she said, trying to remain calm. 'Do you think you can do the reversal ritual?'

Kizzy nodded her head nervously. 'I need to find the book and the herbs, but I'll go as quickly as I can.'

'Good. I'll wait here with Colt,' Mia told her.

And without further ado, Kizzy turned and sprinted across the graveyard, back towards the castle.

Colt's eyelids drooped. 'It's starting to numb,' he said to Mia, 'which is pleasant. I think it's time you left me. The Hunters will sense what's happened to me and track me down. I imagine they'll be here soon.'

Mia traced her hand along his face, soothing him. 'I don't want to leave you,' she said, unafraid.

Colt wheezed for oxygen, like a fish out of water. 'Go!' he said firmly. 'When they find you here, they'll kill you.'

'I can't,' Mia choked. 'I can't leave you when you're in such pain!'

He forced a weak smile. 'I'm not in pain. I can't feel a thing. I'm rather enjoying it in many ways.'

'How can you make jokes at a time like this?' she cried despondently.

He blinked up at her, as though he couldn't quite see her properly. 'Please go,' he said quietly. 'You know how much I loathe to say please. And I did it, didn't I? Just for you.'

Mia shook her head. She could feel her eyes welling with hot tears. 'I don't want to go.'

'Don't worry. It'll be quick,' he assured her. 'And I wasn't exaggerating – I really can't feel a thing. Otherwise I'd throw you on your way.'

'You'll die?' Mia whispered, fighting to hold back the tears.

'Yes. But quickly.'

'No,' Mia defied him stubbornly. 'Kizzy will be back with the antidote soon and then . . .'

'She won't be back in time,' Colt interrupted. 'The poison is spreading. It'll be a matter of minutes. The girl will barely have time to find the correct book, let alone execute the ritual.'

'Well, then, you'll have to hold on.'

'It's not like I have a choice in the matter, darling.' He shuddered as his body throbbed and tautened under the mercy of the poison.

'There has to be another way,' she tried again.

'There isn't. Go!' he barked. 'Listen to me; there's a kind of instinct in a Hunter coven to go to a brother when he's under threat. I'm trying to focus my mind on blocking their senses, but I'm fading fast. I can't keep it up. It takes a lot of concentration, and I want to rest.'

Mia's whole body began to quake. Not in fear of the Hunter coven, but in terror at the thought that she would helplessly watch Colt die.

'Wait . . .' she muddled on, mostly to herself. 'The coven. Blood of the coven,' she said out loud, the familiar phrase ringing in her mind. 'You said blood of the coven can be a loophole in all sorts of rituals.'

'No,' Colt denied her flatly, already predicting where her thoughts were heading.

'Will it work?'

'I'm not taking your blood,' Colt snapped, momentarily revitalised. 'Now, be gone! You're not wanted here.'

'Why won't you take my blood?' Mia persisted.

He convulsed as a brutal wave of pain flooded over him. 'Don't be absurd! You're not even a coven!'

Mia shrugged her shoulders. 'Kizzy's the closest thing I have to a coven. If it's got a chance of working, I think we should try it.'

'No!' Colt snarled warningly at her.

'Why not?'

He closed his eyes, ashamed to divulge anything further. 'Because I'll bleed you dry,' he muttered grudgingly.

'No, you won't,' Mia insisted. In truth, she couldn't be sure of that, but she refused to let him die. Not when there was a chance of healing him.

'Don't be so careless with your life,' Colt advised her sombrely. 'If I start drinking from you, I won't stop.'

'I'll stop you.'

Colt laughed sourly. 'No one could stop me.' The statement, though arrogant, was not said with pride.

But it didn't deter Mia. Even with Colt's harrowing warnings, she twisted her arm and picked at the graze on her elbow.

'Ow, ow, ow!' she grumbled, wincing as the cut reopened and glistened with fresh blood.

By this point, Colt was so weak that he was more or less paralysed.

'No,' he groaned. With great effort he tipped his head away from her.

Mia leaned forward and gently guided his face back towards her. She noticed that his skin was hot and clammy to the touch. His eyes rested upon hers with a wistful intensity.

'Go away,' he said pensively. 'And just say goodbye. I'd like that to be the last thing I hear.'

'No,' she denied him.

'Don't make "no" the last thing I hear! I'm told it far too frequently as it is.' He coughed gutturally. 'That word has been the bane of my life, and now my death, too.'

'Now who's being melodramatic?' Mia uttered under her breath.

'I'm *allowed* to be melodramatic. I'm soon to be dead!'

All of a sudden, Mia felt uncomfortably warm. She knew what she needed to do. 'Open your mouth,' she instructed.

Colt pressed his lips together obstinately. 'Go away!' he garbled, followed by a string of profanities which, as luck would have it, were mostly inaudible behind his sealed lips.

'What a temper!' Mia teased him, tears starting from her eyes. '*I* didn't resort to such foul language when our roles were reversed last night.'

In spite of his suffering, Colt smirked. 'Your memory is selective,' he pointed out. But his mouth remained clamped shut.

Taking charge, Mia pressed her elbow to his lips.

Colt let out a howl of protest and thrashed his head back and forth in an attempt to escape her.

But his efforts were futile. A trickle of blood spilled over into his mouth, and with the taste on his tongue, it was impossible to resist. Reluctantly, his lips parted and so began the exchange.

Mia pulled a face. 'This is disgusting!' she squealed. She could feel the sensation like tiny pinpricks. Contrary to what Colt had said, it wasn't enjoyable in the least.

Before her very eyes, Mia watched Colt's strength return. His limbs flexed and regained their movement and dynamism. Vigorously, he clamped his hands around her arm, securing her elbow to his mouth.

'OK,' Mia spoke shakily. 'I think that's enough.'

But Colt didn't respond to her. He didn't stop feeding, either. In fact, he seemed more rapt by the procedure than ever.

'Stop!' Mia cried. She squirmed to free herself, but his grip was ruthless.

The pinprick sensation rapidly developed into an excruciating sting. Fiercely, his fingers squeezed down upon her arm, as though he would crush her bones with his bare hands.

'Stop!' Mia commanded. Desperately, she used her free hand to push at his face. But it was like trying to dislodge an immoveable object. Just as she began to panic, a strong gust of air whipped over Colt, tousling through the strands of his dark hair. The breeze swirled around him and, in one solid blow, struck his face away from her, breaking the connection.

Mia quickly withdrew her arm, and Colt lay panting on the ground, his face cushioned by the moss of Spangles' grave.

Neither spoke for a moment. They were both shaken from the experience.

'Thank you,' Colt murmured at last. He paused and slanted his head to look up at her. 'You see,' he said puckishly, 'that's the suitable response for such self-sacrifice. Thank you. I believe your response to me was, "You evil, vile monster." Or something to that effect.'

Mia smiled. 'I see you're back to your old self,' she commented wryly, rubbing at her sore elbow. 'My blood worked?'

He lay on the moss, placid but strong. 'Apparently so.' Euphorically, he stretched his arms out around him, relishing in their restored muscle and strength. 'I suppose we're even now,' he noted.

'I suppose we are. Although I think I drew the short straw!'

Colt grinned. He flexed his hands and idly knotted his fingers through the moss. 'You didn't enjoy it? Not even a little bit?' he taunted her wickedly.

'No!'

'Suit yourself. But, on the plus side, you resorted to using your power. Well done.'

Mia beamed, and her joy twinkled all the way up to her silvery eyes. 'I did it!? *I* charged the air to push you away?'

'Yes, you did. And it was quite a powerful force, too,' he admitted.

'As powerful as you?'

Colt chuckled throatily. 'No.'

'But one day I might be . . .'

'No,' he cut her off. 'You're delusional.'

Mia swatted at him good-naturedly. 'Maybe I'll surprise you.'

'You always do,' he replied casually.

For some reason Mia blushed. 'Anyway,' she moved on swiftly, 'will the other Hunters still be tracking you?'

'No. I'm not in pain any more. I'm weary, but under no threat.'

Mia glowed affectionately. 'So you'll be OK?'

Colt closed his eyes. The shimmer of the sunlight lit up his face and for a moment he looked utterly otherworldly, ethereal. 'Yes. I just need to rest for a moment.'

'I should find Kizzy and tell her we don't need the reversal potion,' Mia mused out loud.

'No,' Colt said in a smooth tone.

Mia studied him curiously. 'No?'

'Not yet,' he elaborated. 'You've lost a lot of blood. You're probably feeling light-headed.'

'No. I think I'm OK.'

Colt opened one eye and peered at her. 'Even so, perhaps you should stay here.'

'Why?'

'You know why.'

'Do you want me to stay?' she asked tentatively.

He mulled it over for a second. 'Yes, *please*,' he said at last.

'Well, seeing as though you asked so nicely . . .'

Colt patted the ground. 'Would you like to rest for a while?' he coaxed her, more for his own comfort than hers.

A little unsure, Mia lay down on the moss beside him. She looked up into the clear blue sky.

'Are you tired?' Colt asked her. He was all too aware of how wearing the blood trade could be.

She tilted her head to look at him. 'A little,' she confessed. This close to him, she could see every detail of his face. He looked striking, almost handsome.

'Then you can shut your eyes,' Colt told her. 'I'll make sure no harm comes to you.'

She had to admit she was feeling sleepy. The prospect of closing her eyes was incredibly appealing.

'I won't sleep,' she said softly, 'but I'll shut my eyes. Just for a minute.'

Colt chuckled quietly. 'OK, darling.'

*

The melody of wind chimes gently woke Mia from her slumber. She opened her eyes blearily to find that she was alone in the graveyard. The sun was still high, but there was a distinct bite in the air.

She realised she must have fallen asleep.

Sitting herself upright, she glanced around for Colt. He was nowhere to be seen.

And then she heard the sound of footsteps approaching.

'Colt?' Mia called out.

As the footsteps neared, Kizzy came into view, pacing across the graveyard clutching a vial of translucent liquid.

'Kizzy!' Mia cried.

'I've got the remedy!' Kizzy declared, beaming in triumph.

Mia groaned. 'I'm sorry,' she apologised meekly. 'I should have gone looking for you, but I fell asleep. He's OK. We didn't need the potion.'

Kizzy jogged to a halt and dropped down beside Mia, leaning back against Spangles' gravestone. She wiped her brow with the back of her hand; her cheeks were flushed and rosy from running.

'That's kind of a relief,' she admitted. 'I'm not sure how well this would have worked.' She held up the vial for closer inspection. 'It's not so easy to do the reversal ritual. But how did you manage it without the potion?'

Mia cringed at the memory. 'Do you really want to know?'

'Perhaps not. But go ahead and tell me anyway.'

Mia subtly touched her tender elbow. She feared that Kizzy would be appalled by what she had done, but she didn't want to lie to her again, either.

'I had to give him blood,' she confessed. '*My* blood.' She held her gaze on the ground, avoiding Kizzy's eyes.

'Eugh!' Kizzy shrieked.

'Yeah. It was . . . gross.'

'Eugh!' Kizzy wailed again. 'I'm so sorry, Mia! If I hadn't shot him, you never would have had to do that.'

Mia looked up at Kizzy earnestly. 'It's not your fault. It's my fault for not being honest with you.'

Kizzy leaned over and gave her a little hug. 'Don't be silly. You don't have to tell me everything, you know. Although I am a little surprised that you didn't tell me about Colt.'

'I wanted to.'

'What stopped you?'

'I don't know.' Mia gazed distantly at the wind chimes as they swayed in the afternoon breeze. 'I suppose I was embarrassed.'

'You don't need to be embarrassed – it's only me.'

'I know,' Mia smiled timidly. 'Thanks.'

'You must really like him,' Kizzy guessed intuitively.

'Maybe. Not at first,' Mia mulled it over, 'but now I think I do. In fact, I *know* I do.'

Kizzy chewed on her thumbnail. 'Good. Well, kind of good. I mean, I'm glad you've met someone you like. But, at the same time, I am a little worried. It's Colt.'

Of course, her only interaction with Hunters had been in a negative context.

'Believe me – I was as shocked as you are!' Mia laughed lightly. 'But I know him. He's not who we thought he was.'

'He's still a Hunter though, Mia,' Kizzy pointed out gently.

'I don't care. I'm not afraid of him. They say Hunters are heartless and inhumane, but he isn't. I know he isn't those things.'

Kizzy exhaled submissively. 'I'm on your side, whatever happens. Just be careful, OK? I don't want to see you get hurt.' Her bright-blue eyes brimmed with sincerity.

'Thanks,' Mia said again. 'And thanks for today. You know, for coming to my rescue and all.'

Kizzy grinned. 'Any time.' She paused. 'Sorry I shot your boyfriend.'

Mia chuckled. 'It happens.'

'So, does anyone else know? About you and Colt, I mean.'

Mia shook her head adamantly. 'No way. You think I'd tell Dino? He'd have a fit!'

'I dread to think. I take it that means you're not going to tell him?'

'Why should I? It's none of his business, anyway.'

'OK,' Kizzy concurred impassively. 'Well, your secret's safe with me. Just promise to keep your wits about you. I know you've got close to Colt, but there might be another side to him. One you haven't seen yet.'

'I know.'

A hazy cloud drifted overhead, blocking out the sun and shading the graveyard. The girls fell silent as they contemplated the dull shadows loom grimly over the graves.

That evening Dino and Blue retreated to the library. Alone in the disused room, Blue worked on his power while Dino leafed through a stack of aged books.

'What exactly are you looking for?' Blue asked his friend, somewhat suspiciously.

Dino kept his eyes fixed on the yellowed pages of his current book. 'Anything I can find on Hunter covens.'

'Why?' Blue pressed.

Dino flipped through a few more pages and then slammed the book shut in frustration. 'Damn it!' he cursed.

'OK, what's g . . . going on?' Blue demanded in an uncharacteristically assertive tone. 'You've been acting t . . . tetchy all day. And you still haven't explained about that c . . . cut on your face. I covered for you, remember? You at l . . . least owe me an explanation.'

'I can't explain,' Dino replied vaguely.

'Does this have to do with that guy you met? Tol?'

Dino's coffee-brown eyes darted anxiously around the poorly lit library. 'Shh!' he hushed his friend, despite the fact that the room was completely empty.

Blue obediently lowered his voice to a whisper. 'Either you're insanely p . . . paranoid, or something else has happened. Which is it?'

Dino groaned inwardly. Tol had warned him not to speak of their arrangement, so how could he possibly share his woes? More than anything he wanted to tell Blue of his predicament, but it was far too risky.

'I can't tell you,' he said after a suspenseful pause.

Blue frowned. Waves of sandy blond hair fell forward over his brow. 'Why can't you t . . . tell me?' he asked.

'Because I can't.'

'It has to do with Tol again, doesn't it?' Blue guessed insightfully.

'Shh!' Dino hissed again.

'Then tell me!'

Unwillingly, Dino pushed his book aside and leaned forward in his chair. 'It *is* about Tol,' he admitted in a weak voice. 'But you can't go shouting that around, OK? This guy is serious.'

'I won't say a word,' Blue reassured him.

Dino took a deep breath. 'I saw him again. Last night. And I was right – he is trying to get to my sister.'

Blue's nose twitched nervously.

'He's given me an ultimatum,' Dino went on. 'It's me or her.'

'You or her for w . . . what?'

'He wants me in his coven.'

Blue swallowed. 'Hunters?'

'Yep. Now I need to know whether being a Hunter is really that bad . . .'

'Yes,' Blue cut him off, 'it *is* that bad. You're not a Hunter; you're an Arcana.'

'Am I?' Dino questioned. 'Because Tol seemed to think I was a born Hunter.' At the mention of Tol's name, Dino's voice reduced to an almost inaudible level.

'You're not a Hunter!' Blue protested. 'Why w . . . would you believe anything h . . . he has to say?'

'Argh!' Dino bellowed in angst. He slouched back in his chair, defeated, his hands clutching at his skull. In the shadow, his hair and eyes appeared even darker than usual – more Hunter-like.

Blue picked up a book from Dino's pile and began skimming through the pages. 'There's got to be something in here to deflect him. He can't threaten you like that.'

'He can, and he is,' Dino responded glumly. 'And there's nothing in these damn books that can help me. It doesn't seem like it's all that common for a Hunter to recruit an Arcana.'

'It isn't,' Blue agreed. 'So why does he want you?'

'I don't know.' Dino shrugged helplessly. 'Maybe he needs my power to complete his coven?'

'But you're not the only Sententia around here.'

'He thinks I'm a Hunter. Maybe I am . . .'

'You're not! What about s . . . speaking to Wendolyn? Maybe she can help.'

Abruptly Dino shook his head. 'No way. Tol made it crystal clear that, if *I* start talking, *he*'d start slaughtering.' His stomach lurched at the mental image of the gruesome man harming his sister.

'Then we just n . . . need more t . . . time to find a way around it,' Blue reasoned. 'There's got to be a way to stop . . .'

His sentence was interrupted by the strained moan of the library door. Wendolyn swept into the room, her long white hair flowing loosely over her apple-green dress.

'Time for lights out,' she told the boys.

Dino glanced at his watch. *It's only ten o'clock!* he thought petulantly. At home he had no bedtime or curfew. In fact, he barely had any discipline at all. His mother and aunt weren't exactly the most responsible of parents. Most of the time they were more like children than adults.

But without debate Dino returned the books to the shelves and extinguished the flickering candles.

'Don't worry,' said Blue once Wendolyn was out of earshot, 'you'll be safe here tonight. Tomorrow we'll come up with a plan.'

They left the library and traipsed along the narrow mahogany hallway.

'I hope so,' Dino muttered under his breath.

'It'll be OK,' Blue affirmed supportively.

Their conversation simmered as they ascended the staircase. The fact was, there was nothing more to say. Tol had Dino in checkmate, and finding a way out was a bleak hope.

In the upstairs hallway, the boys went their separate ways. Nodding a quick goodbye to Blue, Dino quietly slunk into his bedroom. The lights were out, leaving only the moonlight streaming in through the window as a guide.

'Mia?' Dino called out in a stage whisper.

A garbled response came from behind her bed curtains.

Dino took a step closer and peeked through a gap in the curtains. Mia was curled up beneath the blankets, her dark hair fanned out over the pillow and her eyes barely open.

'What is it?' she mumbled sleepily.

'Nothing,' Dino replied, his voice dropping to a low murmur. He touched her head with his forefingers. 'I love you, OK?'

Mia opened her eyes. That certainly wasn't a comment she was familiar with. Not from her brother's mouth, anyway. 'OK,' she said softly. 'I love you, too.'

'I know.' Dino took his hand away. 'Goodnight,' he said as he retreated to his own bed. Not anticipating sleep, he lay on top of the covers, fully clothed. How could he sleep when this problem plagued him so intensely?

*

He lay there for almost two hours before something alien entered his subconscious.

'Come to me,' a voice said, so sleek and commanding that it was impossible to ignore. Mesmerised and unaware of his actions, Dino rose from his bed and strode out of the room.

'Come to me,' the voice chanted over and over again. Hypnotically, it drew Dino out of the castle and across the grounds towards the forest. It was an unmistakable voice; it was the voice of Tol.

Dino walked over the cut grass, trampling the flower beds unseeingly. The midnight sky was clouded with a purple fog that had swallowed up the stars.

He descended the embankment, but did not head directly into the forest. Instead he walked along the edge of the forest mist, never quite venturing through it. He walked for miles until eventually the mist dissolved away. Only then did Dino step into the forest.

The moment he crossed the boundaries, Tol was upon him.

'How lovely to see you,' Tol sneered. His tongue flickered in and out of his mouth as he eyed Dino eagerly.

The uncut sound of Tol's voice jolted Dino out of his trance.

In confusion, Dino glanced around at the pine cage he now found himself in. How had he got there? he wondered in alarm. He distantly remembered walking – remembered the simple motion of the act – but he could not for the life of him fathom *why* he had done it.

'I called for you,' Tol said, unwittingly responding to Dino's thoughts, 'and I think you will be glad you came.' His beady eyes bore into Dino malevolently. 'It is time you see who you truly are.'

Out of the trees, two other shadowy men emerged. They surfaced out of the darkness as though they had materialised out of thin air. Both men were of a similar robust build, and both were shrouded in dark robes which covered all but their gaunt, deformed faces. They circled Dino with a heavy yet weightless stride.

'Step forward,' Tol ordered Dino.

But Dino stood unmoving, frozen to the spot – half out of obstinacy, and half out of fear.

Tol locked eyes with him. 'Step forward,' he repeated in a spellbinding murmur.

And this time, Dino obeyed. He inadvertently stepped on to a triangular symbol that had been scratched into the parched soil.

The two robed men continued to circle him with cruel leers on their warped faces.

Dino drew in an urgent breath as the symbol began to morph and mould around his feet. It somehow clamped him to the spot and sent an immense torrent of electricity through his body.

At first he cried out in pain, but as the current worked its way along his arms and out to his fingertips, the sensation became less of a pain and more of a pleasure.

'Do you feel that power?' Tol salivated.

'Yes,' Dino whispered.

'It's waiting for you,' Tol encouraged him menacingly. 'Take it.'

Dino looked down at his hands in terrified awe. His fingers trembled with life and glowed a vibrant yellow-black, the colour of a bruise.

'Become us!' Tol roared, his harrowing voice reverberating among the trees.

'No!' Dino choked. The flow of electricity inside of him started to burn. It became too hot for him to bear. He let out an anguished howl.

Enraged, Tol slammed the palm of his hand down against the ground. On command, the symbol released its hold, sending Dino toppling forwards on to the forest floor.

'We are running out of time,' Tol growled to the other two men. 'We must change him before he belongs to the Arcana.'

'But he is resisting,' one of the shadowed men snarled. The taller of the two, he had milky translucent eyes and saw-like teeth.

Tol stared at Dino, who lay on the ground, broken. 'He is tempted,' Tol judged. 'The power has flowed through his veins, and soon he will crave it. Then he will surrender.'

All three men turned to Dino, tearing him apart with their eyes.

With his heart racing, Dino sprung to his feet and fled from the forest, running at full pelt to escape the nightmare.

'Bring him back!' the second cloaked man shouted.

'No!' Tol stopped them in a toxic voice. 'We cannot take him unless he is willing. But we still have time. His allegiance is undecided, and eventually he will come to us.'

'How?' the man questioned irately. 'You cannot force him to turn.'

'No, but I have his blood,' Tol reminded them. 'I can call to him every night, infecting him with the dark power. And you're forgetting – I'm part Sententia, too. I can plant feelings of desire and yearning in his mind, and he will believe that the thoughts are his own.'

'It had better work,' the taller of the two men scowled. 'We've waited too long to lose him now.'

Tol cackled. 'We won't lose him. He's already ours.'

11

Brotherhood

As the weeks passed by, Mia resolved herself to developing and sharpening her Tempestus power. She hadn't seen Colt since the day in the graveyard. And she missed him. Pined for him, in fact.

During their last conversation, Colt had told her that he could no longer meet with her. But she had presumed, after her sacrifice of blood, that things had changed between them. It certainly had seemed that way at the time. Not now though. Now she was left feeling abandoned and forgotten.

True to her word, she heeded his warning to steer clear of the forest. However, it didn't stop her from returning to the graveyard every day, in the hope that he would eventually appear. But he never did.

On the bright side, Mia's unaccompanied days proved to be a valuable asset in her quest to develop her powers. She often found herself alone in the solitude of nature, the ideal setting to engage and explore her abilities. Sometimes she would sit beneath the wind chimes for hours, channelling the breeze to sway them back and forth and play a soothing melody. She felt connected to everything and wonderfully at peace. Of course, she could not quite match Colt's skills yet, but she was powerful nonetheless.

But even with her new-found sense of serenity, she constantly dwelled on Colt's absence. Questions repeatedly flooded her troubled mind. Where was he? Had he been hurt? Or was it simply a case of him not caring enough to find her?

One sunny Wednesday afternoon she decided to take matters into her own hands. On a whim, she plucked a catkin from the willow tree. She nursed the little flower in her hand as she headed for the embankment. Taking a seat on the grassy ridge, Mia looked down on the forest. There it stood, austere and mysterious as always, hidden behind a veil of mist.

Mia opened out her hand. The catkin sat in her palm, comfortable and pure, awaiting its task.

'Go to Colt,' Mia whispered to the dainty flower. And with a gentle breath, she blew on it.

The catkin lifted and soared, floating effortlessly on the summer's breeze. Mia watched in admiration as it dutifully followed its course and vanished into the labyrinth of the forest.

That was that. The message to Colt had been sent. Now, all she could do was wait for a response – and what better place to wait than Spangles' grave?

Satisfied with her plan, Mia rose to her feet and trotted to the graveyard. The familiar wind chimes welcomed her with their customary tuneful greeting. She strolled beneath them and took her place at Spangles' stone, situating herself comfortably on the spongy moss. Her heart began to flutter with a mixture of nerves and excitement.

Any minute now, she thought breathlessly.

But, as the minutes turned to hours, Mia had to face the reality that Colt wasn't coming. She remained at the gravestone regardless, disheartened yet patiently steadfast all the same.

As she sat alone, she couldn't help but remember his harsh words to her.

Don't feel affection towards me, he had said. Because I will never reciprocate.

'Why am I such an idiot?' Mia reprimanded herself out loud. And yet still she did not leave her post.

She touched the ground where Colt had once lain. Now, he merely seemed like a figment of her imagination. Maybe that was all he'd ever been.

Sadly, Mia began to feel the pain of her loss, and her loneliness. She had never known feelings like this before: they were intense and true, and had been awakened from a part of her soul which up until now had lain dormant. It was as though she and Colt had been destined to meet. As if their story had already been foretold. One thing was for certain – an inexplicable force had connected her to him. Perhaps it was the power they shared, or perhaps it was beyond that. But now he was gone. And somewhere deep in her heart, she feared that he would not return.

It began to rain.

The little catkin brushed against Colt's leg and dropped to the forest floor. Colt recognised it instantly. The scent and the essence were so intoxicating that it would have been impossible to mistake them.

Hesitantly, he lifted the catkin from among the foliage and embraced it in his hand with the delicacy of a giant holding a china teacup.

He sucked in his breath sharply. He had been dreading this moment. The moment in which she'd summon him. He wanted to ignore it, but how could he? She had been calling to him for weeks – he'd felt it – and it was sheer torture. And now, to see her message in front of his very eyes, as clear as day, was the ultimate temptation.

Why am I not stronger? he scolded himself unsympathetically.

A wallop to the back of his head sent him hurtling into a thick tree trunk.

'Colt!' Lotan barked. 'Your mind is elsewhere! Get yourself together.'

Colt staggered to his feet, the catkin still cocooned safely in his hand. 'Minor error,' he said aloofly. 'I lost concentration for a moment.'

Lotan narrowed his dark eyes. 'There is no room for error, minor or otherwise. Not with the intruder Hunter coven on our land.'

Lotan's nostrils flared. 'The girl,' he said, picking up the scent that lingered in the travelling breeze.

Colt tilted his head, his expression unreadable.

'Does she seek you?' Lotan demanded.

'No,' Colt lied expertly.

Lotan bared his teeth, angry at Mia's continuing intrusion into his tight-knit coven. 'If one of us is not alert, then the whole coven will fall,' he warned Colt.

'I *am* alert,' Colt retorted with confident swagger.

'She will destroy you,' Lotan muttered resentfully, 'if you let her.'

'Forget the girl,' Colt said briskly. 'Yes, she requests my assistance, but I'm undisturbed, and eventually she'll grow tired of trying.'

'She affects you,' Lotan said accusingly.

Colt laughed lightly. 'She doesn't affect me! She is simply a temporary inconvenience.'

'If she poses such an inconvenience to you, then perhaps I should kill her,' Lotan suggested casually, though it was more of a test of Colt's response than a real threat.

Never one to be duped, Colt was alert to his ruse. 'Kill her if you wish,' he said. 'But be sure to have good reason, or else Wendolyn will banish us from the castle. *All* of us.'

'I will take her if she steps foot on to our territory again. That *is* permitted.' Lotan eyed his friend confrontationally. 'But, as you know, Colt, she has somehow managed to deflect my enticement.' If he suspected Colt of interfering, he certainly would not say so out loud.

Colt didn't reply. What he had done had been the highest form of treason. To go behind the back of one of his coven was punishable by death.

'Although,' Lotan went on, 'there are other ways in which I can draw her in.'

'Why bother?' Colt snapped. 'She's no threat. Need we continue with this futile conversation when there are more crucial matters at hand? A rival coven is closing in on our terrain, and your concerns are with a harmless girl.'

'My concerns are with *you*!' Lotan retorted.

'Well, I'm at a loss as to why that would be,' Colt grumbled. 'It's not my fault that she calls to me.'

Lotan met his stare. 'Her calls are the least of my worries. Her influence is what troubles me most, brother.'

Colt chuckled jovially. He strolled away with a blasé gait. 'You think I'm not able?' he challenged Lotan. 'If that is the case, then I defy you to test me. Command our coven to track me and contain me; use it as a training exercise. Put them all on me, yourself included. And then congratulate me when I do not falter.' He leapt several metres up into a tree to add to the drama of his statement.

Lotan smiled reluctantly. 'I think your arrogance is your fatal flaw, Colt.'

Colt sat haughtily on a sturdy tree branch, his legs dangling over the edge. 'You know that I'm unsurpassed,' he smirked, looking down upon Lotan. 'A nuisance girl would never sidetrack me from my duty to the coven.'

'Unsurpassed?' Lotan repeated, his tone brightening somewhat. 'I believe you like to *think* you're unsurpassed, but you're still a far cry from me! That is why I lead and you follow, brother,' he teased good-humouredly.

Colt grinned. 'Is that so?' he replied in jest. 'Perhaps one day you and I should duel,' he mused. 'Pit ourselves against one another and see who fairs best.'

'Ha!' Lotan laughed robustly.

'Ha, indeed,' Colt returned with a wry smile. He dropped down from the tree branch, pouncing to the ground with the agility and prowess of a panther.

'Move yourself, Colt,' Lotan ordered, giving him a hearty clip around the ear. 'I want the entire perimeter covered by nightfall.'

'Well, seeing as though you asked so nicely . . .' Colt privately smiled at the pleasure of using Mia's very words.

'Go, boy!' Lotan exclaimed.

Colt sped off through the trees, faster than any human or animal. He returned his focus to his role as a Hunter – because it would have been perilous not to.

The hours passed slowly and Colt did what was required of him. He guarded and secured the forest boundaries like a lion defending its lair. But all the while he clutched the catkin in his palm, grateful for its company.

And then, just when he thought he had made it through another day, the first drops of rain began, and it broke him. For it wasn't normal everyday precipitation. It was *her* rain – Mia's rain. It was saturated with her scent and spilling relentlessly from the bulging purple rain clouds.

Colt recoiled in anguish. He pressed his body flat against a tree trunk, desperate to shelter himself from the onslaught of water. But there was no escape. The droplets trickled over his face and body, soaking his hair and clothes. Like a wounded soldier, he crumpled to the ground in defeat. He trembled as the drops of rain rolled over on to his lips and leaked into his mouth.

In a desperate attempt at fighting it, he used his power to

command the water away from him. But it was too great to combat: he could not keep up with the downpour.

For the first time in his life, Colt was scared.

In the quiet solitude of the library, Dino slouched in an armchair, staring off into space. He felt like he hadn't slept in weeks. And perhaps he hadn't. In all honesty, he wasn't entirely sure – it was such a blur. Each night Tol would call to him, and, like a devoted dog, Dino would comply. He would trudge miles along the forest borders until he reached Tol's camp. Every night Tol would offer him power, and every night Dino would run from it.

But it wasn't the exhaustion that had left him so dazed, because he was beyond tired. It was the confusion. Somewhere along the way, he had lost sight of everything. What was he doing? Why was he doing it? He had even lost sight of who he was. It was as though he existed solely for the purpose of his nightly conflict with Tol. And gradually, he could feel Tol's presence taking up roots in his subconscious, whittling away until Dino was too weak to fight any more.

Numb, Dino wondered if giving in was really such a bad idea. Why was he resisting anyway? Tol had been right – Dino was craving the dark power to be bestowed on him. And in a warped, sadistic way, he sometimes actually found himself looking forward to standing on the triangular symbol and absorbing its phenomenal energy. After all, during those few brief minutes per night, he was a god.

'I think I've got something,' Blue's voice jolted Dino out of his reverie.

'Huh?' Dino glanced at him, only mildly interested.

'Read this.' Blue thrust an open book into his friend's hands.

Dino grimaced. 'Do I have to read it? I'm tired.'

'OK.' Blue rolled his eyes. 'I'll read it to you.' He took the book back.

'Whatever,' Dino yawned. He propped his feet up on the apothecary table. The disused library had become more of a bedroom than his own room was.

Blue cleared his throat. ' "Coven Laws," he read the heading aloud: ' "Young witches' powers are ambivalent until they are sealed. However, unless a witch has been born into a Hunter coven, it is most likely that those who lived as civilians will settle as Arcana. In some cases there is ambiguity, as the use of power is always free-willed, and occasionally a witch will choose to cross over. Any coven – Hunter or Arcana – can offer a place to whomever they desire. But their offer must be accepted willingly. To deflect an unwanted request, the sought-after witch must perform a ritual of refusal. Through this ritual, the witch is protected from unwelcome advances, spells, or attacks commanded by their opponent . . ." '

Dino closed his eyes, barely listening. 'What does that mean?'

'It means that there's a ritual to protect you from Tol's onslaughts,' Blue explained. 'And it also says here that a Hunter can't prey on hallowed ground. Do you understand what that means?'

'Nope.'

'Dino, the Glass Castle is hallowed ground! It belongs to Wendolyn. It means that Tol is magically bound from harming Mia while she's on Wendolyn's land. I'm guessing that there's a pretty big chance he was making empty threats in a ploy to lure you into his coven. We've got him!' Blue cheered.

Miraculously, since his friendship with Dino, Blue's stammer had reduced drastically. It seemed that, as his confidence rose, his stutter dropped.

Dino appeared marginally more enthused. 'How can you

be sure his threats are weightless? And what if he somehow gets to Mia when she's not on this hallowed ground thing?'

'You need to talk to Wendolyn about the details.'

'OK,' Dino replied, as casually as if he had been asked to post a letter.

Blue furrowed his brow. 'What's the matter with you? This is what we've been researching for weeks! If we do this ritual, Tol can't call on you any more!'

Dino gave another sleepy yawn. 'And how is that, again?'

Blue stared at him, utterly perplexed. 'I just t . . . told you. You perform the ritual of refusal to seal your alliance to the Arcana. Tol's threats are just a trick to draw you in. He can't touch Mia while she's at the castle.'

'OK,' Dino said lethargically. He mulled it over in his mind – or, at least, what was present of his mind.

'Tol can only change you into a Hunter if you offer yourself willingly,' Blue added.

'And how would I go about doing that?'

Blue gawped at him.

'Relax. I'm not gonna do it,' Dino clarified. 'I'm just wondering.'

'I don't know.'

'Right.' Dino picked at his teeth with his fingernail. 'So, what's this ritual?'

'The refusal ritual?' Blue didn't feel as though he should have to clarify which ritual, but from the looks of Dino he could just as easily be talking about a ritual to accept Tol's offer.

'Yeah, sure. That one,' Dino agreed, clearly indifferent.

'It's here,' Blue told him. 'In this book. There's an incantation, in Latin I think. You need to g . . . get together a few herbs and plants. I can help you.'

Dino closed his eyes complacently. 'Yeah. Whatever.'

Even in the dim candlelight, Blue could make out the dark, sunken circles forming beneath Dino's eyes.

'Shall we speak to Wendolyn now?' Blue pressed.

'Nah.' Dino opened his eyes; they were blank and empty. 'I think I should do it by myself. Personal, you know?'

'Of course,' Blue nodded. But he couldn't help feeling a little hurt by the remark.

Dino outstretched his arm. 'Can I take a look at the book?'

Relieved to see him showing some sign of interest, Blue handed over the musty hardback book.

'This is the ritual?' Dino asked, pointing at the page the book was open to.

'Yes, that's it. Everything we need to know is on that first page.'

'Cool.' Dino swiftly tore the page from the book. As it broke away, dust sprinkled from the old paper like crumbling bones.

'Whoa!' Blue winced. 'I don't think you're allowed to rip the pages out! These books are hundreds of years old.'

Dino shrugged. 'Oh, well. Who's going to know? Besides, I want to take it away to look it over properly.'

The hairs on the back of Blue's neck bristled. 'O . . . OK,' he stammered.

All of a sudden, the library door heaved open and Wendolyn peered into the room. Dino discretely slipped the yellowed page into his back pocket.

'Time for lights out,' she kindly informed them.

Blue looked expectantly at Dino, waiting for his friend to ask to speak with Wendolyn. But Dino said nothing. He simply gave her a false smile and hopped to his feet, extinguishing the candles as ordered. Well, all but one.

'Goodnight, Blue,' Dino said, blatantly hinting for his friend to leave.

Blue frowned. 'Aren't you coming with me?'

'I'll be up in a minute. I just want a moment to myself to look over this ritual.'

'Right,' Blue said slowly. Despite his mistrust, he left the library and set off along the narrow corridor.

160

Dino was now alone in the library, standing in the flickering light of the one remaining candle. He pulled the crumpled page out of his pocket and unfolded it. It was scrawled with a jumble of words that made no sense to him. Dino scowled and, with a hardened look in his eyes, he held the page over the flickering candle flame, watching with morbid fascination as the paper shrivelled and disintegrated into silver ashes.

12

Mirror Opposites

Mia awoke to a tapping sound. She squinted against the flood of morning sunlight that engulfed her bedroom. Fuzzily, she realised that someone was knocking at the door.

'Dino?' she murmured, half asleep. When there was no response, she tried again, a little louder this time. 'Dino?'

There came three distinct raps against the bedroom door, followed by the softer sound of Kizzy's voice. 'Mia?'

'Kizzy?' Mia replied in a groggy slur.

'Yeah, it's me,' the voice returned to her. 'Are you awake?'

'No.' Mia paused. 'Come in,' she beckoned.

The door swung open and Kizzy skipped in, bright-eyed and full of zest.

'Good morning!' she sang out. Her blonde hair was twisted into two braids, each secured with long red ribbons.

Mia buried her face into the pillows. 'It's *not* a good morning,' she grumbled.

Kizzy perched on the bed and cautiously peeled back the covers. 'Are you still miserable?'

'Yes.' Mia yanked the covers back up over her head, hiding herself from the world.

'Come on,' Kizzy sighed, 'you can't mope around for ever.'

'Why not?' Mia disputed.

'Because it's boring!' Kizzy persisted with the bedcover tug of war.

Eventually Mia gave up. She dramatically rolled to the

edge of the bed and draped her arm over the side, letting her fingertips skim the ruby carpet.

Kizzy folded her arms. 'I knew no good would come of falling in love with a Hunter.'

Mia sucked in her breath, aware that they were not alone.

'Dino?' she called out, warily.

'Sorry,' Kizzy mouthed sheepishly. She peeked out from behind the bed curtains. 'It's OK,' she confirmed. 'He's not there.'

Mia reflected for a moment. This wasn't the first time that Dino had been out of the room before she'd woken up. It was coming to be a bit of a habit. In fact, over the past couple of weeks, she hadn't seen much of her brother at all. He would come to bed late and wake up early, and during the days he would generally keep his distance from the other Arcana. Mia presumed that he'd been working on his power in solitude. As it happened, it was no bother to her – she wasn't feeling much in the mood for company either.

'Forget about Colt,' Kizzy insisted, returning to their original conversation. 'He doesn't deserve you.' There was only so much she could say to cheer Mia up. It had been days since Mia had sent her catkin message, and still Colt was nowhere to be found.

Mia muttered something quietly and let out a forlorn sigh.

'That's not true!' Kizzy consoled her, despite the fact that she had no idea what Mia had said. 'Now, up you get. Wendolyn's called us all to the drawing room. Group meeting or something like that.'

Mia stretched out her stiff limbs. 'What's the meeting about?' she asked, rubbing at her eyes.

'Dunno. Something about something.'

'I wonder if it's important,' Mia mused out loud.

'Don't try to weasel your way out of it! You're going!' Kizzy replied flatly. 'If I have to go, then you have to go, too.'

Mia pulled a face. 'The last group meeting we went to was the one about the Athame – and look how well that turned out!' The memory of her frightening attempt to wear the Athame dagger was still fresh in her mind.

'Oh, yeah,' Kizzy chuckled. 'Why did we ever think that was a good idea?'

Reluctantly Mia hauled herself out of bed and slowly got dressed. She threw on a pair of cropped jeans and a charcoal top. Her dark hair fell in loose waves over her shoulders.

The girls chatted for a while and then casually made their way downstairs to the drawing room.

When they finally strolled into the room, the other Arcana were already there. All but Dino, that is. Wendolyn stood at the front while the girls quietly took their seats.

But before Wendolyn could begin the meeting, the drawing-room door burst open and a familiar breeze swept in. The Hunters marched through the doorway and lined up in formation at the back of the room, just as they had done at the first of Wendolyn's meetings.

Mia felt her cheeks grow hot. It hadn't even occurred to her that the Hunters would be present. She snuck a glance at the back of the room. Colt was there, standing like a soldier, his eyes trained on Wendolyn.

She hastily returned her gaze to Wendolyn, unsure how to react to the situation. She had waited for weeks to see Colt again, and now here he was in the very same room, yet she couldn't bring herself to look at him. It was utterly nerve-wracking.

'Thank you all for coming,' Wendolyn announced.

Mia barely heard the older woman's voice above the deafening sound of her own racing thoughts.

Wendolyn continued: 'I apologise for the abruptness of my request to call you together, but I fear that the issue cannot wait any longer.'

He's just . . . standing there! Mia thought in disbelief, resisting the urge to turn around and stare at him.

'For some time now,' Wendolyn was saying, 'I have been aware of intruders at the Glass Castle. A Hunter coven.'

Surely he sees me. I'm sitting right in front of him! She nudged Kizzy. 'Has he noticed me?'

Kizzy subtly craned her neck. 'I don't know,' she whispered. 'He's looking straight ahead.'

'We are faced with a threat,' Wendolyn said, 'but we're dealing with it as best we can. Our Glass Castle Hunters are covering the forest boundaries. However, there is still an element of danger. Please, Arcana, stay within the castle grounds until the risk is eliminated. I'm not entirely certain why the trespassers are here, but I will employ every means possible to ensure your safety.'

The audacity! Mia fumed, outraged. *I don't even exist to him!*

From across the room, Blue raised his hand 'Are they h . . here f . . . f . . . for an A . . . Arcana?' He painfully struggled to articulate his words.

A group of boys sniggered in the corner.

'B . . . b . . . b . . . buttons!' one of the boys mocked, encouraging the taunting laughter.

Blue bowed his head. He sat alone with only an empty seat beside him.

Kizzy spluttered in fury. 'Those guys are such morons,' she muttered to Mia. Without thinking, she lobbed her pen at the cackling boys.

'Hey!' one of them moaned as it clunked against his head.

Wendolyn eyed them sternly. 'That's enough!' she scolded the boys. Then her voice softened. 'No, Benny,' she said, answering Blue's question. 'It's not likely that a Hunter would want to recruit an Arcana. I imagine they are here to take up residence on our land. But our Hunters are skilled and accomplished warriors, and will guard the territory until the threat has passed. In the meantime, however, I would like the less experienced witches to stay in the designated castle grounds.' She turned to the Hunters, who were hidden among the shadows at the back of the room. 'And you,' she said, addressing Lotan in particular, 'I ask to keep your wits about you, and good luck! Any questions?'

For a moment, Blue looked as though he were trying to speak up, but his voice failed him.

'Thank you,' Wendolyn concluded. 'You are free to leave.'

Mia had never moved so fast in her life. She was out of the room and into the hallway in the blink of an eye. No way was Colt getting past her! She watched tensely as the Hunters marched out in single file.

As Lotan passed her, he gave her the look of a savage animal, warding her off. But she met his stare fearlessly. He was not the one she was waiting for.

'Why have you been avoiding me?' Mia blurted out the second Colt stepped out of the drawing room. The statement had sounded a lot cooler in her head.

Colt glimpsed around furtively, conscious of his coven lingering within earshot. 'I have no further business with you,' he replied simply.

Mia felt a stab of sorrow in her heart. Of course, it was what she had expected, but that didn't make it any easier to hear.

'Oh, don't do that,' Colt groaned quietly.

'Do what?'

'Look all sad and pathetic.'

'I . . . I,' she stuttered, now insulted as well as hurt.

'Oh, Lord!' Colt rolled his eyes melodramatically.

'Don't roll your eyes at me!' Mia exclaimed. 'I'm angry at you.'

'I suppose it can't be helped,' Colt replied. 'I seem to anger people easily.'

'That doesn't surprise me.' Mia turned away from him. 'I

don't know why I bothered stopping you.' She sighed. 'Just go.'

Colt looked over to his coven, which loitered stiffly at the castle entrance. 'I didn't plan on upsetting you.'

'It's OK,' Mia said softly. She glanced to the main entrance. 'You should go. Lotan is waiting.'

'So he is,' Colt noted with a hint of a smirk. 'Perhaps one more meeting wouldn't be the end of the world,' he deliberated in a hushed voice, more to himself than to Mia. 'Would that please you?' he asked her.

Mia pondered it. 'I'd like that,' she admitted.

'Not here,' Colt said under his breath. 'Spangles.'

In reaction to their arrangement, Mia couldn't suppress her smile. Her cherry lips pressed together blissfully and her grey eyes lit up like winter frost.

Colt rubbed his hand over his mouth and jaw in an attempt to conceal his own forming smile. Abruptly, he shook it off and spun around, striding away in a prompt exit.

In the thick of the graveyard, Mia weaved through the stone slabs towards Spangles' plot. The birds chirped overhead and the summer sun broke through the trees, dancing on the ground like spilt glitter.

Planting herself in her usual spot, Mia listened intently to every sound, waiting on tenterhooks for Colt's arrival. Occasionally the wind chimes would whistle and the leaves in the trees would rustle, but other than that Mia was alone.

'Hello!' A smooth voice interrupted the peaceful setting.

Startled, Mia gasped. 'I didn't hear you coming,' she said, twirling around to face Colt.

'I intended it so,' he replied blithely. Beneath the fractured sunlight, his eyes shimmered vibrant green, alight with a sort of mystical enchantment.

'It's good to see you,' Mia told him honestly.

'I imagine it would be.'

Mia paused. 'You're not pleased to see me?'

'I came, didn't I?' Colt answered impassively.

She smiled. 'I'm glad you came. I was worried about you. I thought that something might have happened to you. After the incident with the poisoned arrow, I woke up and you were gone . . .'

'I couldn't stay,' he explained, almost remorsefully.

'I understand. I can accept that you don't have feelings for me in that way. But I missed you. God knows why, but I did. Can't we be friends? Nothing more – just friends?'

Colt laughed scornfully. 'No.'

'Oh.'

'We will never be friends,' he elaborated. 'You want more than friendship.'

Mia blushed, embarrassed by the remark. 'Maybe I did. All the same, I'd be just as happy to be your friend. I know you think you're irresistible, but I'm perfectly able to control myself,' she joked in a mocking tone.

'Well, *I'm* not,' Colt blurted out.

If she'd have been thinking rationally, she would have kept her distance from him. But that was not the case. Instead, she rushed forward and threw her arms around him, relishing the sensation of closeness.

Colt remained rigid. He didn't return the hug, but he didn't pull away either.

Mia stayed in the embrace, listening to the sound of his ragged breathing. Her fingers brushed against the nape of his neck. It was strange being so near to him.

Relenting slightly, Colt allowed one arm to move around her. However, he kept the other rigidly at his side.

Mia familiarised herself with the sensation of being this intimate with him. It felt right to her – as though her whole life had been building up to this moment. It was as if they belonged to one another.

'Stop,' Colt said sharply. Still, his arm didn't move from around her, and she did not attempt to separate herself from him, either. Colt ground his teeth in an unseen battle against a personal inner turmoil. 'Step away from me,' he ordered.

This time Mia did as he said, unnerved by the urgency in his voice. But no sooner was she apart from him than he pulled her back in, using both hands to grip her arms.

Mia looked up. His eyes were no longer light and radiant. In fact, they were black and emotionless, with a thin border of red encircling the engorged pupil.

At that moment, he looked as though he were about to either savagely kill her or passionately kiss her. Mia supposed that, to Colt, the two were one and the same.

She tried to push away from him, but his arms held her as if they were made of unbreakable steel. She could virtually see the aggression issuing from within him. The muscles in his jaw contracted tautly.

'What are you doing?' Mia demanded, her voice surprisingly bold.

Colt didn't respond. Instead, he swiftly moved to kiss her.

'Don't!' Mia snapped. She jerked her head away from him.

'What?' Colt asked, in an innocent yet resentful tone. 'I thought this was what you wanted.'

'No!' Mia scoffed. 'Not like this!'

Colt tensed, hesitant and uncertain.

'I don't want you to kiss me as a substitute for killing me!' she went on furiously.

He gave an aloof shrug of his shoulders. 'Is there really a difference?'

'They're as different as can be!' Mia cried. 'Violence is a terrible, sinister thing . . .'

'So is kissing,' Colt cut her off, amused by his own comment.

'No, it isn't,' Mia scowled. 'You kiss someone when you care for them. Or when you love them,' she added quietly.

Suddenly it wasn't so funny for Colt any more. When he next spoke, his words were slow and regretful. 'I will never love you,' he told her ruefully.

His remark stung.

'Then never kiss me,' Mia whispered, her voice choked by the lump in her throat. She looked up to Colt's eyes and watched as they transformed before her. The pupils contracted, and the ring of red merged once more into that recognisable pine green.

'OK,' he agreed humbly.

Mia blinked back the tears. 'And while we're on the subject, don't kill me either.'

'That's fair,' Colt nodded. His expression was sincere and noble. He released his grip on her arms and stepped back.

Mia stepped back, too – not because she wanted to, but because she respected herself too much not to.

Colt stared down at the ground. 'I didn't want you to see me like that,' he confessed, evidently ashamed of his behaviour.

'I've already seen you like that,' Mia reminded him, 'when I wore the Athame.'

'Well, that was different,' Colt snorted. 'You put on an Athame, for crying out loud! You couldn't even control your own power, and yet you thought you could control a ceremonial tool that dates back hundreds of years!'

Mia placed her hands on her hips. 'I didn't know how powerful it would be,' she defended herself.

'I know,' Colt smiled. 'That's why I came to your rescue. It would have consumed you. It had already begun.'

'You came to rescue me?' Mia scrutinised him dubiously. 'It seemed to me that you were coming to kill me!' She mused over how casually she spoke of such horrors. A few weeks ago, all of this would have seemed preposterous.

'No, no, if I'd planned to kill you, I would have succeeded,' he boasted. 'I came to help you out – although for the life of me I can't think why. And, anyway, I did save you.'

'You saved me from the Athame,' Mia agreed, 'but not from yourself.'

Colt sighed submissively. 'I can't save you from me. I'm my own worst enemy, as it were.' He paused for a moment. 'Actually, that's not the case. I'm rather fond of myself, if truth be told.'

'You don't say.' Mia feigned shock.

'Yes, I think I'm quite superb. And I'm right to think that way. But perhaps I'm *your* worst enemy.'

'Well, you know what they say – keep your friends close and your enemies closer,' Mia replied in jest.

'Not in this scenario. The closer you keep me, the more I detest you.'

'Gee, thanks!'

'I detest you in the most adoring way,' Colt amended. 'It's all passion, isn't it? Love, hate, happy, sad – what difference does it make?'

'A lot of difference.'

'So you say. But only because you were taught to feel and obey emotion. I, however, am a solitary opportunist. My only goal is to satisfy myself.'

'So you say,' Mia retorted. 'But if that were true, why come to my rescue when I took the Athame? Why give me your blood?'

'Because I'm a fool.'

'And so am I!' Mia laughed.

'Yes, you are. You saw how feral I became when I turned. All of that passion – to kill, to kiss, to be – it takes hold of me and I can't fight it,' he divulged openly. 'I lose it. I lose myself to it.'

'But you stopped yourself,' Mia reasoned. 'You didn't harm me, or kiss me. I think you're more in control than you give yourself credit for.'

'Not really. Today, just then, was the only time I have ever managed to master my demons. *Ever.*' He put extra emphasis on the final word.

'Ever?'

'Yes. Once it grips me, there's usually no turning back. Until I've made my kill, that is.'

'How pleasant,' Mia slipped in sarcastically.

'Yes,' Colt agreed, unaffected by her tone.

'So, what changed? What made today different?'

'Hard to tell.' He scuffed at the moss underfoot. 'Perhaps you. Perhaps your voice sedated me. Or perhaps it *bored* me into sobriety.' He chuckled. 'But as I said, I didn't want you to see me in that state.'

'Apology accepted.'

'It wasn't an apology.'

Mia smiled sweetly. 'Well, whatever it was, I accept. And thank you for saving me – both times.'

'Ah! A thank-you! My very first!' Colt cheered.

Mia giggled. 'How does it feel?'

'Overrated.'

Mia laughed again.

Much to his dismay, Colt found the sound quite beautiful. He reached out and touched her cheek with the backs of his fingers.

Mia closed her eyes. She felt a breeze pass gently through her hair. 'That's you,' she said placidly, 'isn't it?'

Colt drew the breeze around her, dusting it over her lips. 'Very perceptive,' he grinned. 'I've noticed your own powers are growing. I got your message.' He dug into his pocket and produced the catkin, which he had cherished secretly.

Mia's eyes fluttered open. 'You kept it!'

'I found it *interesting.*'

She beamed. 'Can I ask you a question?'

Colt heaved a weary sigh. 'I expect you'll do so regardless

of my response, so I might as well pretend that it was on my terms. Go ahead.'

'When you noticed the catkin, did you consider coming to find me? I know you don't love me, but do you think of me at all?'

Colt looked momentarily pained. 'Of course I do!' he cried. 'I wanted to come for you. And even more so when it began to rain. I felt your sorrow.'

'Then why didn't you?' Mia asked tenderly.

'Because it's not who I am.'

'Who are you?'

'A Hunter,' he stated matter-of-factly.

'What difference does it make?'

Colt smiled sadly. 'It's the difference between love and hate.'

The irony of his comment silenced Mia. Silenced her to the point that she wished she had never spoken at all.

Colt dipped his head. 'I should leave.'

'At least this time it'll be a proper goodbye.'

'I suppose it will be,' he said amicably. 'I'd offer you a hug, but . . . we both know how *that* would turn out.'

'I'll take the risk,' Mia chanced recklessly. She rushed to him and enveloped him once again.

This time Colt shared the embrace. His hands pressed against her back warmly, and he buried his face in her hair, indulgently breathing in her scent.

'Goodbye,' Mia said solemnly. She released him and stepped back, restoring the space between them.

'Goodbye,' Colt returned. He reached out and pushed a stray strand of hair behind her ear. 'It's been . . . different,' he said with a husky laugh.

'Yep,' Mia agreed. 'Different and the same.'

With a wistful look about him, Colt began to walk away. But he appeared to be stalling his departure, running his hand along a serrated tree trunk and looking up and down its bark as though it was foreign to him.

'It's a tree,' Mia teased.

Colt stopped and turned back to her. His hands were balled into fists, and one was pressed so firmly to the tree trunk that it started to dent the bark.

'You know,' he said, somewhat grudgingly, 'I shouldn't say this, but if you want to try the Athame again, I will help you.'

Mia's eyes twinkled in delight. She didn't care about the Athame, but she did care about Colt. 'Really?'

Colt licked his lips nervously. 'I can help you. But only if you are mindful that spending time together will only make things more difficult in the long run.'

Mia gave a nonchalant wave of her hand. 'I don't care about the long run.'

'I've noticed,' Colt smirked wryly.

'Besides,' she added, 'like I said, I'm willing to take the risk.'

Colt winked at her. 'Me, too.'

'You see?' Mia grinned. 'We're both fools! When shall we try it?'

He debated silently for several seconds. 'Dusk. I'll patrol the forest until sunset, and then I'll find you. Don't look for me,' he warned. 'I'll find you.'

'But how will you know where . . . ?'

'*I'll find you*,' he reiterated impatiently.

Mia frowned. 'How?'

Colt chuckled as though he were laughing at a private joke. 'Darling,' he drawled, 'I could find you anywhere.'

13

Ascending

As the sun began to set, the Arcana gathered in the dining room for dinner. The only person missing was Dino.

He had other plans.

For the past few hours he had shut himself away in the library. And there he remained, chaotically ransacking the shelves of books. Every so often, he would pull out a book, leaf through it, and then discard it on to the floor.

So engrossed in the task at hand, Dino barely even reacted when the library door opened.

'Dino! What are you d . . . doing?' Blue exclaimed.

'Looking for a book,' Dino mumbled distractedly. Even as he spoke, his attention didn't leave the bookshelves.

'What book?' Blue asked. Witnessing his friend at that moment, he was horrified to see how blackened and bruised Dino's eyes had become. It was unsettling.

'Ascension,' Dino replied, not inviting any further conversation.

But Blue persisted, his honey-coloured eyes wide with shock. 'Why do you want to read about that?' he gawped.

Ascension was a ritualistic practice that would enable a witch to ascend to a higher power. Essentially it was dark magic, so its secrets were kept safe by the Arcana. If the ritual works fell into the wrong hands, there would be a danger of it being used for malevolent purposes. Ultimately, the process would grant its commander the ability to tap into the greatest powers known to witchcraft. It was a gift sought by many, but permitted only to those who were pure-hearted and in a state of mature wisdom.

'Why do you want to find out about ascension?' Blue demanded again.

'I'm just interested,' Dino responded evenly.

Blue looked around at the disarray of the library. He found it hard to believe that Dino was simply just interested. There was something Dino was not telling him.

'Did you do the r . . . refusal ritual?' he asked.

Dino frowned impatiently. 'Huh?'

'The ritual. The one to b . . . block Tol's advances.'

'Oh. Yeah, yeah,' Dino blagged evasively, 'I did it.'

'How did it go?'

'Peachy. No problems.' He continued to pull books out at random, only to toss them aside like worthless junk.

'You won't find it there!' Blue blurted out, cringing as the delicate books collided against the furniture.

Suddenly Dino was ready to listen. He turned around slowly, his dark eyes suddenly focused and severe. 'Where is it?'

'Did you tell Wendolyn and Mia about Tol?' Blue persevered, ignoring Dino's question.

'Yes. Where's the book?'

'What did they say? Because there was a m . . . meeting this morning and Wendolyn had some s . . . serious concerns about Hunters in the area, and she didn't seem to know . . .'

Dino cut him short. 'Where's the book?'

'Ascension is d . . . dark magic. It's not on the shelves with the other books. Has Tol tried to contact you again?'

'Where are the books on dark magic?' Dino snarled, his lips curled upwards like a rabid dog.

Blue backed away instinctively. 'What's wrong with you?'

'Nothing's wrong with me. In fact, I feel fantastic. Better than ever.'

He may have felt it, but he certainly didn't look it. His

appearance was noticeably worn and battered. And what had once been an attractive face was now bruised and dishevelled. But the most perceptible change of all came from within. The plucky spark that used to shape Dino's character had been replaced by a deluded, manic insanity.

'If something's happened, I can help you,' Blue appealed to him.

'I do need your help,' Dino admitted, and for a moment it seemed as though Blue's words might have got through to him. 'I need you to tell me where the book is!' he bellowed.

Blue shrank back. 'No!'

'Then I'll drag it out of you,' Dino threatened in a menacing voice that was no longer his own.

'W . . . w . . . w . . .'

'Button it!' Dino sniped, sneering at his own cruel mockery. 'Now, I should warn you, this might hurt just a little . . .' He raised his hand and twisted his fingers, as though he were picking at an invisible lock.

Blue howled in agony. He clutched at his head as if he were trying to hold his skull together.

'You want to tell me where the book is,' Dino stated in a low, hollow tone.

Blue fought to resist, but Dino was too powerful.

'William Wix's study,' he inadvertently choked out. Dino had planted the desire in his mind, forcing him to share his knowledge, and Blue was helpless to defy him.

Abruptly Dino snapped his fingers and released his hold. 'Thank you,' he hissed slyly.

Blue trembled, staggering backwards against the bookshelves.

'So,' Dino spoke again, 'the dark magic books are stored in William Wix's study. You are a useful friend, Benny Blue.' He tapped his chin thoughtfully.

'You'll never get into the room,' Blue bit back. 'Wendolyn keeps the door locked at all times.'

'Does she?' Dino mused. 'I'm afraid you underestimate me.' He smirked devilishly. 'You forget, the power of the mind can be a marvellous thing. Wanna see?' Without waiting for a response, Dino darted out of the library and slammed the door shut behind him.

Blue raced forward and yanked at the door handle, but the heavy door didn't budge.

'Power of the mind,' came Dino's muffled voice from the other side of the thick wood. 'Bet you didn't know I could do that!' he laughed raucously. 'I can lock a door simply by willing it. The question is, can you unlock it?'

Blue rattled the handle and banged against the solid wood.

Then Dino's stifled voice came again. 'Nah, I'm only messing with you,' he chuckled devilishly. 'I used the key. It was already in the lock. In fact, I think I'll take it with me for safe keeping. See ya,' he taunted in a devious tone.

'Open the door!' Blue hollered, bashing his fists against it. But Dino was already gone.

Distressed, Blue slumped against the door. He drew in several deep breaths in an attempt to calm himself. He had to think rationally.

Trying not to panic, he reached into his pocket and pulled out his vial of ciron thistle. With a shaky hand, he sprinkled a few flakes into his palm and encased them beneath his fingers. The ciron thistle lay dormant, waiting for its command. Blue closed his eyes and envisioned the chunky, brass library key.

Trembling with nerves, he unclenched his fist to inspect the contents.

'No!' he cried in despair as he hopelessly lobbed a small, brown button at the impenetrable door.

Mia sat alone in her bedchamber, perched on the windowsill where she could watch the sun set over the courtyard. The sky bled with dusty blues and pinks as the sun dipped beyond the horizon.

There was a singular knock on her bedroom door.

Mia held her breath. 'Come in,' she called out.

The door opened and Colt hovered in the doorway. He glimpsed up and down the empty corridor like a fugitive. 'Come with me,' he said, extending his hand to her.

Mia hopped down from the windowsill and trotted over to him. He held the door open as she ducked through it.

'Where are we going?'

'Shh!' Colt pressed his index finger to her lips. 'Stay close to me and keep your head down,' he instructed.

They walked swiftly along the corridor – but not towards the stairwell, the direction in which Mia would usually head, but rather away from it, to places unknown.

Colt walked with a brisk, purposeful stride. He gripped Mia's wrist, directing her behind him.

At the end of the unlit corridor, they came to a second stairwell. It was similar to the other, with faded red carpet and an elaborately carved wooden banister. However, this staircase was spiralled and windowless. It was almost like a secret passageway.

All of a sudden, it dawned on Mia where exactly they were going.

'I can't go to the Hunters' quarters!' she cried. Stubbornly, she dug her heels into the stairway carpet, refusing to take another step. 'I'll be flayed!'

Colt gave her a slanted smile. 'Flayed? Really?'

'I don't know what Hunters are capable of! You've already told me that they're out to get me!'

'It'll be fine,' Colt reassured her. 'The others are in the forest. They don't even know I'm gone.'

'Are you sure?'

'Yes. I'm not careless. If we were caught, I'd be the one to pay.'

'Even so,' Mia griped, 'I'm not sure this is such a good idea. What's to stop the others from coming back at any moment?'

Colt slid his grasp down her wrist, catching her hand and knotting his fingers through hers. This time, it was an unspoken reassurance, perhaps more valuable than actual words.

They continued downwards along the snaking staircase.

When they reached the bottom, they plunged into complete darkness. Mia could just about make out the walls on either side of her. She kept her eyes down and placed her trust entirely in Colt's guidance.

Every step felt never-ending. Mia knew that she was in Hunter domain – not merely because she had been told so, but because the whole area reeked of it. For the first time, she was adroitly able to sense the different scents and auras. Quite frankly, it terrified her.

'Here,' Colt said in a husky voice. He heaved open a weathered oak door and hustled her through it.

Beyond the door was not a room as Mia had expected, but another flight of stairs leading upwards. These stairs weren't elegant like the others had been. In fact, they were made simply from uneven stone and were only a foot or so wide.

Mia hesitated.

'Go ahead,' Colt told her. The stone stairwell was so narrow that they were forced to walk in single file. Mia went first.

'I read something once, about civilians,' Colt said, his voice louder and more relaxed now, signifying that they were out of danger. 'It said that men are to walk behind women when climbing up stairs, and in front of them on the descent. Just in case they fall. Chivalry – what a riot!' He was so close behind Mia that she could feel his breath on the back of her neck.

'I don't know much about that,' she said, retaining her

hushed voice. 'I think that's a very dated tradition. Women's and men's roles have changed quite a bit since then.'

'Huh.' Colt contemplated it silently for a moment. 'Well, I'm walking behind you right now, aren't I?'

She smiled. 'Are you planning to become chivalrous, then?'

He mulled it over. 'I'm certainly good at it. Or, at least, better than the human men.'

At the top of the stone staircase Mia came to an abrupt halt.

'There's a door,' she noted.

'Yes, there is.'

She craned her neck to look back at him. 'Well? What should I do about it?'

'What do you think you should do about it?' he exclaimed. 'It's a door – go through it!'

Mia scrunched up her nose. 'You first.'

Colt muttered irritably under his breath. 'Move, then.'

She pressed herself flat against the stone wall while Colt manoeuvred his way around her. As their paths crossed, they brushed past one another at an uncomfortably intimate proximity.

'My, my,' Colt smirked mischievously, 'isn't this cosy?'

He reached for the door handle and pushed the door open. 'See, nothing scary in there. Ladies first,' he said in a sickly pleasant tone.

Mia peered into the room and then gingerly stepped inside. Colt swaggered in behind her.

The room was in the turret, at the highest peak of the castle. It was a large circular space with a vast window overlooking the rolling grounds below.

With the day's light slowly slipping away, so was the illumination of the room. Colt busied himself lighting candles.

As the new glow of flames lit the room, Mia was taken aback by her exquisite surroundings. A red-and-black four-poster canopied bed stood at the centre, as handsome as the bed of a king, while around it was arranged intricately carved furniture, armchairs, tables, a desk.

'Is this your bedroom?' Mia asked in blatant awe.

'Yes, it is. And it's the best room in the castle, if you ask me,' he added immodestly.

Mia couldn't help but agree. 'How long have you been here?' she pried. Based on the treasures and artefacts gathered in the room, it appeared that his collection must have been building for some time. Not like her own room, which boasted only a rack of clothes hanging in the wardrobe.

'In this room?' Colt checked her meaning.

'Yes.'

'Maybe nine, ten years,' he guessed. 'But I had to work my way up to it. I started off in one of the smaller chambers downstairs.'

Mia did a quick mental calculation. 'So, how long have you been living at the castle?' She furrowed her brow, surprised by the fact that he had been in this room alone for an entire decade – not to mention the time he'd spent in a smaller room prior to that.

'Hmm . . . hard to say. As long as I can remember, that's for sure.'

'But, what about your family?' Mia tried to broach the subject as delicately as possible.

'The Hunters are my family. Lotan, Roc and Siren.'

'But . . . your parents?'

'Oh,' Colt registered her point. He ambled over to his dressing table and lifted a framed photograph, which he handed to Mia for inspection. 'There she is,' he said. 'That's my mother. I believe she was a civilian.' He pointed to the woman in the photo with the pride of a dutiful son, although it was clear that he had no extensive knowledge of her.

'You don't remember her?' Mia tried to conceal her utter bewilderment. She knew that Colt's world was a complex one, but this was unfathomable to her.

'No. But I like the picture, don't you?' He gazed lovingly at the photograph.

The woman smiled back at them. She sat beneath a willow tree, wearing a white embroidered dress. She had long blonde hair and forest-green eyes.

'Yes,' Mia replied truthfully, 'it's lovely. What about your father?'

'I understand that he was a Hunter. But he belonged to another coven,' Colt explained. 'I've never met him.'

'Is he still married to your mother?'

Colt laughed. 'Of course not! He was a Hunter! I'm sure they were not married or romantically in love like you would wish it to be. Most likely my mother was needed to carry a child for the new generation of Hunters. It's a fairly common procedure. It's the cycle of life.'

Mia couldn't hide her shock at the coldness of his words. 'What about the others?' she asked. 'Do they know their parents?'

Colt chuckled at the outlandish idea. 'Oh, no! You wouldn't be a Hunter if you had a family outside of your coven. The whole point is that we are detached from human emotion. Detached from humanity itself. We are bred only as warriors.'

Mia watched as he stared fondly at the framed photograph. His was not an expression of someone detached from humanity. In fact, his was more an expression of someone in the clutches of it.

'What about you?' he returned the question, placing the photo back in its spot. 'You have parents.'

'Yes. Well,' she corrected herself, 'I have a mother and an aunt. And Dino.'

'Where is your father?'

Mia shrugged. 'He's around somewhere, but I've never met him. My mother doesn't like to speak about him. I guess their relationship didn't end so well.'

'But that doesn't deter you from love?' Colt noticed quizzically.

Mia's cheeks flushed pink, and she was glad that the poor lighting hid her blushes.

'I suppose love isn't something you can choose. It's out of your control.'

'Like anger?'

'No, not really. Love is something that consumes you. Anger is a reaction.'

Colt studied her curiously. 'And what do you know of love and anger?' he challenged her.

'I know that I've experienced both.'

'And you're still alive to tell the tale,' he joked cheerfully.

'What can I say? I'm invincible,' she grinned.

'Aren't you just,' Colt remarked wryly. 'Care to test that theory?' As he spoke, he lifted a small dagger from an altar-like table covered in a purple cloth.

'The Athame!' Mia murmured.

'*My* Athame,' Colt amended. 'My personal tool.'

Mia edged forward to get a better look. 'What do you use it for?'

'Mostly to develop my powers, or for ritual. Although I've never really been one for rituals.' He rotated the blade to allow Mia a thorough look.

'It's beautiful,' she breathed, examining the detail of its engraved symbols and the sharpness of its pointed tip.

Colt nodded his head. 'Yes, it is. Shall we begin?'

'Now?' She looked up at him timidly.

'Yes. I'm not sure how much longer I can have you in my bedchamber without making up to you,' he teased. 'I believe it's mandatory. Or at least customary.'

Mia tut-tutted. 'It baffles me how you can think you are anything other than a normal guy!'

Colt laughed playfully. 'Take a seat,' he said, gesturing vaguely at the floor.

Mia complied, sitting cross-legged on the crimson carpet. 'What if I can't control it? What if it's like the last time I tried?'

'I'll be your anchor,' Colt told her. 'I'll pull you out at any time.' He systematically arranged four candles around her, caging her in. 'North, south, east and west,' he indicated to the candles. 'Earth, fire, air and water.' Striking a match, he ignited the wick of the north candle. A blue flame twitched but finally settled down as a modest amber triangle.

Mia looked at the candles. They were unlike any she had ever seen before: smooth black cylinders adorned with a cascade of dripping wax.

'May I join you?' Colt asked cordially.

'Please do.'

Colt stepped through the candles, crossing the invisible barrier that he had created for her. He sat down opposite Mia.

'Are you ready?'

'I think so,' she told him. But she wasn't entirely convinced.

Colt focused his gaze on the solitary north candle flame, and in an almighty blaze the flame leapt upwards. It circled them, connecting with the other candle wicks as it went. Soon Mia and Colt were imprisoned in a ring of fire.

Mia squeezed her eyes shut.

'Don't be scared,' Colt said in a soothing tone. 'I'm in complete control. This is my fire, and you are perfectly safe.'

Tentatively opening her eyes, Mia nodded, but she could feel her pulse rate accelerating. The heat radiating from the ring of fire noticeably warmed her skin.

In front of her, Colt held the Athame. Serenely, he was both servant to and master of its power. His eyes locked on Mia's.

'Take my hand.'

She did as he requested. His fingers closed around hers, and his hand felt warm as though it were charged with electricity. With his other hand, he gripped the dagger.

Colt spoke again. 'Envision yourself and your connection to nature. Earth, fire, air and water,' he said between shallow breaths. 'Don't forget, nature is a part of all of us. It is who you are.'

Mia closed her eyes. She could hear the crackle of fire as it looped around her in constant flow. But for once she was not intimidated by it, simply respectful of it. Something cold touched the skin of her free hand. Colt had slipped the Athame into her grasp. Her other hand closed around his even tighter than it had before.

'I'm scared,' she whispered urgently.

'You have no reason to be.'

'You won't let go of my hand, will you?'

'I won't,' he promised her.

Mia held the ceremonial dagger in her palm. She felt its energy shoot along her arm like an electric shock. It coursed through her body with a burning heat, swelling like fire around her lungs.

'I don't think I can do this,' she gasped, short of breath.

'You're OK,' he reminded her. 'The Athame's powers are true. Calm yourself, my sweet. Take a deep breath.'

Mia drew in several slow breaths, inhaling and exhaling in a soothing rhythm. The technique seemed to compose her.

'Shall I take the Athame away?' Colt asked.

Mia took another breath. The energy seemed different now – warm rather than hot. 'No,' she answered, now oddly decisive.

Little by little, the magic of the Athame flooded her with a wonderful strength and understanding. It was as though everything had suddenly become clear: she knew who she was and what her capabilities were – both as a witch and as a young woman. She felt strong, beautiful and wise. It was a glimpse of who she was and who she would one day become. And in that instant, she knew that she was a part of everything – the air she breathed and the fire that surrounded her, so alive and imperative in its own right.

Somewhere in the back of her consciousness, she could feel Colt's hand. It was a relief to know he was there with her. Then, very carefully, she felt him take the Athame from her.

As it left her clutches, the dagger's essence rushed away from her. She slumped forward and Colt caught her, guiding her to lean against him. He placed the Athame on the carpet and cradled Mia's head to his chest.

'There, there,' he said, stroking the hair from her face. 'You are a witch. A powerful girl.'

'Am I?' Mia murmured, drained by the experience.

Colt smiled affectionately. 'Oh, yes. You are magnificent.' He radiated a certain admiration, honoured to have shared such a significant moment with her. The use of an Athame was a momentous step, and he was privileged to have witnessed her abilities evolve before his very eyes. To have watched her was quite remarkable.

'It was the strangest feeling,' she whispered. 'I saw my powers. I feel like I can understand them in a way I couldn't before. They're not separate from me – they *are* me.'

'Your powers are born from the substance that you've possessed all along. They are the fruits of your life. And they will grow as you do. But you are already exceptionally powerful. The Athame shared with you its magic and you were able to contain it. That shows a great strength in your soul.'

'I feel so tired, though,' Mia mumbled drowsily.

187

'Understandable. I forgot how exhausting it can be,' Colt replied smoothly. He absent-mindedly nursed her, rocking her back and forth in a tranquil silence.

'Why is it so tiring?'

'Because it's ancient magic. Magic that you've never really been exposed to before. It took all of your energy to embody it.'

'I feel like I'm falling asleep,' she slurred, glad to have him to prop herself up against.

'Then sleep you shall,' Colt said. Leisurely he rose to his feet, lifting Mia in his arms. Through the command of his eyes he directed the ring of fire to break, and the blazing flames returned to being tiny pyramids dancing atop the candlewicks.

Colt stepped out of the circle and carried Mia to the bed. He placed her down gently and draped a blanket over her. Then he lay down beside her, watching with amorous curiosity as she drifted in and out of sleep.

'Are you dreaming?' he asked her quietly.

'Maybe,' she replied softly. 'I don't know the difference any more.'

Colt grinned. 'I can relate to that. You know, you were very brave today.'

'Brave?' Mia mumbled. 'You told me I was safe.' She managed a weak smile.

Colt laughed softly. 'You *were* safe. Next time you won't find it so draining. And you won't need me around, either.'

'I don't think I could do it without you. I wouldn't want to.'

'Oh, don't underestimate yourself. You are more than prepared, my dear.'

Mia opened her eyes hazily. 'Do you know my name?' she frowned. It was a strange question, but a valid one nonetheless. Even after all this time, she had never introduced herself, nor had she ever heard him use her name.

Colt chortled in amusement. 'Do you think I would go through all of this without finding out your name?'

'I don't know,' she jibed. 'It wouldn't surprise me.' From where she lay she peered at him, his face resting on the pillow beside her.

Colt smiled in humorous delight. 'I know your name, Mia,' he said. It felt good to finally speak it aloud. He had never done it before – perhaps because it would make her real. 'In fact, I knew your name before I knew you.'

'How?'

He touched her nose with his index finger. 'I heard Wendolyn speak it once and I rather liked it. I remembered it. I should have known then that things would go awry,' he joked.

'Things haven't been so bad though, have they?'

'Oh, no, darling. Quite the opposite.'

That was the last thing Mia heard before she fell into a much needed slumber.

Colt lay at her side for some time after that, observing her steady breathing, until eventually he too fell into a comfortable sleep.

An hour passed before Colt was awoken again. A deafening cry jolted him into alertness. He glanced at Mia, who continued to sleep soundly beside him.

The cry grew louder and more agonising. Colt recognised the call at once.

The death of a Hunter.

He sprang to his feet, and in a blur he was gone.

14

The Call of Duty

Colt sped through the grounds, his legs moving with the wind at a speed that tripled that of a normal human. The night sky was dark and layered with an opaque purple fog. Such a congested sky was never a good sign. It meant that heavy magic was at play.

In the depths of his mind, Colt heard the unmistakable cry of a Hunter. Innately, he knew which direction to head. At a nail-biting speed, he weaved in and out of the forest's pine trees, closing in on Lotan.

'Brother!' Colt called out to Lotan, who lay crumpled on the forest floor. 'I am here.' He dropped dutifully to his friend's side.

'Colt,' Lotan responded in a strained breath. 'Where have you been?' His dark eyes were harsh, but not condemning.

'I've been in my chamber,' Colt replied, as honestly as possible. Of course, he had no intention of mentioning his Arcana companion.

'The coven was struck,' Lotan informed him. 'We were attacked by the rival Hunters.' He let out a throaty cough and a trickle of blood spilt over his lips.

Colt staggered for words. He was racked with guilt. He should never have abandoned his coven at such a crucial time. 'And the outcome?' he asked, in barely a whisper.

'They are strong and fast. They picked us off, one by one.'

Colt's heart hammered in his chest. 'They made a kill?' He already knew the answer.

'They took down Roc,' Lotan confirmed. 'I could not stop it.'

The world seemed to move in slow motion as Colt realised that his brother, Roc, was dead.

'And Siren?' he asked meekly.

'Siren set off in pursuit, but he is no match for them. They will slaughter him,' Lotan stated the facts in a sterile, emotionless tone.

'I'll go,' Colt snarled. 'I'll take them down myself.' Avenging Roc's death would not only be an obligation, but a tribute.

'No. You will not survive,' Lotan said flatly. 'Colt, their leader is in the first stages of ascension.'

Colt looked momentarily baffled. 'How can a Hunter perform an ascension? The ritual is protected by the Arcana.'

'They run with an Arcana. A boy from the castle. Dino.'

Dino. Colt's stomach knotted at the mention of the name. Mia's brother.

'Their leader is beyond powerful,' Lotan went on. 'I read his thoughts and felt his capabilities. He has begun the ascension and it has heightened his power. He will render you useless in one strike.'

Colt took a steady breath. 'Then I won't let him get a strike in.'

'You cannot face him alone,' Lotan cautioned.

'OK. When you're sufficiently healed, we'll attack . . .'

'I won't heal,' Lotan cut him off bluntly.

Colt stopped dead. 'What? Of course you will heal. Where are you hurt?' He looked him up and down, scanning for possible injury. There was a small puncture wound just below Lotan's rib cage.

'I've been infected with a poisoned tip. It's spreading quickly, but I held on for your arrival. I needed to warn you not to go up against them.' Lotan clenched his fists in the throes of his death agony. 'If you try, you will fail. Flee from the forest,' he commanded, with a strange nobility.

Colt was temporarily lost for words. 'No!' He shook his head firmly. 'I will never flee. I will track them down and bring you the blood of their coven. It will remedy the poison.' His thoughts returned to his own narrow escape and how effective blood of the coven had been in aiding his recovery.

'They're too powerful,' Lotan argued, struggling to speak as his pain worsened. 'You won't get close enough to make a kill.'

'Then I'll take the boy,' Colt said callously, referring to Dino. As he uttered the proclamation, something tugged at his heart, but he immediately blocked it out. His weakness for Mia was what had distracted him from his duty in the first place. Perhaps if he had blocked her out sooner, he could have prevented this. Or at least he would have been at his coven's side during the attack, like a true soldier.

'No. They protect the boy,' Lotan divulged. 'The leader goes by the name of Tol. I listened to his thoughts. He holds an enticement over the Arcana, which drew him into their coven. If they seal him as their fourth, Tol will be able to complete the ascension. He will be unstoppable.'

'So I'll kill the boy and they'll lose their fourth,' Colt deduced simply. 'The leader cannot ascend without a full coven.'

'True,' Lotan agreed. 'But they guard him. They've almost turned him, and no doubt they'll be anticipating your retaliation.'

'Well, I have to do something!' Colt exclaimed. He felt utterly helpless, and that wasn't a feeling he was used to. He hated it. He'd sooner die with his coven than stand back and watch.

'Foolhardy retaliation will be suicide. Go to Wendolyn and tell her of the Hunters' siege. Tell her they need the boy to join the coven in order to complete the ascension. The boy is the key. Go!' Lotan wheezed.

Colt wanted to obey, but he found that he could not move.

'Go!' Lotan rasped again.

'I . . .' Colt swallowed. He knew that his next words would sound pathetic to Lotan. 'I want to stay with you,' he said simply.

Lotan let out a broken laugh. 'My boy! What has she done to you?' Despite his cold words, their delivery was surprisingly warm.

Colt's lips twitched into a grudging smile. 'Nothing, brother. I wish to stay with you in your final hour. It would be an honour.' He bowed his head as a show of respect.

Lotan smiled curiously. 'Respect is a fine quality, but attachment will be your demise.'

'And if I am attached to you?'

'Then you are truly in a sorry state!'

'Well, then, it's a good thing I consider you expendable,' Colt teased. However, his humour was but an unconvincing mask for the devastating grief that tore him up inside. Although only a few years his senior, Lotan had raised Colt from the day he had arrived at the Glass Castle. Lotan had been a father, brother, leader and friend.

Colt resented being witness to such a distressing end, but nevertheless he refused to leave Lotan's side. It was one last act of devoted loyalty.

'Forgive me,' Colt implored. 'Forgive me for not being with the coven when the enemy attacked.'

'I'm glad you were not with us,' Lotan replied. His body lay limp and his lips were parched and ashen.

'Why?'

'Because you would have been killed, too.'

'Be careful, Lotan,' Colt smiled sadly. 'That sounded like a trace of humanity.'

Lotan smirked. 'Disgusting! It must be airborne.' He paused. 'Although, I dare say, you wear it well.'

Colt sighed. He felt compelled to own up, though he knew he may regret doing so. 'I have lied to you,' he confessed shamefully.

Lotan didn't appear shocked. He continued to smile passively. 'I quite enjoy your lies, Colt.'

Colt frowned. 'You don't know them all yet!'

'Don't I?' Lotan toyed with him like a cat with a mouse.

'No! You would exile me if you knew the treachery I have done!'

'Go on,' Lotan goaded him. 'Surprise me.'

'I . . .' Colt closed his eyes to work up the nerve. 'I gave the girl blood of the coven.'

Lotan laughed good-naturedly. 'The most absurd thing is that you thought I would not know.'

'You knew?'

'Of course!'

'Do the others know?' Colt winced in humiliation.

'No. Only myself.'

'How did you . . . ?' he trailed off. Lotan was a Reader, but Colt had lived with him long enough to adeptly block his power – just as Dino had done with Wendolyn.

'You may think you can fool me,' Lotan chuckled, 'but I know you too well.'

'Why didn't you tell Roc and Siren?'

'Because my loyalty is to you, foremost.'

'I am a traitor.' Colt hung his head in disgrace.

'Yes, you are,' Lotan taunted him with a smile. 'But you are a born protector, also.'

'And yet I could not protect my brothers.'

'Nor could I,' Lotan spoke regretfully. 'But, my boy, you are strong and you will carry on without us. Soon you will find a new coven, and this time *you* shall lead.'

'I can't lead,' Colt choked. 'You are my leader; I follow you. If you die, then so should I. I can't live knowing that you are not here.'

'Brother, take courage.'

'I can't do this without you.' Colt pounded his fist against the soil, and the ground shuddered beneath him.

'My boy, it is your time to lead. I have every faith in you. After all, you learned from a great warrior,' Lotan boasted in jest.

'I will never be the Hunter you are.'

'Probably not,' Lotan joked. 'But you'll outlive me at least.'

Colt didn't laugh. He slumped to the ground and lay beside his friend, looking up into the towering trees. 'I don't want to outlive you,' he muttered desolately.

'You're a born Hunter, and yet you're affected by humanity,' Lotan commented, baffled by the juxtaposition.

'Why me?' Colt grumbled. 'What did I do to deserve such a fate?'

'None are exempt from fate,' Lotan pointed out shrewdly.

'I hate it,' Colt growled. 'You were right – I should not have allowed her to do this to me. She ruins me.'

'Your heart was awakened,' Lotan replied. 'I understand it is a powerful thing.'

Colt grimaced. 'Yes. It's repulsive.'

'Perhaps not,' Lotan murmured, the life slowly leaving him. 'In a way I envy you.'

'Liar!' Colt snorted.

Lotan chuckled and closed his eyes. 'Take care, my boy.'

'Lotan,' Colt snapped fiercely. 'Not yet. Hold on for just a little while longer,' he pleaded desperately. He wasn't ready to lose him. In fact, he supposed he never would be.

'Courage, boy,' Lotan repeated, before his final breath of air escaped him.

Colt froze. Time stood still for him as he mourned his loss.

195

In a mixture of sorrow and rage, Colt let out a shattering howl. Above him, the sky echoed with a strident clap of thunder – a storm commanded by his own will.

As Colt stood beneath his vengeful sky, the rain poured down over him like never before. It was Colt's rain – terrifying, viscous and merciless.

Yes, Colt thought venomously, *now it is my reign.*

The rumble of thunder awoke Mia from her sleep. For a moment she forgot where she was. The unlit room was strange and unfamiliar to her. But then the memories of the eventful evening came flooding back.

She rolled over in the bed, her eyes slowly adjusting to her dim surroundings. The four candles remained on the floor where she had sat amidst their confines just hours earlier.

Mia shuddered as she listened to the thrashing of the rain outside. High up in the turret room, it sounded as though the roof would cave in from the onslaught.

'Colt?' she called into the darkness.

When there was no response, she sat upright, still clutching the blanket to her chest.

'Colt?' she tried again.

A rupture of lightning illuminated the room in a flash.

Mia crawled out of bed and stood before the vast window, looking out at the aggressive storm. She had never seen such torrential weather before.

All of a sudden, the bedroom door burst open.

Mia gasped. The person shadowed in the doorway was not Colt.

'What are you doing here?' she asked, visibly startled by his presence.

'Come with me,' Dino ordered. He marched into the room, kicking away the arrangement of candles.

Mia backed away from him. 'How did you know I was here?'

'I tracked you,' he replied expressionlessly.

'You tracked me?' She creased her brow. As far as she was aware, only a Hunter had the ability to track a person.

'Yes,' he snapped. 'Now, come!' He extended his hand to her, but it was not a loving gesture.

Mia stared at his outstretched hand. 'What's wrong with you?'

'Nothing is wrong. I need you to come with me.' Dino's eyes were hollow and unblinking.

'Where?' Mia asked guardedly. She hardly recognised him. He looked worn and detached – almost inhuman.

'I need you,' Dino said in that unnerving, robotic voice.

She took a step closer to him. 'Why? What's wrong?'

'I need you,' he repeated. 'It won't take long.'

Although she could have persisted with her questions, she knew they would get her nowhere. The bottom line was that he needed her. The only question that remained was, would she go?

'OK,' she accepted, succumbing to his request.

'Follow me.' He turned and stalked out of the room with a stride that would crush anything in its path.

Mia followed, wary but trustful all the same.

They descended Colt's stone stairwell and emerged into the dark Hunter corridor. In silence, they paced swiftly along it. Mia presumed that they were heading back towards the Arcana wing, but instead Dino led her to a bolted oak door. He slid the bolt across and opened the door, which led out into the courtyard.

'Dino!' Mia held back as her brother stepped into the pouring rain. 'It's a thunder storm! Where exactly do you plan on going?'

He glared at her. 'Follow me.'

Obstinately, she folded her arms. 'No way. Not until you tell me where you're taking me.'

Dino reached through the doorway and grabbed her arm, yanking her into the lashing rain. She wriggled to free herself but he held her tightly, dragging her across the courtyard.

Mia stumbled to keep up with him as they passed beneath the arched hedge and emerged into the gardens.

'Let go of me!' she cried. 'Have you lost your mind?'

Dino stopped walking for a moment. 'Lost my mind? No. Quite the opposite, in fact.'

'It's raining!' she protested. As the water drenched her skin and hair, she began to realise that it was no ordinary rain. It was Colt. She could sense him in every drop. And he was in pain. Mia dug her heels into the mud and tugged her arm free.

'I need to go!' she cried, overcome with the urgency to find Colt. She spun around, but before she took a step Dino was in front of her, blocking her path.

'No,' he said. 'You have to come with me.'

'Dino, not now!'

'It has to be now.' He grabbed her arm again.

'Stop it!' she yelled at him. She shoved him forcefully, but he remained glued to the spot.

'Keep walking,' he barked.

The rain continued to plummet down, streaming through the sodden garden.

'You don't understand!' Mia wailed.

'No, *you* don't understand!' he shouted back at her. 'I need you.'

Mia took a shaky breath, calming herself. 'OK,' she reasoned with him. 'You keep saying that, but you won't tell me anything. What do you need me for?'

'I need to rid myself of you,' Dino explained, as though his justification would make perfect sense.

198

She gawped at him. 'What does that mean?' Now she wondered if maybe he really had lost his mind.

'I need to free myself from humanity,' he rambled on. 'You're my humanity, Mia. You're what makes me human. If I can rid myself of you, then I'll be free.'

Mortified, Mia clouted him around the head. 'You're talking like a psychopath!' she exclaimed.

'No.' He shook his head, causing a spout of rain to spew from his ebony hair. 'I'm sorry, but it's the only way. Come with me.'

'I'm not going anywhere with you!'

In one swoop Dino hoisted her up and carried her across the garden, just as he had done when she was a little child – except, now, his intentions were sinister.

Mia kicked and screamed, but Dino heard and felt nothing. One way or another, this would end tonight.

15

Facing Demons

Colt tore through the grounds, his fury focused into every stride. The sky rumbled above and the rain lashed down upon him. It was as though he had opened up a wound that would not stop bleeding. With each step he took, the ground quivered beneath him. He wanted revenge, and he intended to get it.

Like a tornado, Colt burst into the castle. He charged towards Wendolyn's private chamber. But the chamber door swung open before he had even reached it. Wendolyn stood in the doorway wearing a pale-blue dressing gown over a floor-length cotton nightgown. Her white hair was combed and swept to the side.

'Come in,' Wendolyn beckoned. She ushered Colt into the chamber and guided him to a regal chair that stood in front of a smouldering log fire.

Shaking, he sat down and gripped the velvet arms of the chair.

'Make yourself comfortable,' Wendolyn told him kindly. She busied herself around the fireplace, heaping wood on to the glinting embers.

Colt shivered as his body adjusted to the change in temperature. The crackling flames warmed his wet clothes.

'You'll catch a chill,' Wendolyn fussed. She bustled over to him carrying a small, yellow towel. Without warning, she began towel drying his hair like a mother caring for a toddler.

Colt let her, his body numb and his face blank. She used a corner of the towel to blot the water from his face, as though she were wiping away a tear. Rain, tears – it was all the same to Colt.

'Lotan is dead,' he said at last, his voice noticeably fragile.

Wendolyn hung the yellow towel on the fire grate.

'I know,' she replied empathically.

'Murdered,' Colt elaborated. He stared into the fire, watching the amber flames dance up into the chimney.

'Yes,' Wendolyn nodded her head sombrely. 'I'm sorry.'

'Sorry is no use to me,' he said brusquely.

'No, I suppose it isn't.' Wendolyn took a seat opposite him. She lowered herself into the chair slowly, her aged bones stiff and tired.

'The rival Hunters attacked,' Colt went on. 'They killed my brothers . . .' He stopped talking and covered his face with his hands. He couldn't continue. It was too painful.

Wendolyn nodded in an unspoken understanding. 'May I?' she asked, aware of his struggle to speak.

Colt knew that she was asking to read his thoughts.

'Go ahead.' It would certainly be easier than saying it aloud. Although, by reading his thoughts, there was a chance that Wendolyn would find out about his bond with Mia. But Colt didn't care.

Moments later Wendolyn's expression turned grave. 'Their leader is ascending?' she checked, almost in disbelief.

'According to Lotan, yes.'

Wendolyn concentrated once more on something beyond their verbal communication. 'Dino,' she uttered regretfully. 'They must change him in order to complete their coven.'

'But why?' Colt practically hollered. 'What do such powerful Hunters want with a young Arcana? A useless Arcana, scarcely in his first weeks!'

Wendolyn's gaze rested on the fire. 'It's much easier to turn a young witch. Their alliance has not yet been sealed.'

'Why him?' Colt spat resentfully.

'Who can say why a witch's power is sought after.'

'He has no great power!' Colt scoffed. *Not like his sister*, he added silently. 'I request permission to take him.'

'No,' Wendolyn denied him outright. 'You will not harm the boy.'

'Why not?' Colt raged. 'The Hunters will turn him, and their leader will use his power to ascend! It's either the boy or all of us,' he stated frankly.

'No, Colt,' Wendolyn affirmed, her decision unwavering. 'Harming the boy is not an option.'

'It's our only option!' he conflicted.

'Your judgment is impaired by your desire to seek revenge.'

'And?'

'And, you are forbidden to attack an Arcana.'

'He's a Hunter!' Colt argued.

'No, he is not. Not yet. We will stop the transformation.'

'How?' Colt demanded. As far as he was concerned, their attempts would be wasted energy.

'To become a Hunter, Dino will need to sacrifice his humanity . . .' she trailed off, as though a realisation had suddenly dawned on her.

There was no need to vocalise it because the same thought was crossing Colt's mind.

'His sister,' he murmured. In a split second Colt was gone. His feet barely skimmed the floor as he raced to his bedchamber.

Exploding through his bedroom door, his heart leapt to his throat. The room was empty.

'Mia!' he called, flinging the bedcovers back as though perhaps she was unnoticed beneath them. The four candles lay sideways on the crimson carpet, overturned from where Dino had trampled through them just a short while earlier.

Colt darted to the window, looking down upon the

grounds. He knotted his hands through his hair. She was nowhere in sight.

In a flurry, he turned and darted back down the stone staircase. Speeding through the castle, he made a beeline for Mia's bedroom. From the other direction, Wendolyn was heading the same way.

'He's taken her!' Colt exclaimed. He flung open Mia's bedroom door. The room was empty.

'Perhaps not,' Wendolyn reasoned, puffing as she reached the room. 'Perhaps she is with friends.'

'No. He's taken her,' Colt choked. 'I can't sense her.'

The colour drained from Wendolyn's lined face.

'I request permission to kill him,' Colt hissed. His teeth were clenched ferociously.

'No!' Wendolyn scolded. 'Under no circumstances will you hurt the boy. Do you understand me?'

Colt snarled.

A new voice broke through the tension. A girl's voice, but not Mia's.

'Wendolyn!' Kizzy cried, galloping up the staircase in her oversized dungarees. 'You need to come, quick! Dino has locked Benny Blue in the library! Blue says Dino's gone mad!'

Wendolyn turned to Colt. 'The spare key is in my bed-chamber,' she told him. 'Go!'

Colt vanished in a flash. Minutes later he joined them at the library, brass key in hand.

Hastily, Wendolyn unlocked the door and Blue burst out. In a garble, he told her everything he knew. Including how Dino had been searching for the books on ascension.

'It's as I feared,' Wendolyn muttered grimly.

'I think Dino is being p . . . possessed by a Hunter named Tol,' Blue explained.

At the mention of the name, Wendolyn froze. 'Tol?'

Blue nodded his head.

For a moment, Wendolyn seemed sickened. 'Then I'm afraid things are worse than I had imagined,' she said. 'We must act fast. I need to contact Cassandra and Madeline Bicks.'

'Dino's family?' Blue looked on, wide-eyed.

'Yes. I will require their assistance.'

Colt fidgeted restlessly at the library door. 'Let me go,' he implored Wendolyn. 'I won't kill the boy.' At that point, he didn't know if he was lying or not. And he didn't care, either. All he cared about was finding Mia.

'Go,' Wendolyn said. 'Find them. Try to stop the sacrifice. But be careful – if Tol *is* ascending, his power will be beyond what you have experienced before.'

'I'll stop it,' Colt swore.

'I meanwhile will search for ways to protect Dino from Tol's power. We must release him from the hold Tol has over him.'

'Will that stop Tol?' Kizzy pressed.

'No. For that we will need Cassandra and Madeline.' She turned to the Hunter. 'Colt, delay the sacrifice for as long as you can.'

'There will be no sacrifice,' Colt vowed resolutely. And with one last righteous look, he was gone.

Colt paced agitatedly around the flooded courtyard, confused as to which direction to go. His rain continued to spill relentlessly from the oppressive purple sky. Distressed, he stood at the mercy of the downpour, lost and helpless. It was surreal; he had brought the rain more times than he could remember, and had crossed through that courtyard near enough every day of his life, but never had he felt so frantic, hopeless and afraid.

It was exasperating. Attempting to track Mia in a down-pour this torrential was an impossible task. The sheer quantity of water had swallowed every other scent in the surrounding area. Ironically, the more unsuccessful Colt was, the wilder the storm became.

He growled viciously, his frustration and anger rising by the second. His eyes were as black as soot. Even the whites of his eyes were now swollen jet black.

'Compose yourself,' he reprimanded harshly. But it was an unattainable wish. He had lost all control, and could not regain it.

Fury drove him now – it consumed him. He was addicted to it, he was filled with the urge to destroy whatever was misfortunate enough to cross his path. He longed to make a kill, to satisfy the savage demon baying inside of him.

There was only one thing that held him back, only one thing left that stopped him from surrendering to the darkness. He needed to find Mia. And the only way he could do that was by beating the anger that absorbed him.

I can't do it! I have never been able to control it. How can I expect to overcome it this time?

'But . . . *she* did,' he said aloud, suddenly recounting his run-in with Mia earlier that day. She had brought him back from the brink of ferocity with the greatest of ease.

He closed his eyes, savouring the pleasure of envisioning her. With immaculate precision, he pictured every detail of her face: the curve of her cheekbone, the cherry red of her lips, her slate-grey eyes, and the dimple of her smile. With a wave of relief, he felt his rasping breath steady somewhat.

Stay with me, he asked the image that resided in his mind's eye.

'Don't,' he muttered out loud, his eyes still closed.

Bizarrely, he found himself reciting the conversation that had sedated him only twelve hours before. The words were a wonderful comfort; it was as though she were right there at his side, scolding him from her own lips.

'What a foolish man to yearn for a lecture!' he said, chuckling quietly.

The rain, though still present, had started to relent.

Spurred on by the effectiveness of his ramblings, Colt persisted to run though their earlier conversation. 'I will never love you,' he mumbled to himself. 'Then never kiss me . . .' Colt opened his eyes. He rolled the words over one more time. 'Then never kiss me,' he repeated.

And then, he picked up a scent. It was faint and distant, but it was Mia.

Colt jerked his head in the direction of the forest. The night was eerily quiet, but Colt knew that it was rife with activity. He would stop at nothing to uncover it.

He began to run, empowering the wind to work alongside him. It aided his legs, heightening their speed until they were nothing more than a blur. Tearing through the land like a bullet, he weaved in and out of the trees, leaving only a trail of dust in his wake.

That night Colt ran faster than even he imagined possible. Lives depended on him, and this time he wouldn't be late.

A large diamond had been drawn into the soggy mud. Tol stood at the northerly point, while his two robed minions stood at east and west. Dino took his post at the southern point. In his arms, Dino clasped Mia in front of him. She struggled, but he restrained her so closely to him that her movements hardly made any impact at all.

Dino peered over her head at Tol's sneering face opposite them. The grotesque man seemed morbidly fascinated by the siblings.

'What a sight,' Tol leered menacingly. 'How very similar you look.'

'Actually, we look nothing alike,' Mia shot back boldly.

Dino tightened his grip on her, as though he were punishing her for speaking out of line.

'Ouch!' Mia grumbled. She lowered her voice for only Dino's ears. 'Snap out of it, Dino. You've been brainwashed by that . . . monster!'

He heard her, but her words barely registered. His attention was too focused on Tol to be distracted by his sister.

Tol's snake eyes flickered between the members of his coven, and then, like clockwork, the three men began chanting in an unfamiliar tongue.

'I can't believe you're really going through with this,' Mia hissed under her breath. 'I was wrong about you. You're not my brother – you're just an evil demon, like them.'

'Exactly,' Dino whispered back into her ear. 'This is who I am.'

Mia kicked back against his shin, but it caused no reaction. He was numb to it.

'I've changed my mind,' she spat. 'It's not who are you. Being who you are would be too convenient an excuse, and I'm not letting you get off that easily. Who you are is my brother, and you're going to kill me. I want you to feel very, very guilty. You are officially the worst brother in the whole world.' She kicked him again.

Dino blocked out the sound of Mia's voice and listened instead to the ritualistic, monotone chanting of the coven.

'You realise,' Mia went on, 'that I'm going to haunt you for ever. I'm going to haunt you until it drives you insane, like in that movie, *Ghost Fever*.'

Dino paused. 'I haven't seen it.'

'That's not the point! The point is, I'm going to dedicate my life – or my afterlife, or whatever – to making your life hell. You thought I was annoying before? Well, get ready to meet me as a ghost.'

Dino laughed involuntarily and Tol glared at him.

'Stop talking,' Dino snarled, his sharp breath prickling against Mia's ear.

'I most certainly will not!' she exclaimed. 'If anyone should stop what they're doing, it should be you!'

'I can't stop. I have to rid myself of my humanity.'

Dino's grasp grew tighter and tighter.

'Argh!' Mia wailed in frustration. 'Cassandra and Madeline are never going to forgive you for this,' she added heatedly.

Cassandra and Madeline.

Dino stiffened. It had been weeks since he had thought about his mother and aunt. It was strange to hear their names.

Unbeknownst to Dino, Tol had invaded his mind. He had exhaustively suffocated all of Dino's own thoughts until only Tol's influence remained.

But now, a new influence crept into Dino's subconscious. And it wasn't Tol's, or even his own. It was Mia's. His Sententia power detected the recognisable sound of Mia's emotion. She had always been louder to him than anyone else – evidently Tol included.

'You love me,' he uttered in disbelief.

'No, I don't!' Mia objected. 'You're evil!'

'How can you still love me?' Dino stammered. 'I'm about to kill you.'

'You're so infuriating!'

The Hunter chanting grew louder and faster.

All of a sudden Dino's head started to throb. There were so many conflicting emotions all battling to be heard. His mind told him that he wanted Mia dead, but simultaneously his heart told him otherwise.

Then Tol spoke to Dino in a deep, guttural voice. 'Make your sacrifice,' he commanded, his beady eyes blazing.

Dino gulped uncertainly. He placed his hands on Mia's head.

'No, Dino! Don't!' she cried.

You can do it! Tol planted the affirmation in Dino's mind. *You are a Hunter.*

Dino's fingers twined into Mia's hair. He breathed steadily. It would be over in seconds. She would feel no pain.

Suddenly they were not alone. A warm breeze tousled Mia's hair, coiling around it and sweeping the strands from her face.

Colt.

Tol tensed. 'Kill the girl!' he roared. Then something almost undetectable shot past him.

In a cyclone of wind, Colt appeared. He stood staunchly just outside of the ceremonial border, his eyes fixed on Tol.

'So, you're the big bad wolf who murdered my brothers,' Colt remarked brazenly. 'You don't look all that intimidating.' He sized him up with arrogant disdain.

'And you must be the fourth Hunter of the Glass Castle,' Tol sneered back. 'The only one left.'

'Still standing,' Colt provoked him.

'Not for long.' Tol raised his hand and shot a blast of yellow light in Colt's direction.

With impeccable speed, Colt dodged the spear of light. He grinned tauntingly.

'Colt, run!' Mia screamed. Dino's hands remained clasped to her head, as though he would crush her skull like it was nothing more than a tiny grape at any moment.

'I'm not going anywhere without you,' Colt assured her calmly, his eyes constantly fixed on Tol.

'They'll kill you!' Mia cried. 'Just go!'

'No,' he replied in a surprisingly level voice. 'I'm not leaving you.'

'Funny you should say that,' Tol remarked shrewdly. 'Because that's precisely how we captured her in the first place. Who knew it would be so easy to take you away from her?' His laughter pierced the night air like the screeching caws of a crow.

'That's why you killed my coven?' Colt deduced. 'To take me away from Mia?'

'It worked, didn't it?' Tol cackled.

'Well, guess what? There's none of them left for you to kill. I suppose that means I'm staying this time.'

'Of little use it'll be! You're not at the Glass Castle any more. You're on *my* ground now.'

'Ha!' Colt snorted. 'There is no such thing. All ground is my ground. And I'll kill every single one of you before I let you harm the girl.'

Dino dipped his head to Mia's ear. 'What is this? Are you in some sort of relationship with a Hunter? Mia, what are you thinking? He's too dangerous for you!'

Mia spluttered at the absurdity. 'Are you serious? Now is not the time to play the protective brother! You're about to kill me, remember? It doesn't get much more dangerous than that!'

Groping for time, Colt persisted in distracting Tol from the ritual. 'You went to great effort to get me out of the way,' he goaded in a risky jeer. 'Sounds like you might be afraid me.'

'Afraid of you?' Tol scoffed. 'You are nothing!'

'Then take your best shot.' Colt extended his arms, inviting a challenge.

Tol raised his hand and shot a second bolt of light at his opponent – faster and more forceful this time. But again, Colt ducked aside, using his Tempestus agility to his advantage.

In terms of strength, Colt was no match for Tol, but nevertheless he was a distraction. And an effective one at that.

'Leave now,' Tol warned him. 'You have no business here.'

'Actually, you're wrong.' Colt laced in and out of the trees, trying not to stay in one place for too long. 'I *do* have business here.' He disappeared behind a pine tree and resurfaced somewhere else entirely. 'And I'd go so far as to say that my business takes precedence over yours.' His voice echoed, its origins indistinct.

'Pah!' Tol bellowed. 'I beg to differ.'

'No, *I* beg to differ.' Colt paused and looked intently at Mia. 'I have to kiss that girl,' he announced.

Even in the midst of warfare, Mia couldn't help but feel elated.

'Because I love her, and I believe that was the deal,' Colt elaborated. He smiled proudly.

'You have got to be kidding me,' Dino muttered under his breath.

'And I love him!' Mia returned fervently.

Tol let out a rippling, thunderous laugh. 'Falling for a Hunter?' he ridiculed, addressing Mia for the first time. 'Just like your mother. Foolish little girl!'

Colt frowned. 'Where are your manners?' he mocked scornfully. 'That's no way to speak to a lady.'

Tol glared at Mia, his expression vindictive and bitter. 'I shall speak to her any way I choose,' he hissed. 'She *is* my daughter, after all.'

16

The Unseen

Mia felt Dino's grip instantly slacken. Her stomach flipped.

'Liar!' she screamed at Tol, her grey eyes smouldering with resentment.

Tol guffawed spitefully. 'You are just as I imagined. Pure. Nothing like my son.'

'You're my father,' Dino murmured.

'Surprised?' Tol asked lightly.

'Don't listen to him!' Mia cried. 'He's lying! Our father could never be a monster like that!' Looking into Tol's loathsome face, she saw only evil – not the wholesome man that she had always pictured to be her father.

The man whom she had dreamed of had gone away on a covert mission, which kept him from returning to the family home. This wonderful, imaginary man would one day return wearing a tweed suit and carrying a leather briefcase. He was worlds apart from the fiend she saw before her now, his face so warped with malice that he was barely human, let alone a father.

'Mia,' Dino whispered, 'he's not lying.' Suddenly everything seemed to make sense. Of course Tol had wanted Dino for his coven. What greater asset was there than the direct descendant of Tol's very own blood – Tol's heir?

'I'm shocked that your mother never spoke of me,' Tol mused in a taunting voice. 'I wonder why she chose not to?' He laughed wildly.

Mia gawped at Tol in revulsion. 'You make me sick!'

'Mia, calm down,' Dino implored her. His arms remained sealed around her, although now it was more for comfort than containment.

Colt watched the scene in utter bewilderment while Tol's two minions stood motionless, hidden beneath their dark robes.

Mia grimaced. 'You know, I always wondered why you never tried to contact us, or why you never sent me a birthday card. Now I know it was because you were too busy plotting my death!'

'You're of no interest to me,' Tol said icily. 'It's the boy whose powers I seek.' He cast his eyes upon Dino. 'My son, join me.'

'No!' Colt shouted. 'He's got into your mind somehow! He's tricking you into thinking you want to become a Hunter . . .'

Tol threw a spear of light at his antagonist. Colt dived out of the way, but it was a near miss.

'Has he taken your blood?' Colt asked Dino hurriedly. 'Think!'

'Quiet!' Tol roared.

Dino tentatively ran his fingers over the raised scar across his jaw line. Tol had taken his blood.

'You see?' Colt responded to Dino's unspoken thoughts. 'You don't want to kill your sister. You're being possessed. He's probably working all sorts of magic on you . . .' His sentence was cut short. A powerful burst of light exploded into him, lifting him from the ground and hurtling him through the air like a rag doll.

'No!' Mia cried as Colt's body collided with a tree trunk and plummeted down to the ground.

'Dead,' Tol sneered in satisfaction. 'Now we can proceed.'

'No!' Mia screamed again. She pushed away from Dino and ran to where Colt lay unmoving on the forest floor. She dropped to the ground, shaking him, but his head hung limply in her hands.

'Now!' Tol barked. 'It is time.' He scowled at Dino. 'Bring her back,' he ordered.

Dino froze. 'Why don't you bring her back?' he tested cautiously. It had suddenly occurred to him that, even with all of his power, Tol had never directly approached Mia. Tol was keeping his distance from her, just as he had done with Dino – until Dino had inadvertently accepted Tol's offer, that was.

'It must be you,' Tol spat.

'Because you can't touch her,' Dino guessed. 'She's magically protected from you. And so was I until I invited you in. You're in my mind, aren't you? The Hunter was right – you're controlling me.'

'You belong to me,' Tol snarled.

Dino glanced at his sister, who now lay buckled over Colt, crying breathless, heartbreaking tears.

'Mia,' Dino murmured, 'you're hurting.' It made no difference whether or not she had been physically harmed; she was in irreparable ruins – or at least her heart was.

'This isn't real,' Mia choked pitifully. She repeated the words over and over again until they distorted into nothing more than earth-shattering sobs.

Dino didn't know if it was her words, her tears, or his own consciousness breaking through, but he was suddenly guided by a new strength. It was as though his mind was reborn to him at long last. He focused his concentration on blocking Tol's power, just as he had done with Wendolyn so many times before.

In a counterattack, Tol's determination hardened as he desperately fought to retain his influence over Dino.

With a strained breath, Dino stepped out of the ceremonial diamond and raced to Mia's side. For once, he ignored every reflection and emotion that crossed his mind and only thought of her. He dropped to his knees and grabbed her shoulders.

'Please forgive me,' he begged her urgently. He pulled her into him roughly, rent by his own ragged sorrow.

'Let me go,' she wept. Even when enveloped in Dino's unwelcome hug, Mia's fingers remained coiled around the collar of Colt's shirt. Her fingertips touched his skin as though their connection gave him a link to a life force.

Tol and his incomplete coven watched this display of human passion with heartless curiosity.

'Come on,' Dino said in a gentle yet imperative voice. 'We need to get out of here.' He took her elbow, urging her to leave, but she shook herself free of him, clinging to Colt's lifeless body.

'No!' she cried

Dino bit his lip. 'I'm sorry,' he whispered. 'I'm so sorry.'

Grief-stricken tears were her only response.

Tol let out a deafening bellow. 'I may not be able to touch her, but you, on the other hand, are fair game.' His eyes bore into Dino vengefully.

'Mia, please,' Dino rasped. 'We have to go.'

'I can't leave him here alone,' she whimpered. 'I don't want him to be alone.' With one of her hands, she protectively shielded Colt's serene face. 'You go,' she said to Dino briefly, looking up at him through her blinding tears.

Dino crouched over her, stroking her hair softly. 'No,' he said in a tender voice. 'I won't leave you.'

With his coven looking on impatiently, Tol stepped away from his post and lunged towards his victim. But his opening assault was not on Dino. Instead he grabbed Colt by the scruff of the neck and hoisted him upright. Colt slumped forward, his eyes shut and his body limp.

'No!' Mia screamed, as Colt was ripped away from her.

With astonishing ease Tol tossed Colt aside, hurling him into the thick of trees.

Mia fell back, dismayed.

Next, Tol moved on to Dino. Backed against a tree, Dino had nowhere to run. Tol gripped his throat and lifted him to his feet.

Dino wheezed as Tol's knife-like fingernails pierced his skin. Their eyes met, and slits of ruby-red blood began to appear on Dino's throat as his attacker's nails penetrated his flesh.

Mia retched at the sight. She was torn, riddled by her conflicting needs to both stay with Colt and help her brother. But she knew what she had to do. Colt had taught her the meaning of strength and sacrifice, and now it was her time to use it.

With tracks of tears staining her face, she staggered to her feet. As Tol wrung the life from Dino, Mia turned her palms down to the ground. Progressively, the earth beneath her feet began to rumble, shuddering in an underground eruption. Mia's earthquake.

The shaking ground jolted Tol off balance. He stumbled backwards and dropped Dino to the ground.

Mia looked at her brother, whose blood was trickling down his throat and on to the lapel of his T-shirt. In a profound moment, the siblings locked eyes intently, communicating by instinct rather than words.

Without missing a beat, Dino sprung to his feet. Taking Mia's hand, he began to run. They darted through the maze of trees, racing at full pelt through the forest, driven by the knowledge that Tol would be upon them at any moment.

A rusty blue station wagon pulled up to the dark courtyard. The purring engine let out a final splutter before cutting out entirely. Now only a ghostly silence engaged the courtyard.

'Cassie,' Madeline said from the front passenger seat of the car, 'before we go inside, I want to promise you that, whatever happens, we'll get through this – just like last time.'

'It can be nothing like last time, Maddie!' Cassandra exclaimed, her slender hands still resting on the steering wheel. 'Last time we lost our brothers to Tol. I will not lose my children, too,' she said adamantly.

Madeline held up her hands submissively. 'That's what I'm saying – we'll find a way. We've stopped Tol before . . . eventually.' She scraped her mane of red hair into a high ponytail, letting it bob at the crown of her head.

'Yes, we stopped him,' Cassandra agreed, fixating on the positive, 'and we will do it again.'

'Sure,' Madeline flipped down the vanity mirror and inspected her appearance. 'And look how well that worked out,' she added dryly.

Cassandra glared at her. 'It worked for sixteen years, didn't it? I'd say that's a pretty successful spell.'

'He must have found a loophole,' Madeline muttered, twisting her head from left to right to get a thorough look at her attractive profile.

Irritably, Cassandra pushed the vanity mirror back into its place, regaining her sister's focus. 'I imagine he's searched many years to find a way around our curse.'

Without her reflection to distract her, Madeline was suddenly re-energised. 'And now he's taken baby Dino!' she shouted, outraged.

Cassandra chuckled in spite of the sombre mood. 'How much longer are you going to call him baby Dino? He's seventeen years old. That's practically a grown man!'

Madeline pouted. 'He'll always be a baby to me. I liked him as a baby – he was cute. As a man he's sullen and petulant. Just like his . . .'

'Madeline! Don't you dare say, just like his father, or so help me God . . .'

'Easy, tiger,' Madeline gave her an aloof glance. 'I was going to say, just like his mother.'

'Oh!' Cassandra retracted her claws. 'I'm not sullen,' she slipped in as an afterthought.

Before another word could be exchanged, the castle door lurched open and Wendolyn bustled into the courtyard, followed by Kizzy and Blue. The rain had stopped, but the ground was still damp and puddled in places.

Cassandra and Madeline unfastened their seatbelts and hurried out of the car to greet the newcomers.

Wendolyn, still in her nightwear, hugged and kissed the two women.

'How can I show my face to you?' she sighed remorsefully. 'You trusted me with your children and I have failed you.'

'Oh, nonsense!' Cassandra exonerated her immediately. 'You are most certainly not to blame for any of this.'

'That's absolutely right,' Madeline chimed in. 'Besides, I think we all half expected Tol to return sometime.'

Blue peered at the women inquisitively. 'So, you knew that T . . . Tol would come f . . . for Dino?' he asked meekly.

Cassandra and Madeline looked at Kizzy and Blue as though they had only just noticed them standing there.

'Well,' Madeline shrugged, 'it was always at the back of our minds. I suppose it was only a matter of time.'

'What does he want with Dino?' Blue asked her. He fidgeted tensely, shifting his weight from left foot to right.

Madeline took the liberty of explaining. 'I'm a Seer,' she pointed to herself, causing her array of colourful bracelets to clang against each other noisily, 'and when Cassandra was pregnant with Dino, I foresaw a powerful heir. Of course I told Cassandra and Tol about their unborn child . . .'

Kizzy and Blue gasped in unison.

'Tol's child?' Kizzy repeated, her blue eyes as wide as saucers.

Cassandra and Madeline shared a private glance.

'Tol is Dino's father,' Cassandra confirmed, a little shame-fully. 'Mia's, too.'

'Anyway,' Madeline went on, skipping over the stunned silence, 'Tol became obsessed with Dino's imminent power. He wanted to raise the child in the dark arts, but we didn't know it at the time. You see, Tol wasn't always evil. I mean, personally, I never liked him . . .'

'He was a Hunter,' Cassandra interjected, 'but he was noble and I fell in love with him. I was young, and so was Tol. But the idea of having such power within his grasp turned him for the worse. It drove him insane with ambition.'

'Of course, he hid it well,' Madeline jumped in. 'It was almost two years before we began to notice how sinister he was becoming – by which time Dino was a toddler and Mia was a newborn.'

'Everything about him changed,' Cassandra said, speaking directly to Wendolyn now, finally able to unload the burden that she had been carrying for years. 'His voice, his appearance, his manner. *Everything*. I loved him so dearly, and it broke my heart to watch. But Tol – my Tol – was gone, and what was left was a shell, driven only by greed.'

'So, we did what we had to do,' Madeline spoke softly. 'We performed a binding spell, banishing Tol from our land and protecting the children from him.'

Cassandra smiled sadly. 'And the irony of it all is that Dino isn't the powerful heir that Maddie saw – Mia is. Of course, Tol doesn't know that.'

Kizzy and Blue looked at one another, bewildered and amazed all at once.

'And now he's got them both,' Kizzy said quietly.

Cassandra flinched at the remark.

Quickly, Madeline draped her arm over her sister's shoulders. 'Not for long,' she assured Cassandra. 'All we need to do is find a binding spell . . .'

219

Wendolyn stopped her. 'Madeline,' she said delicately, 'Cassandra, there's something you both should know.'

The women regarded her carefully, their matching azure eyes clouded with anxiety.

Wendolyn took a calming breath. 'Tol is ascending.'

Cassandra let out an involuntary cry.

'Wait!' Madeline raised her hand, her fingers bejewelled with chunky rings. 'Ascend*ing*, or ascend*ed*?'

'As far as we know, he hasn't ascended yet,' Wendolyn filled them in. 'He needs a complete coven to execute the ritual. That's why he has taken Dino.'

Madeline frowned. 'If Tol needs Dino for his coven, then it'll require a sacrifice of humanity. He needs Dino to sacrifice Mia!' She pieced together the information with grim logic.

'He won't do it!' Cassandra blurted out. 'I know my son, and he will not harm Mia. He cares too deeply for her.'

Nobody dared challenge her statement.

'If Tol hasn't yet ascended,' Madeline went on, brainstorming ideas, 'then he is still manageable. What if we upped the game and did a power-stripping spell?'

'We'd need a strong coven for that,' Cassandra pointed out.

The three elder witches looked dubiously at the two youngsters.

'They're not ready,' Wendolyn said, confirming what they had all been thinking.

'But we *need* a fourth!' Madeline wailed. She placed her hands on her hips. 'Why am I *never* part of a coven?' she complained grouchily. 'It doesn't make sense. I'm beautiful, I'm powerful, everybody loves me . . .'

'Be quiet, Madeline!' Cassandra snapped.

Madeline pulled a face.

'There is one way,' Wendolyn interrupted, mulling a thought over in her mind. 'But, Kizzy and Benny, we will need your help.'

Kizzy and Blue unquestioningly agreed, but their apprehension was obvious. As young witches, they were way out of their league.

Wendolyn cleared her throat and straightened out her shoulders. 'We must raise my husband, William Wix.' She stood staunchly, her long white hair spiralling over her shoulders like a coat of armour.

Kizzy grimaced. 'Raise him from the . . . ?' She couldn't bring herself to utter the final word.

'What a fabulous idea!' Madeline clapped her hands in glee. Then she eyed Kizzy and Blue uncertainly. 'You *have* raised a spirit before, haven't you?'

Again, Kizzy and Blue looked dumbfounded.

'Uh . . . no,' Kizzy answered on behalf of them both.

Madeline waved her hand nonchalantly. 'Oh, it's no bother. It's great fun. In fact, it's to die for!' she giggled infectiously.

Kizzy and Blue smiled politely, but they were clearly overwhelmed.

'So,' Cassandra said, forming a plan out loud, 'the three of us will find Tol, while you two work on raising William. With any luck, by the time we get to Tol, our coven will be four and we can perform the power-stripping spell. But we'll have to move fast. If he already has Dino and Mia, then every second is vital.'

Wendolyn nodded in concurrence. 'We should head into the forest. As a guess, I'd say that he's somewhere along the borders.'

'That forest stretches for miles!' Madeline shrieked. 'It'll take us hours!' She looked down at her glamorous high-heeled shoes worriedly.

'Then we are already wasting time,' Cassandra said stiffly. 'Let's go.'

The three women spun around and marched away from the castle, leaving Kizzy and Blue alone at the entryway.

221

'Wait!' Kizzy cried. 'We don't know how to raise William Wix!' She clung to Blue's hand in sheer panic.

'Stay calm,' Wendolyn called back soothingly. 'The ritual spell is in a book kept in the library, *Gateways of the Spirit World*.'

'I know the book!' Blue shouted back.

'Good,' said Wendolyn, smiling warmly at him. 'The spell you will need is called The Crossover. William is buried in the Glass Castle cemetery. You will need to light four candles around his grave, which will act as a sort of portal. Chant the spell once the candles have been lit.' She eased a silver chain from around her neck, displaying the amber pendant hanging from the end. 'This amulet will draw William's spirit to me. All you need to do is say the spell.'

'We can do it!' Blue assured her in a hoarse voice. Behind his curtain of sandy blond hair, his complexion was ashen.

'And if we can't?' Kizzy called out timidly to the departing women.

'Then we'll all die,' Madeline chortled. 'Just kidding! Who knows what'll happen. It's anyone's game.' Something about her amended sentence was even more alarming than the original statement.

17

Soulmates

Dino raced blindly through the forest, dragging Mia along behind him. He felt her stumble as she ran faster than her comfortable speed, but he yanked her back upright and kept moving forward.

'Just a little further,' he encouraged her. 'We have to get back to the castle. Tol can't touch us on hallowed ground.'

Mia gasped for breath, exhausted from the gruelling run and choking on her tears.

'Nearly there,' Dino said sympathetically. In actual fact, his comment was simply wishful thinking. The truth was, he didn't know how far away from the castle they were. And the deeper they plunged into the forest, the more lost they became. But Dino refused to stop running. He had witnessed Tol's capabilities first-hand, and they frightened him to his very core.

Then Mia let out a cry of pain. She tripped over a fallen tree branch and tumbled to the forest floor.

Dino caught her elbow, but it was too late.

'My ankle!' she sobbed.

Dino stooped over her. 'Can you walk?' he asked hurriedly. Every second they wasted was potentially life-threatening. He cautiously helped her to her feet.

Mia let out an involuntary yelp and crumpled back down to the ground like a wilting flower.

'Damn it!' Dino cursed.

She couldn't put weight on it, let alone run on it. He could attempt to carry her, but it would slow them down so drastically that it would most likely render their efforts pointless.

Mia sat on the ground, nursing her rapidly swelling ankle. Her eyes welled with a fresh batch of tears, glistening silver like two rock pools. 'I can't,' she whispered. 'I'm sorry.'

Dino crouched down in front of her, placing his hands on her knees and fixing his eyes on hers. 'Don't *you* apologise, Mia. You've got nothing to be sorry about.'

'I can't walk,' she mumbled in a tiny voice.

'That's OK,' he told her. 'We can rest here for a while.' The prospect of stopping chilled him to the bones, but he hid his fear well.

'We have to keep going,' Mia said, silent tears spilling from her brimming eyes.

Dino lifted his hands to her face, wiping the tears away with his thumbs. 'No, we don't,' he said, feigning composure. 'We'll be fine right here.'

Mia began to cry openly now, weeping for everything that she had lost – and gained. Colt was gone. Just like that. And the man who'd killed him was her father.

'Hey, hey,' Dino soothed, trying unsuccessfully to pacify her. 'No more tears.'

'I feel like I'm in a nightmare and I can't wake up,' she rasped in uneven breaths.

Dino nodded his head benevolently. 'I know.'

'I loved him,' Mia murmured. 'Colt.'

Dino didn't respond, but he listened compassionately as her heart poured out.

'I did,' she said. 'I don't know why, but I did. I thought he was my soulmate. Isn't that stupid?'

'I don't think it's stupid,' Dino replied gently.

'It's pathetic,' Mia went on. 'There's no such thing as soulmates,' she said bitterly.

Dino sat down on the floor opposite her. Absent-mindedly,

he twined his fingers through a stray tuft of grass. 'I think there is such a thing. I think there's a place reserved for those few people who you love in a special way. I always thought our dad would be my soulmate,' he laughed ironically. 'Now *that*'s stupid.'

Mia blotted the tears from her eyes. She smiled understandingly. 'What a disappointment,' she said quietly. 'That man's not your soulmate, Dino.'

'I know,' he agreed. 'Hey, Mia,' he added hesitantly, 'if you're still looking for one, I'll be yours. Your soulmate, I mean.'

She laughed sadly. 'Thanks.'

'Yeah, why not? I'll hang out with you in our future lives – for my sins!' he joked. 'And maybe in the next life, Colt will be there, too. Then you'll have two soulmates. That can't be bad.'

She closed her eyes, trapping the tears behind an eyelid prison.

A mild breeze wound among the trees and laced through Mia's hair. Such a breeze was unnatural in the sheltered depths of the forest.

Dino froze. 'Tol!' he grimaced. Instantly, he sprung into action, hauling Mia to her feet. 'We've got to get out of here! I'll carry you.'

'Wait!' she stopped him. She knew that breeze, and it wasn't Tol.

The air grew stronger. It spiralled around Mia, sweeping her chocolate-brown hair back from her damp face.

Mia's heart fluttered. 'Colt!' she called out.

A stream of air rustled through the leaves, and in a blur Colt appeared before them. He placed his hand on Mia's tear-stained cheek.

'Colt,' Mia breathed. She touched his hand where it rested on her face, half expecting him to be an illusion. 'I thought you were . . .' she trailed off.

He stared at her, his eyes an identical colour to that of the forest around them. 'It's not *that* easy to take me down,' he smirked conceitedly.

Mia blinked. 'But you were . . . dead.'

'Was I?' he mocked her. 'That's news to me!'

'You're alive?' she stammered.

Colt shook his head in jest. 'Oh, dear! My love, so very quick to jump to conclusions. A person can't lose consciousness for five seconds without someone calling time of death!' He winked at her. 'I woke up just as you were leaving. I distracted Tol's coven for as long as I could, then I tracked you.'

Mia threw her arms around him. 'I'm so glad you're alive,' she said tearfully.

'Of course you are. You would have missed me so very terribly.'

Mia clung to him, nuzzling into the groove of his neck. 'Yes!'

Colt smiled. 'You're fond of me,' he observed. 'I'm awfully fond of you, too.' He rubbed his hand up and down her back, besotted by the sensation of it. Then he spoke again, his voice more uncertain this time. 'In the graveyard, you told me not to kiss you unless I loved you.'

Mia laughed. 'I vaguely remember,' she said as she tilted her face to look up at him.

'Well, I do love you,' Colt said virtuously. 'So I would also very much like to kiss you.' He pulled away from their embrace, a self-satisfied smile on his lips. 'May I?'

Mia nodded her head shyly.

And Colt kissed her with the passion of a man starved.

For what felt like a lifetime, Dino stood back, averting his eyes from the private scene. Then at last he spoke up. 'OK,' he said, clearing his throat. 'I think that's enough.'

The star-crossed lovers parted like impish children caught

in an act of mischief. They shared a secret smile before turning to Dino.

'Colt,' Dino said, addressing the stranger with awkward humility. 'Thanks for helping out back there.'

Colt eyed him warily. 'It would have been easier just to kill you,' he pointed out.

'Probably,' Dino agreed, unperturbed by the remark. 'In fact . . .' He paused. '. . . That's not such a bad idea.'

'What?' Mia gawped at him.

Dino elaborated. 'Tol wants me, right? He can't ascend until I join his coven. And he won't stop until he gets me. So, what's the one guaranteed way to stop him from getting me?'

Colt mulled it over, somewhat amused.

'No!' Mia said flatly. 'No way.'

'Look,' Dino reasoned, 'Tol will stop at nothing to get me. He'd kill you all.'

'But he won't get you,' Mia insisted. 'He's lost his hold over you.'

'For how long?' Dino argued. 'He's too powerful. As soon as he gets near me, he can get back inside my head. I know because I recognise it. I've done it myself. I think Tol is a Sententia.'

Colt frowned. 'Strange. I detected a Tempestus power in him. It was faint, but present.'

Dino looked at Mia. 'Like you,' he noted, drawing the genetic comparison. Suddenly he remembered one of his earlier encounters with Tol, when Tol had used his power to split a tree trunk in two. 'Can a Tempestus rupture a tree in half?'

Colt nodded. 'Yes. From the root. We have command over the earth. Why?'

'Because Tol did that!' Dino explained. 'That's what he threatened to do to Mia if I didn't consider the offer of his coven.'

Colt snorted. 'Party tricks! He couldn't have done that to Mia – she's a human. In order to fracture a tree, he would have manipulated the ground to shatter its roots.'

Dino cringed. He felt utterly duped. 'So, is it possible he's part Sententia and part Tempestus?' he asked Colt.

'Yes. But a combination of powers would involve a very weak strain of each. No wonder he's so keen to get your power in his coven. You're the thoroughbred he probably yearned to be.'

'Weak strain or not, he's definitely a force to be reckoned with now,' Dino concluded pessimistically.

Colt rolled his eyes. 'That's because you handed over the ritual of ascension, and now he's halfway down the road to being all-powerful!'

The memories of his behaviour and actions came back to Dino in a haze.

'My death is the only way to stop him,' Dino declared. 'You have to end it here.' He looked to Colt.

'That does sound like fun,' Colt mused.

'No!' Mia repeated, her voice wildly aggressive.

'It's the only way!' Dino protested. 'All of this is my fault, and I want to fix it.' He turned to Colt. 'Kill me,' he requested valiantly.

Colt smiled. 'As much as I'd love to oblige, I'm afraid I can't. You see, I've been cursed.' Mia and Dino looked on wide-eyed, and Colt let out a forlorn sigh. 'I've caught humanity. And it's a real kicker. I can't kill you – not today, anyhow.'

'But you're a Hunter,' Dino furrowed his brow, baffled.

'Yes,' Colt snapped sharply. 'And I'm the best around. Don't you forget it! I'm just . . . *ill*.'

'All right,' Dino accepted. 'Then I'll do it myself.'

'Another fine idea,' Colt commented wryly. 'But there *is* one other option.'

'What's the other option?' Mia pressed urgently, happy to move away from the current plan.

'Bring him down.'

'Tol?' Dino was clearly dubious. 'Impossible.'

'Not impossible,' Colt corrected. 'You will need to get to Wendolyn. I can track her and lead you to her,' he suggested.

'Are we far away from the castle?' Mia asked him.

Colt inhaled the air as though he were tasting it. 'Not really. A mile, maybe two.' To him, that distance was a mere drop in the ocean. However, to Mia and Dino, it didn't sound quite so easy – especially with Mia's injured ankle.

'I won't be able to make it that far,' she told them despondently. She displayed her inflamed ankle.

'Oh, good Lord!' Colt exaggerated his sympathy. 'How will you live?'

Mia placed her hands on her hips. 'I can't walk. And I certainly can't walk two miles!'

Colt grinned roguishly. 'Then, darling,' he drawled, 'you shall fly.' He lifted her up and slung her on to his back like a cloak.

Mia wrapped her arms around his neck securely 'Are you sure you'll be able to carry me all the way?' she questioned doubtfully.

Colt chuckled at a joke that only he understood. 'You won't even slow me down,' he said confidently. 'All I ask is that you hold on, dear. I wouldn't want you seeing stars for the next week.'

Mia had never actually experienced Colt's supreme speed, but she was aware from his abrupt entrances and exits that he was faster than most. 'Should I be wearing a crash helmet?' she quipped, a little nervously.

Colt plucked a leaf from a nearby tree. He reached over his shoulder and settled it on Mia's head. 'There you go, safe and sound.' He gave Dino a sideways glance. 'Boy,' he said, 'follow me. And try to keep up.' Then, in a flurry of air, Colt was gone.

I'm not wearing suitable shoes for this kind of thing,' Madeline grumbled, her high-heeled stilettos sinking into the soggy mud.

Cassandra tucked her red tresses behind her ears and looked down at her sister's footwear. 'Why on earth did you wear such ridiculous heels?'

'Because they look fabulous!' Madeline argued defensively. 'And you're clearly jealous.'

'Jealous!' Cassandra exclaimed. 'I don't think so, Madeline. I can't for the life of me think why you would choose to torture yourself in such unwise shoes,' she tut-tutted.

Madeline gasped melodramatically, affronted by her sister's slur. 'Well,' she huffed, 'I can't for the life of me think why you would choose to procreate with such unwise men!' she shot back.

'Tol wasn't always evil! And you know that, Madeline.'

'Girls!' Wendolyn stepped in. 'Stop this, please,' she implored them. 'You are grown women.'

'Oh, wake up, Cassie!' Madeline laughed raucously, ignoring Wendolyn's remark. 'Tol was a soulless Hunter! Even on a good day, he was still evil.'

'No, he wasn't!' Cassandra yelled.

'Yes, he was!'

'Girls!' Wendolyn interjected again. 'Enough! Please.'

Madeline sniggered quietly. 'Sorry, Wennie!' she chirped in a sickly sweet voice.

'I too remember Tol as a young man,' Wendolyn reminded them. 'He was strong-willed and ill-tempered at times, but he was not evil.'

'But he was a Hunter,' Madeline objected.

'Hunters are not evil beings,' Wendolyn said setting her

straight as they trudged through the forest. 'And you'll do wise to remember that,' she added, now aware of the budding relationship between Mia and Colt.

'Tol was,' Madeline muttered under her breath, always a contender for the last word.

'No, he wasn't!' Cassandra threw up her hands. 'Not at first.'

'I'm sorry, Madeline, but Cassandra is right,' Wendolyn reflected. 'Being a Hunter did not warp Tol – it was his greed and thirst for power that turned him into what he is today. I believe everyone is born equal – a blank canvas. And it's the choices we make that will ultimately define who we will become. Not just as witches, but as men and women alike.'

'Madeline is still a blank canvas,' Cassandra teased. 'Aren't you, Maddie?'

'Wennic! Can you fathom the way she speaks to me?' Madeline wailed, outraged. 'And after everything I do for her.'

'Everything you do for me?' Cassandra chortled at the ludicrousness. 'You mean lounging around my house, eating my food, and making a mess?'

'And raising your two rug rats,' Madeline pouted.

Cassandra's expression softened. She smiled warmly at her sister. 'Oh, don't pretend that you don't love them as much as I do.'

Madeline sulked like a spoilt child. 'The girl, perhaps. But not the awful boy.'

'Madeline!' Cassandra exclaimed. 'That's a horrible thing to say! Take it back immediately.'

Wendolyn frowned in disappointment. 'Maddie, that was terribly unkind.'

Madeline folded her arms obstinately as she walked through the pine trees. 'Not really. He's got a vile temper.'

'So have you,' Cassandra accused with a good-natured nudge.

'Oh, puh-lease!' Madeline drew out the word theatrically.

Abruptly Wendolyn stopped walking.

Cassandra and Madeline looked at one another, fearing that their bickering had pushed the older lady too far.

'I hear him,' Wendolyn murmured in a hypnotic voice.

Cassandra became rigid. 'Is he near?'

'Deeper into the forest,' Wendolyn confirmed. 'He is searching for Dino.'

'Dino got away!' Madeline cheered, her obvious relief contradicting her earlier disparaging comments.

Wendolyn closed her aged eyes, listening to sounds unheard. 'Yes. But Tol is angry. He is more determined than ever.'

Forcefully, Madeline unstuck one of her heels from the ground. 'Well, let's just see who's more determined – Tol or us!'

18

United We Stand, Divided We Fall

'Are you sure we're heading in the right direction?' Madeline asked for what felt like the hundredth time. She stomped through the forest, huffing loudly at every opportunity.

'Yes, Maddie,' Cassandra replied tiredly. 'We must be close, because I can sense him.' Her stomach flipped at the realisation.

She hadn't seen Tol since they'd banished him sixteen years ago. The day was still so vivid in her mind. It had all seemed very sudden – one moment they were happy and in love with two beautiful children, and the next she was banishing a demon from her life. It broke her heart. And somewhere deep inside, she knew that she would never love again. Tol *was* her heart.

No. My Tol is gone, she reminded herself sternly. There was no room for weakness.

'We're on the right path,' Wendolyn confirmed. 'I only hope that William is with us by the time we reach Tol.' She clutched the amber amulet that hung around her neck. That small orange stone was the sacred portal which would draw William to her.

'Oh, a race against time!' Madeline noted with a spark of excitement. 'Russian roulette! Do you think those kids are up to it?'

Wendolyn was quiet for a moment. 'I think they are able,' she answered at last.

'I don't know . . .' Madeline studied her fingernails. 'The boy looked like a startled rabbit and the girl looked like she was one plate short of a dinner set.'

'You're very rude, Madeline,' Cassandra scolded. 'You know, you're not so perfect yourself, little sister.'

Madeline ran her fingers along her defined cheekbone, posing for an invisible camera. 'I'm more or less perfect,' she uttered dreamily. 'Besides, I wasn't being rude. I was merely playing the odds.'

A rustle in the trees stopped the three women in their tracks. They bristled, preparing themselves for battle.

And then, in a whirlwind, Colt stood before them. He carefully placed Mia down on the ground, holding her arm to steady her.

'Mia!' Cassandra and Madeline hooted in delight, elated to see her alive and well.

'You're here!' Mia cheered in surprise.

'Yes, Wendolyn sent for us,' Cassandra explained. 'Where's Dino? Is he with Tol?'

'No, he's right behind us. He's OK, but Tol can get inside his mind and use him like a puppet.'

The women nodded to one another knowingly.

'But Dino has not yet joined Tol's coven?' Wendolyn checked.

'No.'

'So Tol hasn't ascended?' Madeline asked, affectionately taking Mia's hand in her own.

Mia looked confused.

'No,' Colt answered for her.

Cassandra and Madeline slowly turned to Colt. Their eyes narrowed critically.

'You're a Hunter,' Madeline remarked, a hint of disapproval in her tone.

'The very best,' he retorted, parrying her disapproval with arrogance.

Madeline smiled sarcastically. 'That's what they all say.'
She swapped an amused expression with her sister.

'Ha!' Colt exclaimed. 'Then they are all lying. And on that
note, no need to thank me for saving your children from
certain death ... It seems that to get a thank-you from an
Arcana is like pulling teeth – which, quite frankly, I'd prefer.'

Cassandra eyed him suspiciously. 'Thank you for saving
my children,' she replied cagily. 'May I ask why you would
do such a thing?'

'You may. I have been infected by love,' he told her, as
though it were a terminal disease that he had recently come
to terms with.

Madeline's jaw dropped open in horror. 'Good God!' she
cried. 'Please tell me that's a joke!'

Colt bowed his head commiseratively. 'I'm afraid not. I
was very upset about it, too. But I suppose no one is exempt.'
He remembered Lotan's words as he spoke.

Cassandra turned to her daughter. 'Mia, is this true?' she
asked gently.

Mia smiled sweetly, and an innocent dimple appeared in
her cheek. 'It's true.'

Madeline fanned her face with her hand. 'I feel faint,' she
declared in an over-the-top voice. 'It's like history repeating
itself.'

'Try not to judge,' Wendolyn advised kindly.

'I think I'm getting a stress-related aneurism,' Madeline
rambled. 'This is what's going to kill me, you know. Stress.
I'm too young to be dealing with this.'

Mia and Colt grinned puckishly at each other.

'Oh, don't tell me,' Madeline gasped, regaining a somewhat abrasive tone. 'Please don't tell me you're bearing his
child! I refuse to go through this again, Mia. *I refuse!*'

Mia flushed in embarrassment. 'Of course not!'

'Well, that's one thing, at least,' Madeline grumbled. 'But
that'll be next. I'm warning you now, Cassandra, that'll be

next!' She wagged her finger at her sister, although she wasn't entirely sure who to direct her anger towards.

'Oh, don't be absurd, Maddie!' Cassandra laughed brightly.

Wendolyn jumped to Colt's defence. 'Colt is a fine young man, and a gentleman at that.'

Colt beamed with pride. 'Well, I'll be damned! A gentleman. Isn't that something! How very mundane I must be,' he chuckled to himself.

Footsteps approached and Dino jogged out from the trees.

'Cassandra!' he smiled warmly at his mother. 'Aunt Maddie!'

Madeline scuttled over to him and gave him an impromptu hug. 'I'm glad to see you safe, you terrible wayward child.'

Dino hugged her back. 'It's good to see you, too. My God, Maddie, you've aged since I last saw you,' he teased mercilessly.

'You see!' Madeline shrieked to Wendolyn. 'What a horrible little pest! He's so cruel to me, I can hardly stand it.' She rubbed her temples for dramatic emphasis. Despite her irritation, Madeline herded Dino and Mia as closely to her side as possible.

Cassandra joined the huddle. 'Dino, Mia, there's something you need to know,' she confessed earnestly.

They gave her their undivided attention, curious about what her admission would be.

Cassandra continued, 'You're probably wondering why Tol has taken such an interest in you.' She paused. 'This may shock you, but Tol is . . . your father.' She braced herself for their mortified reactions.

'Is that it?' Mia asked charily, as though she were waiting for another bombshell to be dropped.

Cassandra and Madeline frowned.

'He's your father,' Cassandra repeated. 'Tol. He's your father.'

'We know,' Dino replied, mildly disinterested.

Cassandra glanced at Madeline. 'Oh. Well, there we are then.'

Colt smirked. 'And may I just say, excellent choice in spouse,' he goaded, unable to resist a sardonic crack. 'He seems like a wonderful man.'

Right on cue, a hissing, snake-like voice suddenly broke in. 'What's this? A family reunion? Seems my invitation was lost.'

Madeline made a noise of revulsion. '*You!*'

'How lovely to see you, Cass,' Tol sneered. 'You're looking well. Or as I remember you, at least.'

'I wish I could say the same to you,' Cassandra replied hotly. Standing before her was a distorted version of the man she had once loved. It was like looking at a watercolour that had been ruined by a sudden shower. Time had warped him into a monster.

Tol glanced disdainfully at Madeline. 'Cassandra, I see you still insist on bringing that troll with you everywhere you go,' he remarked.

'Troll?' Madeline screamed. 'How dare you! I'm going to enjoy bringing you down.'

'Ah-ha,' Tol mused. 'So, you have a little plan up your sleeve?' He spoke only to Cassandra now. 'I'm sure you won't be surprised to find that I do, too.'

'Tol,' Cassandra said remorsefully, 'what have you become?' Even in his toxic state, she couldn't help but try to reach out to the human part of him – the part that still held her heart. 'How can you harm our child?'

'Harm him?' Tol laughed hauntingly. 'I will improve him!'

'By leading him into darkness?' Cassandra argued. 'By taking away his life? This, what you are now, is a fate worse than death. And this is what you want for him – to live like you, a demon in the shadows? *My* Tol would never have wanted this. Not for himself, or for his son.'

'I was never *your* Tol,' he said scornfully. 'I belong to the power, and the child belongs to me.' He turned his attention to Dino. 'Come to me,' he commanded.

Dino robotically walked towards him, his eyes glazed over in a trancelike state.

'No way!' Madeline grabbed hold of Dino, hauling him back. 'You are not taking my boy!'

'He's not your boy,' Tol spat. 'He is my son.'

'He's just as much my son as he is yours,' Madeline disputed. 'I raised him from a baby – long after you were out of the picture.'

Wendolyn sneaked a glimpse at her pendant. The amber stone remained dormant, meaning that William Wix was not yet with them.

Come on! she urged Blue and Kizzy silently.

Time was running out.

'I can't find it!' Kizzy wailed in despair. 'We've searched every gravestone here and none of them are William Wix's!'

She and Blue raced frantically around the moonlit cemetery in a mad hunt for the grave. The wind chimes clattered in cheerful fashion, mocking their failure.

'It's got to be here somewhere,' Blue reasoned. 'This is the only g . . . graveyard.'

'But we've checked every stone, and we're running out of time!'

Blue ran his hands through his hair. 'Then we must have missed one.' In his arms he cradled four white candles and a scroll of yellowed paper.

Kizzy hopped up and down on the spot manically. 'We don't have time to search again!'

'Well, we're going to have to,' Blue told her assertively. 'You take the north side, I'll take the south side.'

Kizzy chewed on her thumbnail. 'OK,' she agreed, although she feared their attempts would be futile.

As Blue spun around to leave, a candle fell from his arms and rolled across the moss. He bent down to pick it up from where it lay at the foot of a gravestone. Blue looked up at the stone slab.

'*Spangles*,' he read aloud. 'Wait . . .' he murmured. Setting the other candles down, he peeled back the weeds growing at the base of the gravestone. And there, in tiny italic writing, was the name William Wix.

'I found it!' Blue cheered. 'Spangles was William's nickname! This is it!'

'Here lies William Wix,' Kizzy recited the words that were etched into the stone. 'May he rest in peace.' She smiled satirically at her companion. 'Time to wake up, Spangles!'

She and Blue dropped to the ground on either side of the grave and set to work arranging the candles at the north, south, east and west points.

Kizzy beamed joyfully at Blue, and he returned the look.

Then there was an extended pause.

'Go ahead,' Kizzy said at last.

'Go ahead with what?'

'Light the candles.'

Blue scratched his head. 'I don't have the matches. You've got them.'

Kizzy's smile vanished. 'No, I haven't. You've got them.'

'Oh, no!' Blue bellowed. 'We have to go back to the castle.'

'We don't have time!'

'But we have to light the candles! The spell won't work without them lit.'

Kizzy wrinkled her nose as though a debatable idea had occurred to her. 'Blue,' she said, somewhat reluctantly, 'you're a Conjurer. Can't you, maybe, conjure us some matches? Maybe?'

'I only make buttons,' he muttered. The very question emasculated him shamefully.

'No,' Kizzy contested, 'that's not true. You're a Conjurer,' she enunciated the title with profound emphasis. 'You're one of the most powerful and rare witches around.'

'I'm not a Conjurer,' Blue replied apologetically. 'I'm a button factory.'

'I disagree.'

'How can you disagree? You've seen it with your own eyes. And you hear what they all call me – Benny Buttons.'

'Forget them.' Kizzy glowered at the memory of the taunts. 'You're not Benny Buttons, you're Benny Blue. And you're a *Conjurer*.'

Blue closed his honey-brown eyes, already accepting defeat.

'Blue,' Kizzy implored, crawling across the grave and plonking herself down beside him. 'I know you can do it.' She took hold of his hand and unthinkingly kissed him on the cheek.

He opened his eyes and cast his gaze upon her. 'I don't want to let you down, Kizzy. I don't want to let anyone down.'

'Forget them,' Kizzy said earnestly.

'I can't,' Blue whispered.

'Benny, it's OK if you make buttons. That's still a power to be proud of.'

Blue snorted bitterly. 'Tell that to my f . . . family.'

'Are they Conjurers, too?'

'My great-grandfather was. He passed away before I was born, but apparently he was one of the most powerful witches of all time. I suppose everyone in my family wanted to be born with the Conjurer gene, but I was the only one. My parents expect me to be fantastic – as good as my great-grandfather – and I guess they're kind of disappointed that I'm n . . . not.' He hesitated for a moment, looking up to the purple sky. 'I've been coming to the Glass Castle for a year, Kizzy. I've read practically every book in the library and I work on my power every day . . . It's just not going to happen for me.'

Kizzy put her arm around him. 'Then that's who you are, and I think that's pretty awesome. I think you are incredible.'

Blue smiled shyly. 'I think you are, too. I'll run back to the castle and get the matches. OK?'

'OK.' Kizzy gave him a final hug, and before she knew what she was doing, she leaned over and kissed him on the lips.

They stared at each other for a moment, unsure of what to say.

'Sorry!' Kizzy grinned sheepishly.

'No, no, I liked it.'

Kizzy giggled. 'Quick! You have to go and get the matches.'

With a deep breath, Blue changed tactics. He dug through his jeans pocket and drew out his vial of ciron thistle like a knight drawing his sword. He sprinkled the grains into his hand and enclosed them.

'Matches,' he whispered. Unfolding his fingers, he examined the contents of his palm.

'Well?' Kizzy pressed.

'It's not matches,' Blue confirmed.

'Button?' Kizzy asked, trying to hide her regret.

'Yeah, it's a button.' Blue studied it curiously. 'But it's on fire!'

Kizzy cheered and clapped her hands fervently. 'I knew you could do it!'

Without wasting a second, Blue used the flaming button to light the candles.

Kizzy crawled to the other side of the grave and looked across at him. His expression, highlighted by the glowing candlelight, was strong and powerful.

'Let's raise the dead,' Blue said with a smile, the pulsating flames reflecting in his eyes.

*

241

Wendolyn, can you hear me? Cassandra asked silently.

Wendolyn glanced at her briefly. *Yes, I hear you,* she replied to Cassandra's voice, communicating through murmurs of the mind. The two Readers had become adept at conversing beyond the ears of others.

Is William with us? Cassandra asked.

Wendolyn traced her frail fingers over the amulet. *I'm afraid not,* she returned.

I don't know how much longer we can hold Tol off, Cassandra admitted grimly.

Tol circled the Arcana and Colt, flocking them like lambs. But his focus was constantly on Dino, relentlessly chipping away at his mind with an intensity undetected by the others. The struggle to resist wore Dino down to the point of exhaustion.

'Say the words,' Tol hissed. 'Tell me that you want to join my coven, and this will all be over. I know you want to accept. Can't you feel it?'

Dino could feel it. The desire to become a Hunter was stronger than anything he had ever experienced before. It devoured him. Something in his subconscious reminded him that Tol had planted these feelings, but it barely mattered. The urge was so extreme that it was almost impossible to resist.

'Mia, keep talking to me,' Dino begged, desperate for an anchor to pull him back.

'Don't listen to him,' she pleaded. 'It's all a trick. You don't want to be a Hunter.'

'Come with me,' Tol persisted in a lulling voice. 'I'm your father.'

Dino flinched. Throughout his entire life he had dreamed of meeting his father. He had often fantasised about running away to find him and escaping the household of women. Now the option was a reality – although it wasn't quite the fishing trips and sports events that Dino had imagined.

'Say the words,' Tol seethed.

So far, Dino had honourably resisted such a dominant force, but like a fraying rope he soon would snap.

'If you will not succumb to the desire,' Tol went on sadistically, 'then perhaps you will submit to pain.' He contorted his hand into a fist, and Dino cried out in agony. Tol was invading his mind so furiously that the pain in his head was now unbearable.

I need to act now! Cassandra cried to Wendolyn frantically. *He's torturing him!*

'Ah,' Tol let out a satisfied breath, momentarily releasing Dino from his clutches. 'It seems my army has arrived.'

The Arcana waited on tenterhooks as Tol's two followers surfaced from the shadows. Shrouded behind dark robes, their sunken, hollow faces resembled skeletons rather than humans.

'Oh, look what the cat dragged in,' Madeline scoffed. 'This really *is* a family reunion. And a family reunion just isn't complete without my two treacherous brothers.'

'My uncles?' Mia uttered, aghast.

'Anton and Phillip,' Cassandra confirmed. 'Good heavens, Phillip! You used to be such a handsome boy. I see that evil has spoiled you, too. You look quite rotten, my dears.'

Anton and Phillip hardly registered their sisters. Sixteen years of greed and poison had turned them into blank minions, emotionless drudges that did Tol's biddings.

Tol turned to his two underlings. 'Slaughter them all,' he instructed.

Anton and Phillip lunged forward like hounds, their razor-sharp teeth glinting in the moonlight.

In a reflex action, Colt raised his hand. He charged a gust of air at the Hunters, bowling them over like dominoes.

Tol directed his hand towards Colt. 'You are a nuisance, Hunter. I'll will enjoy watching you die.'

'Likewise,' Colt retorted.

243

Taking advantage of his distraction, Madeline raced forward and leapt on to Tol's back, digging her nails into his shoulders.

Tol roared and flung her off him. She hurtled through the air and landed on the ground with a smack.

'Maddie!' Cassandra screamed, rushing over to her sister's unconscious body.

A vibrant blush of scarlet light warmed Wendolyn's hand. She looked down at the glowing amulet. 'Hello, my love,' she whispered to the pendant.

Cassandra, she beckoned. *William is with us. It's time.*

Maddie's hurt, Cassandra responded noiselessly. *I can't wake her up!*

While Anton and Phillip slithered in and out of the trees circling Mia and Colt, Tol summoned Dino to him.

'Stand before me,' Tol demanded.

Dino edged forward until they were just a foot apart.

Cassandra, Wendolyn said silently and calmly. *We need to do the spell at once. If you cannot wake Madeline, then we must use Mia in her place.*

Mia! She's not ready for such a powerful spell, Cassandra objected, worried as a witch and foremost as a mother. *It will consume her!*

Take my hand, Wendolyn told her smoothly.

Cassandra left Madeline's side and returned to Wendolyn. Anxiously, she grasped the older woman's hand. They both looked at Mia.

Colt stood protectively in front of her, warding off their two attackers.

'Mia!' Wendolyn called. 'Join us.'

Mia gripped Colt's sleeve. 'I can't,' she whispered to him, already anticipating Wendolyn's intention.

Without response, Colt sent a burst of air to clear her pathway. 'Go to your mother,' he said resolutely.

She didn't move from his side.

'Sweet girl,' he laughed lightly, 'this is your time to shine. Don't hide behind me. You surpass me.'

Mia smiled nervously. 'I thought you were unsurpassed?'

'Don't make me say it again! Just go!' He gave her a little shove and within moments Mia was positioned between her mother and Wendolyn.

Cassandra took hold of her hand. 'Mia, you must be brave. Follow our lead.'

The three women joined hands, and Wendolyn's amulet radiated brightly over her cotton dressing gown.

'Colt!' Mia cried, as Anton and Phillip pounced upon him. She tried to run to him, but Cassandra held her tightly.

'Don't let go of my hand,' she beseeched her daughter. 'No matter what happens, we must not break the connection.'

As the mother held the daughter, the father held the son. Tol clasped Dino's face between his crooked fingers.

'Say it,' he snarled.

Dino opened his mouth, but his words faltered.

Hastily, Wendolyn withdrew an Athame from the pocket of her dressing gown. She held it to the sky and then used its tip to sketch a square into the mud.

With her index finger she tapped each point of the square. 'From the four corners, I call on thee, to protect us from our enemy . . .' She handed the blade to Cassandra.

Mia looked on in horror as Anton and Phillip overcame Colt and pinned him to the ground.

And then, by glory of a miracle, another dark figure dived from the tree tops. A Hunter. But not one of Tol's – one of Colt's.

It was Siren. He had survived.

Filled with vengeance, Siren leapt on to Anton, snapping his neck in the blink of an eye.

Now the tables had turned, and it was Phillip who cowered as the two young Hunters took back their rightful place as the forest coven.

Oblivious to the outside world, Cassandra tapped the corners of the square with the Athame. 'Earth, air, fire and sea, banish Tol's power away from he.' She passed the dagger to Mia.

Mia cringed as her fingers touched the cold blade. What was her mother thinking, handing her the Athame like that? She didn't have the strength to master it – not without Colt, anyway.

She looked over at him. He stood back casually as Siren drove Phillip into the forest.

'I can't do it,' she mouthed to him.

He smiled at her, his eyes shining with the colours of the forest. At that moment, she saw his soul: beautiful, strong and free. Exactly as he was on the exterior.

'Yes, you can,' he mouthed back to her.

Mia clutched the Athame. She brought it to the ground and used its point to tap the corners of the square, just as her mother had done. Inexplicably, the Athame let itself be known to her. It felt true in her hands, as though she shared a secret understanding with it. She could sense it working alongside her, not exceeding her own power, merely aiding it.

Then Mia spoke, the words flowing as if she had used them a thousand times before. 'With love, strength and the powers of we, end evil's reign, so shall it be.'

A clap of lightning sounded overhead and Dino dropped to the ground.

'Dino!' Mia cried.

He scrambled to his feet and stumbled to his mother and sister.

Tol let out an almighty roar. His body blazed with a dull, purple light.

The others watched in awe as a stream of yellow and black light poured out of his mouth, gushing like a faucet of luminous water.

The ground shuddered and the trees trembled. And with a splintering crash, Tol crumpled to the floor, lifeless.

For a moment nobody moved.

Cassandra was the first to break the stillness. She stepped gingerly towards the motionless body. However, the man she saw on the ground was not the man who had tormented them just minutes before. Instead, she saw the young man whom she had loved for so many years. Tol's former features had been restored.

Cassandra dropped to the forest floor and rested her head on his chest. There she wept.

Her Tol was gone.

Epilogue

Mia limped across the courtyard to the old blue station wagon. Even at summer's end, the sun was strong and the sky was brilliantly blue.

'Hurry up, hobbles,' Colt said, rather impatiently. 'You know, if you were a Hunter that ankle would have healed days ago.'

'Oh, well, in that case, maybe I'll become Hunter,' she replied in jest.

'You wish!' Colt scoffed. 'You're not what we're looking for.' He dumped her rucksack on to the ground, propping it up against the car tyre.

Savouring their final moments together, they stood alone at the station wagon. The others would be out shortly for the customary farewells.

'So,' Colt sighed, his blithe tone altering drastically. 'I'd prefer not to be here when the Arcana are around. I suppose I should say my goodbyes now.'

Mia smiled sadly. She had hoped that Colt would be there until the very last moment. In fact, she had hoped that he would be the last thing she saw as she left the Glass Castle.

'You'll come back one day, won't you?' he asked rather vulnerably.

Mia nodded her head. She was afraid that, if she spoke, her tearful voice would betray her. She hated the thought of leaving Colt, but school would be starting soon for her, and, as a Hunter, Colt was obliged to stay at the castle with Siren and their new coven.

'Good,' he said. 'But don't forget, I'll be coven leader with two new rookies to admire me, so don't you go embarrassing me in front of them,' he joked flippantly, but in truth it was hard for him to imagine his coven with anyone other than Lotan and Roc. Yet it was even harder to imagine the days passing without Mia's company.

'Embarrass you?' Mia exclaimed. 'The other way around, more like!'

Colt softened. 'I'm teasing. You don't embarrass me. I'm proud of my illness. I'd shout it from the rooftops – provided that nobody was around to hear it, that is.'

'How very romantic,' Mia mocked. 'You won't forget about me while I'm gone?' she asked, pretending not to know the answer.

'Yes, I'm afraid I will,' he replied coolly.

'No, you won't!' She enveloped him in an amorous hug.

Colt nestled his face into her hair. The action was now like second nature to him.

Mia felt a lump forming in her throat. She would miss him desperately.

'Don't cry,' he soothed.

'How could you tell?' She gave him a melancholy smile, pulling away to look up into his eyes.

'What makes you think I was talking to you?' he grinned wryly.

Their moment was interrupted by a commotion at the castle entryway.

'That's my cue to leave,' Colt told her. 'Go with care. And if you ever need me, call for me.' He dipped his head and kissed her lovingly. But the kiss was bittersweet.

Mia nodded her head again, trying in vain to hold back the tears.

And then, Colt was gone.

Alone in the courtyard, Mia felt his breeze encompassing her. She closed her eyes to relish in it.

'I can't believe it's all over!' Another voice cut through the silence. It was Kizzy. Her blonde hair was tied up in a shoelace and her long, patchwork dress was trailing along the gravel.

Mia gave her a warm hug. 'We'll come back again. We have to. Christmas and next summer, maybe?'

'Definitely.' Kizzy gave her a loud kiss on the cheek. 'And I'll phone you tonight when I get home.'

'Yes. As soon as you get home!' Mia beamed.

Emerging from the doorway, Dino appeared on the scene, his heavy rucksack slung over his shoulder. Behind him were Wendolyn, Blue, Cassandra and Madeline.

Dino busied himself loading the rucksacks into the car, muttering something about being lumbered with the hard labour. Beside him, Blue gave Kizzy a private smile.

'Thanks for everything,' Dino said at last, stepping out from behind the station wagon. 'All of you.' It was clear from his bashful stance that he had been building up the courage to say it for some time.

There was a chorus of humble responses.

'Yes, thank you,' Mia chimed in. She realised that she was crying openly now. Her time at the Glass Castle had gone way above and beyond anything she could ever have imagined. Even with the difficulties, she wouldn't change a second of it.

'Come back any time,' Wendolyn prompted sincerely.

Dino smiled at her with a look of respect and reverence. Then he turned to Blue and extended his hand.

Blue accepted the gesture and shook Dino's hand meaningfully.

'Benny Blue,' Dino said graciously, 'you are a loyal friend. And I am honoured to know you.'

'Aw, don't get all slushy on me!' Blue punched him playfully in the arm.

Dino smirked. 'I'll see you around, buddy.'

'Count on it,' Blue grinned. He had an air of poise and strength that had not been present until now. And he knew that was partly due to the friends he had made at the castle. Before the summer, he had never known true friendship. And Dino, for the good and the bad, was a true friend. Their comradeship would be one that would sustain the test of time.

As the friends said their emotional goodbyes, Cassandra and Madeline hugged Wendolyn and then climbed into the front seats of the car. Dino hopped into the back and fastened his seatbelt.

Before retreating to the station wagon, Mia gave Wendolyn a kiss. As an afterthought she said, 'When I first arrived here, you read my tea leaves. You said you'd tell me what you saw when I was more able to deal with it. After everything we've been through, am I able enough now?'

Wendolyn chortled. 'I'd say so, dear! The leaves foretold your destiny. And your destiny is with Colt.'

The corner of Mia's mouth curved upwards in amusement. Of course she wouldn't have been able to fathom that in the early days. She had lived in fear of Hunters – especially Colt.

'So, you knew all along?' she asked Wendolyn.

The older lady winked genially. 'Let's say I had an inkling.'

From inside the car, Madeline reached over to the driver's side and honked the horn, hurrying her niece along.

Obediently, Mia climbed into the back seat beside Dino. She blew one last kiss to her friends as the engine spluttered to life.

With her hands rested loosely on the steering wheel, Cassandra drove through the meadow, heading away from the Glass Castle. She glanced at her children in the rear-view mirror.

'I'm sorry I didn't tell you about your father,' she said bravely.

'That's OK,' Mia replied. 'I think I preferred not knowing,' she added playfully.

Cassandra smiled thoughtfully. 'How about you, Dino? How do you feel about all of this?' As a Reader she could have glimpsed into his mind, but she decided she'd rather hear it from his mouth.

Dino shrugged. 'I always dreamed of having a father . . .' He trailed off.

'And now?' Cassandra pressed.

'And now, I suppose I won't ever have one,' he concluded simply.

Cassandra looked repentant, as though she had deprived him of that birthright.

'Although', Dino went on, 'Aunt Maddie has a fairly masculine energy, so I guess she'll do,' he jibed in good nature.

'Oh, you dreadful child!' Madeline shrieked. She swatted at him from her front seat.

Dino laughed as he dodged every one of her swipes. 'Don't worry, Mother. I'm not pining for Tol if that's what you think.'

Cassandra's face lit up – not because of what he had said, but because of one word mentioned within it. 'You called me mother!' she gushed.

Dino smiled reluctantly. 'OK, OK. Let's not make a big deal out of it.'

Mia reached over to him and ruffled his hair. 'Aw, how cute!' she teased.

He shoved her hand away. 'Women!' he uttered, exasperated.

Giggling quietly, Mia turned her gaze to beyond the car window. Soon they would leave the castle behind, erasing it into nothing more than a memory. She squeezed her eyes shut, imploring herself not to think about Colt. She couldn't allow herself to surrender to that yet, because, when she did, she feared that she would shatter into pieces, never to be repaired.

Was that my destiny? she wondered reflectively. *And if that was it, is it over now?*

All at once, Cassandra and Madeline let out shrill screams and Cassandra slammed on the brakes. The tyres screeched and polluted the air with the stench of burnt rubber.

It was Colt. He had appeared in front of the car, as if he had materialised from thin air.

He rapped on the bonnet of the car. 'Cutting it a bit close, wouldn't you say?' he accused the driver. 'You near flattened me! Crazy females!'

Madeline shook her fist at him. 'The nerve to jump out in front of our car like that. He scared me half to death!'

Mia unbuckled her seatbelt and thrust open the car door.

'You came back!' she cried, rushing to him and flinging her arms around his neck.

He grinned frivolously. 'Yes. I decided I should be the last person to say goodbye to you. Seeing that I'm your favourite.'

Mia kissed him. 'I wanted that, too,' she declared breathlessly. 'You know, Wendolyn told me that you were my destiny,' she blurted the words out, feeling a little self-conscious afterwards.

But Colt's response eased her uncertainty. 'That doesn't surprise me. After all, what's love without destiny?' he noted rhetorically.

'Do you think we were fated to meet?'

'Absolutely. And we will continue to meet,' he assured her. 'It's out of our hands.' He gently took her palms in his grasp and lifted them skyward. A shower of pink tree blossoms sprinkled over them like snowflakes.

Mia gasped as the silken petals landed on her nose and in

her hair. She dropped her hands down, letting the blossoms scatter around them.

'*Destiny*,' Colt dissected the word astutely. 'You never know where it will take you.'

'It took me to you,' Mia mused.

'Then I am in its debt.'

She pondered it wistfully. 'How long does destiny last?'

Colt chuckled. 'Not long enough.'

'What if it lasts for ever?'

'For ever? Still not long enough.' Colt smiled roguishly.

'But at least there's more to come.'

'Oh, I have no doubt.' Colt regarded her with a mixture of adoration and curiosity. 'I suppose we'll find out in due course,' he added cryptically. 'As they say, the writing is on the wall.'

Mia thought back to the day that she'd found out she was a witch, months ago, in the basement of her family home. *Addo Vis Vires.* The writing was on the wall. She met Colt's gaze.

'To give power,' she muttered, more to herself than to him.

'What was that?'

'Nothing,' she said, her voice more distinguishable this time. 'It's just, I think I understand it now. The writing was on the wall.'

Colt flashed her an alluring smile. 'And so begins another fairy tale.'

Rules

Second Year at Downey House

JANE BEATON

SPHERE

First published in Great Britain as a paperback original in 2009 by Sphere

A CIP catalogue record for this book
is available from the British Library.

ISBN 978-0-7515-4061-1

Typeset in Palatino by M Rules
Printed and bound in Great Britain by
Clays Ltd, St Ives plc

Papers used by Sphere are natural, renewable and recyclable
products sourced from well-managed forests and certified
in accordance with the rules of the Forest Stewardship Council.

Mixed Sources
Product group from well-managed
forests and other controlled sources
FSC   www.fsc.org Cert no. SGS-COC-004081
© 1996 Forest Stewardship Council

Sphere
An imprint of
Little, Brown Book Group
100 Victoria Embankment
London EC4Y 0DY

An Hachette UK Company
www.hachette.co.uk

www.littlebrown.co.uk

For my father. A great teacher,
and an even better dad.

Acknowledgements

Thanks to the board; W. Hickham; every teacher (and pupil!) who took the time to write to me and tell me a little bit about their life; Ben Ward, for finding David's poem; and my beloved Beatons, large and small.

Characters

Staff

Headteacher: Dr Veronica Deveral
Administrator: Miss Evelyn Prenderghast
Deputy Headteacher: Miss June Starling
Head of Finance: Mr Archie Liston
Matron: Miss Doreen Redmond

Cook: Mrs Joan Rhys
Caretaker: Mr Harold Carruthers

Physics: Mr John Bart
Music: Mrs Theodora Offili
French: Mademoiselle Claire Crozier
English: Miss Margaret Adair
Maths: Miss Ella Beresford
PE: Miss Janie James
Drama: Miss Fleur Parsley
History: Miss Catherine Kellen
Geography: Miss Deirdre Gifford

Pupils

Middle School Year Two

Sylvie Brown
Imogen Fairlie
Simone Kardashian
Andrea McCann
Felicity Prosser
Zazie Saurisse
Alice Trebizon-Woods
Zelda Townell
Astrid Ulverton

Chapter One

Maggie was dancing on a table. This was distinctly out of character, but they *had* served her cocktails earlier, in a glass so large she was surprised it didn't have a fish in it.

Plus it was a beautifully soft, warm evening, and her fiancé Stan had insisted on watching the football on a large Sky Sports screen, annoyingly situated over her head in the Spanish bar, so there wasn't much else to do – and all the other girls were dancing on table tops.

I'm still young, Maggie had thought to herself, pushing her unruly dark hair out of her eyes. *I'm only twenty-six years old! I can still dance all night!*

And with the help of a friendly hen party from Stockport on the next table, she'd found herself up there, shrugging off any self-consciousness with the help of a large margarita and grooving away to Alphabeat.

'Hey, I can't see the game,' Stan complained.

'I don't care,' said Maggie, suddenly feeling rather freer, happy and determined to enjoy her holiday. She raised her arms above her head. This was definitely a good way to forget about school; to forget about David McDonald, the English teacher she'd developed a crush on last year – until

1

she'd found out he was engaged. To just feel like herself again, instead of a teacher.

'Isn't that Miss Adair?' said Hattie.

They'd been allowed down into the town for the evening from the discreet and beautifully appointed villa they'd been staying in high on the other side of the mountain. Her younger sister Fliss turned round from where she'd been eyeing up fake designer handbags, and glanced at the tacky-looking sports pub Hattie was pointing out. Inside was a group of drunk-looking women waving their hands in the air.

'No way!' exclaimed Fliss, heading towards the door for a closer look. 'I'm going in to check.'

'You're not allowed in any bars!' said Hattie. 'I promised Mum and Dad.'

'*I promised Mum and Dad*,' mimicked Fliss. 'I am fourteen, you know. That's pretty much the legal drinking age over here.'

'Well, whilst you're with me you'll obey family rules.'

Fliss stuck out her tongue and headed straight for the bar. 'You're not a prefect now.'

'No, but we're in a position of trust, and . . .'

Fliss stopped short in the doorway.

'Hello, senorita,' said the doorman. Fliss had grown two inches over the summer, although to her huge annoyance she was still barely filling an A cup.

Maggie and the girls from Stockport were shimmying up and down to the Pussycat Dolls when she saw Fliss. At first she thought it was a trick of the flashing lights. It couldn't be. After all, they'd come all this way to leave her work behind. So she could feel like a girl, not a teacher. So surely it couldn't be one of her—

'MISS ADAIR!' shrieked Fliss. 'Is that you, miss?'

Maggie stopped dancing.

'Felicity Prosser,' she said, feeling a resigned tone creep into her voice. She looked around, wondering what would be the most dignified way to get down from the table, under the circumstances.

Normally, Veronica Deveral found the Swiss Alps in summertime a cleansing balm for the soul. The clean, sharp air you could draw all the way down into your lungs; the sparkle of the grass and the glacier lakes; the cyclists and rosy-cheeked all-year skiers heading for higher ground; the freshly washed sky. She always took the same *pension*, and liked to take several novels – she favoured the lengthy intrigues of Anthony Trollope, and was partial to a little Joanna for light relief – and luxuriate in the time to devour them, returning to Downey House rested, refreshed and ready for the new academic year.

This year, however, had been different. After her shock at meeting the son she gave up for adoption nearly forty years ago, Veronica had handled it badly and they had lost contact. And although there were budgets to be approved, a new intake to set up and staffing to be organised, she couldn't concentrate. All she seemed to do was worry about Daniel, and wonder what he was doing back in Cornwall.

She was staring out the window of her beautiful office, before term was due to start, when Dr Robert Fitzroy, head of Downey Boys over the hill, arrived for their annual chat. The two schools did many things together, and it was useful to have some knowledge of the forthcoming agenda.

'You seem a little distracted, Veronica,' Robert said, comfortably ensconced on the Chesterfield sofa, enjoying the fine view over the school grounds and to the cliffs and the sea beyond, today a perfect summer-holiday blue. They weren't really getting anywhere with debating the new computer lab.

Veronica sighed and briefly considered confiding in her opposite number. He was a kind man, if a little set in his ways. She dismissed this thought immediately. She had spent years building up this school, the last thing she needed was anyone thinking she was a weak woman, prone to tears and over-emotional sentimentality.

Robert droned on about new staff.

'Oh, and yes,' he said, 'we have a new History teacher at last. Good ones are so hard to find these days.'

Veronica was barely listening. She was watching the waves outside and wondering if Daniel had ever taken his children to the seaside for a holiday. So when Robert said his name it chimed with her thoughts, and at first she didn't at all understand what she'd just heard.

'Excuse me?'

'Daniel Stapleton. Our new History teacher.'

'Mom!'

Zelda was throwing ugly things in her bag. Ugly tops, ugly skirts, ugly hats. What the hell? School uniform was the stupidest idea in a country full of stupid ideas.

'Did you know I have to share, like, a bathroom? Did they tell you that?'

Zelda's mother shook her head. As if she didn't have enough to deal with, what with DuBose being so excited about the move and all. Why they all had to go and up sticks and live in England, where she'd heard it rained all the time and everyone lived in itty-bitty houses with bathrooms the size of cupboards . . . well, it didn't bear thinking about. She doubted it would be much like Texas.

4

'Don' worry, darlin,' DuBose had said, in that calm drawl of his. He might get a lot of respect as a major seconded to the British Army, but it didn't cut much ice with her, nuh-huh.

'An' we'll get Zelda out of that crowd she's been running with at high school. Turn her into quite the English lady.'

A boarding school education was free for the daughters of senior military staff on overseas postings, and Downey House, they'd been assured, was among the very best.

As Mary Jo looked at her daughter's perfect manicure – they'd been for a mommy/daughter pamper day – so strange against the stark white of her new uniform blouses, she wondered, yet again, how they would all fit in.

Simone glanced at Fliss's Facebook update – *Felicity is having a BLASTING time in Spain!* – and tried her best to be happy for her. The Kardashians weren't having a holiday this year. It just wasn't practical. Which was fine by Simone, she hated struggling into her tankini and pulling a big sarong around herself, then sitting under an umbrella hiding in case anyone saw her. So, OK, Fliss might be having great fun without her, and Alice was posting about being utterly miserably bored learning to dive with her au pair in Hurghada, and she was jealous and she did miss them – but she was doing her best to be happy for them.

Thank goodness she'd been invited to Fliss's house for the end of the holidays, so they could all travel back together. Simone had tried not to let slip to her friends just how much she was looking forward to it – and even worse, to admit how much she was looking forward to going back to school.

It had been a long seven weeks, with not much to do but read and try to avoid Joel, her brother, who had spent the entire time indoors hunched over his games console.

5

She'd spent the summer dreaming of school and reading books whilst eating fish finger sandwiches. Her mother had tried her best to get her involved in some local social events, but it wasn't really her thing. She winced remembering an unbelievably awkward afternoon tea with Rudi, the ugly, gangly teenage son of one of her mother's best friends. His face was covered in spots and his hair was oily and lank. They were shuffled awkwardly together on to a sofa.

Simone's misery on realising that this was the kind of boy her mum thought she might like was compounded by the very obvious way Rudi looked her up and down and made it clear that he thought he was out of her league. She cringed again at the memory.

'You go to that posh school then,' he'd muttered, when pushed by his mum.

Simone had felt a blush spread over her face, and kept her eyes tightly fixed on her hands.

'Yeah.'

'Oh. Right.'

And that had been that. It was pretty obvious that Rudi, over-stretched as he was, would much rather be upstairs playing Grand Theft Auto with Joel.

Simone sighed. It would have been nice to go back to school with at least some adventures to tell Alice and Fliss. Still, maybe she could share theirs.

'Tell me about her thighs again,' said Alice, leaning lazily on shady manicured grass, watching tiny jewel-coloured lizards scrabble past and running up an enormous bill on the hotel phone.

'Jiggly,' said Fliss, under a cherry tree two thousand miles away in Surrey, tickling her dog Ranald on the tummy. 'Honestly, you could see right up her skirt and everything.'

6

'I never really think of teachers having legs,' mused Alice. 'I mean, I suppose they must and everything, but . . .'

'But what, you think they run along on wheels?' Fliss giggled.

'No, but . . . oh, it's so hot.'

'FLISS!' The voice came from inside.

'Oh God, is that the heffalump Hattie?' drawled Alice.

'I'm not going to answer,' said Fliss.

'FELICITY!' Hattie huffed into the orchard garden, her tread heavy on the paving stones. '*Felicity*.'

'I'm on the *phone*,' said Fliss crossly.

'Well, I have news.'

'Is she pregnant?' said wicked Alice.

'Ssh,' Fliss told her.

'Fine,' said Hattie, turning to go. 'So I guess you DON'T want to hear who's starting at Downey Boys this year?'

Fliss turned and looked at her.

'What are you talking about?'

'Just that I was down in the village . . . and was talking to Will's mum . . .'

And just like that, Alice was talking to an empty telephone.

'Come on.'

Stan was nuzzling her neck. 'Just one more cuddle.'

'I've got to pack!' Maggie was insisting. It wasn't too long before she had to go back and she wanted to be ready. Her clothes were strewn across the room, along with several books she'd wanted to collect to take back for her girls. Stan had a day off from his printing job.

Also, she felt nervous. Last year had been her probation year at the school. This year she'd be expected to perform.

'Cody and Dylan are quite something, aren't they?' asked Stan, moving away. Her two nephews had been playing with

7

them all day, and seemed to get more rambunctious every time.

'Quite brats, you mean,' said Maggie, who'd had to lift them bodily out of the biscuit tin at ten-minute intervals.

'Oh, they're just boys,' said Stan. 'That's what I used to be like. That's what ours'll be like.'

He tried to drag Maggie back on to the bed, but she resisted.

'Once you're Mrs Cameron, you're going to want little Codys and Dylans all over the place.'

'Yes, maybe,' said Maggie, extricating herself. 'But ours won't be allowed to do that to the neighbour's cat.'

Stan laughed. 'Boys will be boys.'

'I think that's why I only teach girls.'

Maggie softened. 'I do love Cody and Dylan, you know. I just worry – they're so crazy, and I know Anne is working all the time.' Anne, Maggie's older sister, ran a thriving hairdressing practice in Govan and was single-handedly raising her two sons. 'Sometimes I wonder what they're doing at that school.'

'Well, it was good enough for us,' said Stan.

Maggie gave herself up to his kiss, thinking about the rough Holy Cross where she and Stan had met, and where she'd later taught. It wasn't really a good school at all. Now, going back to Downey House for her second year there as an English teacher, she felt as nervous and excited as one of her girls when she thought of its four forbidding towers looming out of the hills over the sea. She fingered her new academic diary carefully.

'I suppose,' she said.

Fliss was nervous about having Alice to stay – she loved their large rambling house, but Alice was used to grand residences, and she hoped it would be smart enough for her. She needn't have worried. Alice's parents being in the diplomatic corps meant they moved every couple of months. Anywhere that had a lived-in feel, with a calendar on the kitchen wall and family pictures scattered on every surface, was heaven to Alice.

Simone, on the other hand, was far more intimidated. Felicity's house was HUGE! The garden alone was about the size of a park. There were loads and loads of rooms. In their terraced house in London there was a front room, a back kitchen and three tiny bedrooms. She and Joel had to share when there were visitors staying, which was all the time.

Fliss's mum and dad were delighted to meet her friends, if a little intrigued by the chubby girl who could barely utter a word at mealtimes. Fliss was embarrassed too. Why did Simone have to act so frumpily all the time? Why couldn't she show people how fun she could be? What, did she think Fliss's parents would look down on her? That was insulting!

The first night there all three had sat up gossiping late into the night. Mr and Mrs Prosser had finally let Fliss start drinking coffee, which to Simone, used from childhood to thick sweet grounds you could stand a spoon up in, was no big deal, but it made the girls feel grown up.

Biggest topic of the night was, of course, Will Hampton. Fliss had had a crush on him for a year, ever since he'd started playing in a local band. In fact last year she'd nearly managed to get herself thrown out of school for trying to see him. And now he was going to be at the boys' school just over the hill from Downey House! Fliss could hardly contain her excitement.

'Well, we'd better see this chap,' said Alice. 'See if he passes muster.'

'He still sings in the church choir,' said Fliss.

'Well, that will do,' said Alice.

It was some surprise to Felicity's parents when the girls announced on Saturday morning that they'd like to go to church on Sunday.

Mrs Prosser raised a heavily botoxed eyebrow.

'*Church?*' she said, in the same tone as she might have said '*The casino?*' Hattie was on the youth guidance committee for their local parish, but she'd had to drag Felicity there under the threat of dire torture since she was nine years old.

'Why on earth do you suddenly want to go to church?'

Felicity pouted. 'To give thanks and all that.'

'Yes, I'd like to go too, Mrs Prosser, if that's OK,' said Alice, with her usual adult assurance.

'And me,' squeaked Simone, promising Jesus in her heart that she didn't really mean it by going to a protestant church.

Hattie harrumphed loudly, but Felicity tried to ignore her. Undaunted, Hattie harrumphed again.

'Are you trying to say something, Harriet?' asked her mother, unable to keep the sharp edge out of her tongue. She loved her eldest daughter to distraction, but she could be terribly pi.

'I wonder,' said Harriet. 'I do WONDER if the male voice choir is singing harvest festival this Sunday.'

Fliss instantly coloured, and Alice spotted it.

'Are they?' she said. 'Actually, it was my idea to go. I do like to give thanks.'

Fliss's parents glanced at each other.

'We'll all go.'

In the event, not even Hattie's hateful sniggering could spoil Fliss's view, and she stood rapt in the third pew, watching Will's dark head as he bowed to his hymnal. His band had broken up over the summer, but he still loved to sing. *Notice me*, Fliss begged in her heart. What was wrong with her? Was she too short? Too fat? In fact, Fliss was blonde and pretty, with delicate features that could often be overlooked for the more striking dark looks of her friend Alice, but at fourteen she couldn't see beyond a touch of puppy fat and the occasional pimple. With all her heart she wished she was as confident as pert, cheeky Alice, with her dark shining hair and neat figure. Even Simone had big breasts. What did she have? Nothing! Oh, how she longed to look like a model.

Afterwards they filed out, Simone bobbing and crossing herself when she thought nobody was looking. Normally Fliss couldn't bear her mother hanging around to talk to the vicar and anyone else she came across, but today she lingered anxiously, wondering if she could find the courage to ask Will about his move.

Suddenly her heart stopped as she caught his floppy brown hair – and he was growing so fast, he must be nearly six foot already and he was barely sixteen – as he came out of the beautiful old church, so in demand for weddings from people who'd never even lived in the village.

As if in a dream, she watched as he slowly walked towards her. She bit her lip nervously. He couldn't be, could he? He couldn't be coming to talk to her? She felt like she was sinking underwater. Could she speak to him? Could she?

He stopped in front of her, and Fliss found she'd lost her breath.

'Uh . . . hi . . .' she stuttered. She felt like the whole congregation was watching them.

'Hi,' said Will. He had an easy, smiling manner about him, which made you feel like you were the only person he'd been waiting to speak to all day. Of course, he was like that with everyone.

'Have a good summer?'

'Uh yeah.'

Fliss's heart was pounding. Why couldn't she say anything interesting? Make a joke, say anything?

'Cool,' said Will. He looked around, to where Alice and Simone were trying to hover not-too-closely. Wow. Fliss's friend was really really hot.

'Hey, those your friends?'

Fliss couldn't do anything but nod dumbly. Will walked towards Alice.

'Hi,' he said, putting out his hand. 'I'm Will. Do you go to Downeys? You may need to fill me in on all its evil ways.'

Alice gave him a curt look, hiding her massive curiosity. She could certainly see what Fliss saw in him. Out of the corner of her eye she caught sight of her friend.

'Oh, I'm sure Fliss can help you out with all that,' she said. Will nodded his head.

'I'm sure,' he said.

'Oh come *on*, Fliss.'

They were four hours into the drive, and Alice had yet to persuade her friend she hadn't been flirting with Will on purpose. Hattie was smugly sitting up the front, reading a book about lacrosse. Simone was in the middle – she'd volunteered – trying to stave off the tension. And Fliss was staring out of the window, thinking about Will and also the last thing her mother had said before she'd left that morning: 'Now, Felicity, you *will* be careful with all that stodge they serve at school, won't you?' She'd leant down out of earshot of everyone else. 'You don't want to end up like Hattie, do you?' 'What's that?' Hattie had said crossly, bounding down the stairs like an inelegant carthorse, her boater, schoolbag, hockey shoes and tennis raquet unraveling in her wake. 'Nothing, my gorgeous girls. Have a wonderful term!'

12

Maybe she would avoid the stodge, mused Felicity. Maybe that would help.

Alice sat back with a sigh, just as the sleek Audi crested the hill and, for the first time, the girls caught sight of the turreted, castle-like building that would be home for the next nine months.

'School! School!' shouted both Hattie and Simone. Simone's spirits lifted fully. Even Alice smiled. It did look like something out of a story book, the four towers of the main houses – Tudor, York, Wessex and their own, Plantagenet – nestled in the hills, with the cliffs behind, leading down to the still turquoise sea.

Chapter Two

'*Mon dieu*,' was the first thing Maggie heard as she stepped down from the railway carriage – this year, Stan had won the battle for the car.

Just ahead, her friend Mademoiselle Crozier, the impetuous French mistress, was wrestling with an elegant suitcase which had discharged its contents on to the platform.

'Claire!' she yelled excitedly, but didn't reach her before the guard and three passing men had all stopped to help. Maggie reflected that she could probably lose a leg under the train wheels before she could attract the attention of three passing men, but put the thought to the back of her mind.

'Hello,' she called. '*Bonjour!*'

'Maggie!' Claire ran up to her and gave her a big kiss. 'Eet eez *disaster*!'

Actually, her case was now being tidily zipped up by the hefty guard.

'Here you are, love,' he was saying. 'Can I help you down to your car now?'

The man was so overweight it didn't look like he'd make it much past the platform, but Claire just gave him her widest smile.

'Thank you zo much! That eez perfect, thank you!'